THE BRIAR'S VEIL

Jason Bramble

OneSparked Publishing

OneSparked
—PUBLISHING—

ISBN-13: 979-8-9915769-1-8

Cover design by: Jason Bramble
Library of Congress Control Number: 2024919968
Printed in the United States of America

In shadows deep where brambles creep,
The Briar's Veil in silence weeps,
A shroud of thorns in darkness spun,
Where ancient spirits hide from the sun.

Beneath the cloak of tangled shade,
Where night and dread in whispers trade,
The veil conceals a secret pain,
Where spectral echoes softly wane.

Through thorny paths the lost ones stray,
In moonlit realms where shadows play,
Their mournful cries the night reveals,
A dance of woe behind the veils.

Those who dare to cross this line,
To the shadows, they will be consigned,
No mortal eye shall pierce this seam,
No light shall touch this spectral dream.

For in the Briar's Veil they dwell,
Eternal bound, where secrets swell,
So heed the woods where shadows play,
And tread with care, or lose your way.

CONTENTS

CONTENTS

PROLOGUE

Environmental Protection Agency
Office of Regulatory Compliance and Investigation
1200 Pennsylvania Avenue, NW
Washington, D.C. 20460

Date: January 12, 2024

To: Mr. Daniel Price
Chief Executive Officer
Sunshine Homes Co.
789 Horizon Drive
Jupiter, Florida 33458

Subject: No Further Action (NFA) Determination
EPA Case Number: EPA-2023-01482

Dear Mr. Price,

The Environmental Protection Agency (EPA) has completed its review of Case Number EPA-2023-01482. Following the necessary investigations, assessments, and inspections, the EPA has determined that no further action is required in connection with this case.

Sunshine Homes Co. has complied with all regulatory requirements, and the EPA now considers the case closed. No additional measures are needed at this time, and no further oversight will be applied unless new information arises.

As part of the settlement, Sunshine Homes Co. is required to disclose the details of this action to all new home buyers of the properties impacted by Case Number EPA-2023-01482. These disclosures must be provided to ensure that future homeowners are fully informed of the property's history and any potential past concerns. Failure to comply with these disclosure requirements may result in further regulatory action.

This No Further Action (NFA) determination is based on the information available as of this letter. Should any new evidence or circumstances arise, the EPA reserves the right to revisit this determination and take any appropriate measures as necessary.

For any further inquiries regarding this matter, please contact Ms. Laura Jenkins, Senior Environmental Compliance Officer.

Sincerely,

Laura Jenkins
Senior Environmental Compliance Officer
Environmental Protection Agency

CC: Samuel Redford, Counsel for Sunshine Homes Co.

CHAPTER 1

Welcome To Briar Vale

The morning sun cast its pale light over the newly paved roads of Briar Vale, illuminating the fresh asphalt that gleamed darkly, like black glass under the gentle touch of daybreak. The air was crisp, still clinging to the lingering coolness of night, yet already whispering promises of the warmth to come. Briar Vale was a place where nature and human ambition met in an uneasy truce, where the ancient earth was smothered by the gleam of new development, like a fading lady's wrinkles concealed beneath a heavy mask of powder.

The community stretched out, a testament to the force of human will that sought to carve order from the wild. Rows of houses stood in cold, silent formation, their sharp edges and clean lines marking them as products of the initial Phase 1 construction boom, completed in 2021. Each home, with its immaculate façade and identical manicured lawns, seemed to declare uniformity and promise. Yet, in the bright morning light, they stood like soldiers in a hollow parade, ignorant of the shadows gathering within their walls.

To one side of the entrance, a modest sign rose from the earth, its polished wood and stone base standing as though to lend an air of permanence to this fragile place. The inscription, in elegant gold lettering, proclaimed: "Welcome to Briar Vale – A Sunshine Homes Community." But the paint was barely dry, much like the houses themselves, and even the land beneath it still seemed to remember the scars of its recent upheaval. Phase 1 had been completed years ago, but beyond its limits lay Phase 2, a different story altogether. Construction there had ground to a halt in 2022, leaving behind a ghostly array of half-built homes, skeletal frames, and plots overtaken by wild growth. Now, in 2024, after the long-forgotten project was acquired by Sunshine Homes, the first completed houses were only just being sold.

Beyond the sign, the road forked, one path curving away into the tidy familiarity of Phase 1, while the other led toward the seclusion of Phase 2, winding through a dense conservation area. The trees stood sentinel on either side, their branches stretching overhead, creating a darkened corridor where nature whispered in the shadows. It was a long, lonely drive, the wild pressing close as if to remind all who passed that here, nature had not been entirely subdued. The houses of Phase 2, handsome in their newness, felt hollow. Few of them were occupied, their driveways holding the occasional car, yet most stood vacant, their windows dark and unseeing, like the empty eyes of forgotten sentries. A strange stillness hung over the place, as if the land itself held its breath, waiting for something unseen to stir within the empty shells.

The unfinished state of the neighborhood only heightened the sense of isolation. While a few homes stood complete, the rest were little more than spectral frames or barren dirt plots, now reclaimed by the wilderness. Briar Vale's Phase 2 felt as though it were cut off from the world entirely, hidden behind the dense conservation area and a long, empty road that wound away into the distance. The nearest trace of civilization, the occupied homes of Phase 1, lay far out of sight, as if lost in another world.

As the road twisted deeper into the heart of Briar Vale, it neared the boundary of the conservation area, where man's fleeting efforts clashed with the eternal persistence of the natural world. The line was clear; on one side, the neat lawns and measured symmetry of Phase 2's houses, and on the other, wild grasses and ancient trees that had weathered centuries of change. The trees, towering oaks and cypress, swayed gently in the breeze, their rustling leaves speaking in low voices, too faint for all but the keenest ear. It was as though they conspired against the new structures that dared to encroach upon their domain.

Here, Phase 2 seemed forgotten by time. Even now, with the promise of new buyers, the houses stood in defiance of their surroundings, the few occupied homes stark against the desolation of overgrown lots and abandoned skeletons. The contrast was jarring, a clash between life and neglect, as though nature were biding its time, waiting patiently for the moment to reclaim what was rightfully hers.

The conservation area, thick with underbrush and shrouded beneath the broad canopies of oak and cypress, stood as a monument to endurance. The air here was different, cooler, heavier with the scent of decomposing leaves and damp earth. It was a reminder of what had once been, an ancient memory preserved in the heart of the land, untouched by the relentless march of time. To those who paused long enough to listen, the conservation area seemed to hum with a life of its own, a pulse that echoed the deep stillness of Briar Vale's empty streets.

Even now, as the sun climbed steadily into the sky, casting long, slender shadows from the trees that bordered the houses, a peculiar calm hung over Briar Vale. It was the calm of anticipation, like the still air before the gathering of a storm. The few souls who had taken residence in Phase 2 were early risers, perhaps drawn from their beds by the same subtle unease that permeated the atmosphere. They moved quietly, glancing out from behind their windows, each one feeling a faint, nameless dread stirring in their hearts. Perhaps it was the isolation, the unsettling silence that clung to the place like a shroud.

Briar Vale's Phase 2, for all its newness and promises, remained unfinished - an incomplete vision suspended between birth and decay. The area's history of delays and neglect clung to it like a shadow, a heavy presence that waited, as if the very ground beneath it demanded more before it would allow the place to breathe and come to life.

And so, Briar Vale lay in the morning light, an unfinished symphony of silence and sound, of new life and old secrets. The sun climbed steadily, indifferent to the whispers of the trees or the emptiness of the homes. The neighborhood waited, each house a silent sentinel in the rows, each shadow a reminder of the past that could not be entirely forgotten. Briar Vale, a place so new yet already so heavy with the weight of what it held, stood on the cusp of becoming, unaware of the darkness that would soon seep into its very foundations.

The sound of tires crunching over gravel announced the arrival of the Miller family, their SUV coming to a gentle stop in the driveway of their new home. The engine's hum ceased, leaving only the quiet murmur of the mid-morning breeze and the rustle of leaves from the distant conservation area. The house before them stood proudly, its fresh white paint gleaming under the sun's rays, as though it were a beacon of new beginnings.

Emma Miller, stepping out of the car, felt a mix of excitement and a touch of nervousness as she took in the sight before her. The house was magnificent, far more spacious than their cramped city apartment had ever been. Its two-story facade loomed before them, with large, mullioned windows that gleamed like the eyes of some great, watchful creature. The front door, painted a cheerful red, stood as a welcoming smile. An expanse of emerald lawn stretched out from the porch, flanked by neatly planted shrubs and a couple of young maple trees, their leaves whispering secrets to the morning air.

Emma inhaled deeply, savoring the fresh air, so different from the exhaust fumes and the staleness of city life. There was a hint of salt carried on the breeze from the nearby ocean, mingling with the earthy scent of grass and the faint perfume of the newly planted flowers lining the walk. She let out a sigh of contentment, her earlier anxieties melting away. This was what they needed, what she needed - a fresh start, a chance to leave behind the suffocating press of city crowds and the whispers that haunted the corners of her mind.

Beside her, John Miller closed the car door with a solid thud and stepped up to her side. He was a tall man, his hair dark with a touch of gray at the temples, his face showing the lines of years spent in the corporate grind. Yet here, in the open space of Briar Vale, there was a lightness about him, a sense of freedom that had been missing for far too long.

"Well, here we are," John said, his voice filled with a mix of satisfaction and relief. "What do you think, Emma? Our new home."

Emma smiled up at him, her green eyes shining. "It's beautiful, John. It really is. So much space…and the air! It smells so…clean."

She glanced around at the empty street and the stretch of untouched greenery beyond. "It's so far away from everything," she added, a note of awe in her voice. "But it's beautiful. I still can't believe we got all of this for the price." She shook her head, still marveling at their luck. "Feels like we're in our own little world."

John nodded, pride swelling as he took in the front yard. "Yeah, hard to believe we found something like this. But it's what we needed - a chance to slow down, take things at our own pace. The kids will have so much room to run around, and look," he pointed toward the edge of their lawn, "the conservation area is right there. It's like having a piece of wilderness in our backyard."

Emma's gaze wandered over the yard, taking in the peaceful quiet that surrounded their new home. As she turned her head toward the conservation area, she caught a flicker of movement. Two sleek, dark shapes darted across the lawn, moving with quick, silent grace. "Look, John," she whispered, pointing toward the trees at the edge of their property. "Cats." The pair of cats, almost identical in their sleekness, paused for a brief moment, their eyes glowing faintly in the morning light before disappearing into the thick brush of the woods. Emma watched them vanish into the shadows. "I guess we have some neighbors after all," she said with a small smile.

The children, freed from the confines of the car, were already exploring their new surroundings. Emily, the eldest, had her phone out, capturing the scene to share with her friends back in the city. She was a striking young girl, with long brown hair tied back in a ponytail, her expression a mix of teenage indifference and curiosity. Jack, her younger brother, had already darted across the lawn, inspecting the garden beds with a critical eye, while Owen, the youngest, stood at the edge of the driveway, staring up at the house with wide-eyed wonder.

"There aren't many neighbors, are there?" Emily remarked, looking up from her phone to survey the street. Indeed, the road was lined with empty houses, their driveways barren, their windows reflecting the sky like blank, unseeing eyes.

"No, not yet," John replied, "but that means more peace and quiet for us, right? And when the neighborhood fills up, we'll have a chance to make some new friends."

Emma nodded, though her eyes lingered on the empty houses for a moment longer. She couldn't shake the feeling that they were being watched, even though there was no one around. The sense of emptiness was almost palpable, the silence pressing in on her ears. Shaking off the feeling, she turned to her husband.

"I just hope this is the fresh start we've been looking for," she said softly, her voice tinged with a hint of uncertainty.

John smiled reassuringly, wrapping an arm around her shoulders. "It will be, Emma. This is a new chapter for us, away from the city, away from everything. We'll make it work. I promise."

Emma leaned into his embrace, finding comfort in his presence. She wanted to believe him, to trust that this new home would be a haven, a place where they could finally find peace. The sun casting long shadows over the front yard, as she tried to imagine the laughter of their children filling the house, the warmth of family dinners, the quiet evenings spent together.

As they stood there, a car approached, gliding smoothly along the newly paved street. Emma nudged John, nodding towards the sleek sedan that was pulling up to the curb. "That must be her," she said, a note of excitement in her voice.

John nodded, his eyes following the car as it came to a stop. A moment later, Mary Kendrick stepped out, her bright smile as welcoming as the morning sun. She was a woman of late thirties, with shoulder-length blonde hair and a professional demeanor that managed to be both reassuring and efficient. In her hand, she held a small leather folder, and on a keyring, the brass keys to the Miller's new home gleamed in the sunlight.

"Good morning, Mr. and Mrs. Miller!" Mary called out as she approached, her heels clicking smartly on the walkway. "I hope you're ready to make Briar Vale your new home."

Emma beamed at her, extending a hand. "Good morning, Mary! We've been looking forward to this day. The house looks beautiful."

Mary shook Emma's hand warmly, then turned to John. "And Mr. Miller, it's a pleasure to see you again. I've got everything you need right here." She held up the keys and the folder with a flourish. "Shall we go inside?"

John returned her smile, feeling a mix of relief and excitement. "Absolutely," he said. "Let's see our new home."

Mary led the way to the front door, the keys jangling in her hand. She unlocked the door with a practiced motion and pushed it open, stepping aside to let the Millers enter first. The door swung open with a soft creak, revealing the spacious, sunlit living room beyond.

Emma stepped inside, her eyes wide with wonder as she took in the sight. The room was filled with light, the large mullioned windows offering a view of the front yard and the distant conservation area. The hardwood floors gleamed underfoot, polished to perfection, and the high ceilings gave the room an airy, open feel. It was a perfect canvas, ready to be filled with their lives, their memories.

John followed, his gaze sweeping over the room. He could already see their furniture in place, pictures on the walls, the sound of their children's laughter filling the space. It was everything they had hoped for, a fresh start away from the hustle and chaos of city life.

Mary entered behind them, her smile growing as she saw their reactions. "It's lovely, isn't it?" she said, pride evident in her voice. "This house has a great layout, lots of natural light. You'll find it's perfect for family living. And the neighborhood is quiet, just a few other families for now, but it'll grow. Briar Vale is really going to be something special."

She handed the keys to John, who took them with a nod of thanks. "Here are your keys," she said, "and this is the final paperwork." She offered the leather folder to him. "Just a few things to go over, some disclosures and acknowledgments. It's mostly formalities, and things you have already seen, but it's important to have everything in order."

John opened the folder, his eyes skimming the documents. He paused on a page marked "Disclosure of materials used in construction." His brow furrowed slightly as he reread the disclosure concerning a notice of environmental regulation action. A small knot of unease formed in his stomach. He glanced briefly at Emma, who was walking around the room, touching the walls and peering out the windows, a smile on her face.

"Everything looks in order," he said, as he signed it, and turning to Mary with a smile. "Thank you, Mary. You've been a great help."

Mary's smile widened, though there was a flicker of something behind her eyes, a brief hesitation that vanished as quickly as it had appeared. "Of course, Mr. Miller. If you have any questions or need anything at all, please don't hesitate to call. We want to make sure your transition into Briar Vale is as smooth as possible. You know, your neighbors next door, George and Ethel Thompson, are wonderful people. They just retired here, and I sold them their house about three months ago. Very friendly. I'm sure you'll get along well."

Emma returned to John's side, her face glowing with happiness. "It's perfect, isn't it?" she said, looking up at him. "I think we're really going to be happy here."

John nodded, slipping an arm around her shoulders. "Yes," he said, the words coming more easily now, "I think we are."

Mary watched them with a soft smile, then excused herself, leaving the Millers to their new home. As she walked down the front steps and towards her car, John closed the door behind her. The sound of the door clicking shut echoed through the empty house, settling into the silence that followed.

The living room, bathed in the warm glow of the late morning sun, seemed to embrace them, promising peace and comfort. Yet, as John slipped the keys into his pocket, the faintest whisper of unease brushed against his thoughts, like a shadow passing over the sun. He pushed it away, focusing on Emma's smile, on the promise of a new beginning.

The house stood quietly around them, its walls solid and strong, its floors gleaming. Outside, the wind rustled through the trees, a soft sigh that went unheard. The Millers were home.

It wasn't long before the stillness gave way to a new rhythm, the quiet solace replaced by the shuffling of boxes and the clinking of furniture against the walls. The sounds of movers echoed through the open door, their efficiency underscored by murmured conversations and the occasional scrape of heavy objects. After months of silence, the house was coming to life again, embracing the hustle and bustle of a family settling into its bones.

John Miller, sensing the mounting chaos of the moving process, decided it was time to give his sons a respite from the clamor. He called out to Jack and Owen, who had been peering curiously into every open box, their youthful excitement barely contained. "Boys, come on out! Let's take a break," he said, waving them towards the back door. The prospect of fresh air and a break from unpacking was met with eager nods.

John led the way, pushing open the sliding glass door that led to the backyard. It glided open with a smooth, whispering sound, revealing the expanse of green beyond. The backyard was wide and open, a stark contrast to the cramped spaces they had known in the city. The lawn stretched out before them, bordered by a low wooden fence, beyond which lay the edge of the conservation area. Tall trees loomed in the distance, their branches swaying gently in the afternoon breeze, casting long, shifting shadows over the grass.

Jack, the older of the two boys at thirteen, was the first to step onto the lawn. His eyes widened as he took in the space, a grin spreading across his face. "This is awesome!" he exclaimed, running a few steps ahead. Owen, his eleven-year-old brother, followed, his face lit with a similar excitement. The two boys had been yearning for a place to stretch their legs, to run and play without the confines of concrete walls and busy streets.

John chuckled at their enthusiasm, a sense of satisfaction warming him. "Pretty great, isn't it?" he said, pulling a small package from his back pocket. The boys turned to look, curiosity piqued. John held up a sleek BB gun, its metal barrel catching the light. He had bought it in anticipation of this moment, knowing how much his sons would enjoy the freedom of the outdoors.

"Wow, a BB gun!" Jack exclaimed, his eyes wide with delight. Owen's face mirrored his brother's excitement, his hands reaching out to touch the gun. John handed it to Jack, his fingers guiding the boy's hands to hold it properly. "Careful now, it's not a toy," he said with a fatherly tone, though there was a twinkle in his eye.

John led them to the far end of the yard, where he had set up a few empty cans on an old wooden stump. The makeshift targets stood stark against the green of the grass, waiting to be knocked down. He showed Jack how to load the BB gun, the small pellets dropping into the chamber with a satisfying click. Owen watched intently, his eyes never leaving his father's hands.

"This is a good spot for target practice," John said, his voice carrying a note of contentment. "Plenty of space, no one around to bother us. It's far different from the city, boys. Here, we can do things our own way."

Jack raised the BB gun, his hands steady under his father's guidance. He squinted, taking aim at the nearest can, and pulled the trigger. The gun let out a sharp pop, the pellet flying through the air. It hit the can with a satisfying ping, sending it tumbling from the stump. Jack let out a triumphant cheer, his face lighting up with pride. Owen clapped his hands, his laughter ringing out in the quiet of the afternoon.

John smiled, watching his sons, a sense of peace settling over him. This was what he had envisioned - a place where they could be free, where they could grow and learn without the constant constraints of city life. The backyard, with its open space and quiet solitude, felt like a sanctuary.

He turned to Owen, handing him the BB gun. "Your turn, buddy. Remember, keep it steady and take your time." Owen took the gun, his small hands gripping it with determination. John guided him, standing behind him to help with his aim. The boy took a breath, focused on the can, and pulled the trigger. The pellet missed, landing harmlessly in the grass, but Owen laughed, undeterred by the miss.

As the boys took turns shooting, their laughter filling the air, John's mind drifted to the real gun he had brought with them, now safely placed out of reach in the bedroom closet. It was a different kind of power, one that held a sense of responsibility and danger. He knew the importance of teaching his sons respect for such things, the balance between freedom and safety.

Casually, he mentioned it, his tone light but firm. "You know, I've got a real gun in the house, I keep in our closet. It looks a lot like this BB gun, but there's a big difference. That gun is not a toy - it's for protection, and only for the most serious emergencies. If you see it, you boys are never to go near it, not even out of curiosity. Guns aren't something to play around with; they're dangerous, and the consequences can be life-changing.

Even this BB gun here - it may seem harmless, but it still needs to be handled with respect and caution. You don't ever point it at each other, even as a joke, and you always need to know exactly where it's pointing at all times. That's how accidents happen, when people stop paying attention. From now on, treat this... treat every gun like it's loaded and dangerous, because that's how serious this is. Understood?"

Jack nodded solemnly, the weight of his father's words sinking in. Owen, though younger, mirrored his brother's expression, his eyes wide with understanding. They both knew their father meant what he said, that this was a matter of trust and safety.

"Good," John said, his voice softening. "Now, how about we see who can knock down the most cans?"

The challenge was met with eager grins, the boys turning back to their targets with renewed focus. As the afternoon sun cast long shadows across the yard, the sound of BBs hitting cans and the laughter of children filled the air, mingling with the whispering of the trees. It was a moment of joy, a glimpse of the happiness they hoped to find in their new home.

John watched his sons, his heart light. Here, in this quiet backyard, far from the noise and bustle of the city, he felt a sense of contentment he hadn't known in years.

Several hours hence, the movers completed their laborious task. What had been a void of emptiness now lay transformed into a sprawling empire of boxes, each one a silent sentinel of the new domain. The sun had begun its descent, casting a warm, golden glow through the windows of the Miller's new home. Shadows stretched long and thin across the freshly painted walls, the light slowly retreating as evening settled in. The once bustling activity of moving day had quieted, leaving an air of calm that permeated through the house. The movers had gone, their work complete, and now the Millers found themselves alone in their new domain, each settling into their own corner, embracing the routines that brought them comfort.

John Miller moved quietly through the hallways, his footsteps softened by the plush carpet underfoot. He had always enjoyed this time of day, the transition from the busy hours of the afternoon to the quiet promise of night. It was a time when the house seemed to breathe, taking in the events of the day and letting them fade into the shadows. He felt a sense of satisfaction, a deep, quiet joy in seeing his family adapting to their new surroundings.

He paused at Owen's room, the door slightly ajar. Pushing it open gently, he peeked inside. The room was awash with the soft light of a small lamp, casting a warm circle around the boy, who was engrossed in his play. Owen was seated on the floor, surrounded by pieces of his Gravitrax set, his fingers deftly arranging the tracks and marble runs. His tousled brown hair fell over his eyes as he worked, his face a mask of concentration. The marbles clicked and clattered as they sped through the course he had constructed, looping and spiraling with precision.

John smiled to himself, leaning against the doorframe. Owen was lost in his own world, his imagination taking flight with the twists and turns of the marble run. There was a peacefulness to the boy's absorption, a contentment that spoke to the innocence of childhood. Here, in the quiet of his room, Owen was safe, untouched by the worries that troubled his parents.

"Having fun, buddy?" John asked softly, not wanting to break the spell of concentration.

Owen looked up, his eyes bright with excitement. "Dad! Look at this! I made a new track, and it goes all the way around!" He pointed eagerly to his creation, his small hand tracing the path the marbles would take.

John stepped into the room, crouching down beside his son. "That's impressive, Owen," he said, his voice filled with genuine admiration. "You're really good at this. Maybe one day, you'll be an engineer."

Owen beamed at the praise, his worries and doubts melting away. "Yeah, maybe," he said, already turning back to his task, his hands moving with renewed purpose.

John watched him for a moment longer, his heart swelling with affection, before standing up and quietly stepping out of the room. He pulled the door to a near-close, leaving it ajar just enough to hear the soft clicks of the marbles as he moved on down the hall.

Next, he made his way to Jack's room. The door was firmly shut, but the faint, muffled sounds of electronic gunfire and eerie music seeped through the wood. John knocked lightly, then opened the door to find his son seated on his bed, his eyes glued to the screen of a handheld gaming console. Beside him, perched on a stack of boxes, was Jack's laptop, streaming a movie. The unsettling sounds of a man trapped in a deep, dark pool added an eerie ambiance to the room. Jack's face was illuminated by the blue light of the handheld device, his expression one of intense focus. He wore a pair of large headphones, the kind that completely covered his ears, shutting out the rest of the world.

Jack was deeply engrossed in a horror video game, his thumbs dancing over the controls with practiced ease. The screen flashed with scenes of dark, haunted corridors, the protagonist moving stealthily through shadows, ready to confront whatever ghostly terror awaited.

John watched his son for a moment, amused by the sight. Jack was at that age where he craved the thrill of the unknown, the adrenaline rush of facing imaginary dangers. It was a phase John himself remembered well, though it sometimes worried him how drawn Jack was to the macabre.

"Hey, Jack," John called out, raising his voice slightly to be heard over the sounds emanating from the headphones.

Jack, startled, looked up, pulling one earphone aside. "Oh, hey, Dad," he said, his voice distracted. He glanced back at the screen, fingers twitching to return to the game.

John grinned. "Just checking in. Everything alright?"

Jack nodded, his eyes still flicking to the game. "Yeah, everything's fine. This place is kinda cool, I guess. A lot of space. It's just...kinda quiet."

John chuckled. "You'll get used to it. Give it time. And maybe take a break from the screen once in a while. Go outside, get some fresh air."

Jack nodded again, but John knew the boy's thoughts were already back in his game. He backed out of the room, leaving Jack to his virtual ghosts. Closing the door, John continued down the hallway to Emily's room, the last stop on his round.

Emily's door was partially open, and John could hear the faint hum of conversation. He knocked lightly before pushing the door open. Her laptop was opened in the corner of the room on a box, streaming "The Pool" as Emily sprawled on her bed, her phone held up above her face, her long brown hair spread out like a halo on the pillow. She wore a slight frown as she talked, the light from her phone casting a soft glow on her features.

"Ugh, it's so boring here," Emily was saying, her voice laced with teenage exasperation. "There's nothing to do. I mean, I can't even get decent Wi-Fi half the time." She listened to the response on the other end of the call, rolling her eyes dramatically. "I know, right? I miss the city already. At least there was stuff going on."

John leaned against the doorframe, a smile tugging at his lips. "Complaining about our new home already, Em?" he teased gently.

Emily glanced up, not surprised by his presence. "I'm just saying, Dad, it's kinda dead here. I mean, what am I supposed to do all day?"

John shrugged, stepping into the room. "Give it a chance. You might find you like the quiet. And hey, you've got all this space to yourself. Think of it as a personal retreat."

15

Emily sighed, but there was a hint of a smile on her lips. "Yeah, maybe," she conceded, sitting up. "I guess it's kinda nice to have my own room."

John nodded, satisfied. "See? It's not so bad. You'll get used to it. And you've got your phone, your friends..."

"Yeah, yeah," Emily said, waving him off with a laugh. "I'll survive."

John smiled, content. He backed out of her room, giving her a wink before closing the door. He moved back down the hallway, his rounds complete. Each of his children was safe, settled into their own world, finding their place in this new house. The house, with its quiet rooms and stillness, felt more like home with each passing hour.

As John made his way downstairs to continue unpacking, the evening shadows deepened, and the house, now gently illuminated by the soft glow of lamps, was filled with the comforting sounds of family life. Owen's marbles clinked, Jack's game buzzed faintly, and Emily's voice drifted through the walls, a soothing murmur of youth settling into the new environment.

The night pressed closer, wrapping the house in a quiet stillness that seemed to welcome the end of the day. As time passed, the sounds of the children gradually faded, each settling into the calm of sleep. John's footsteps echoed softly as he made his way to the master bedroom, ready to join Emma and leave the day's concerns behind. The subtle chill he had felt earlier now seemed absorbed by the night's embrace, replaced by a soothing sense of peaceful normalcy.

"The kids are finally in bed," John said softly as he stepped into the master bedroom, closing the door behind him with a quiet click. He leaned against the doorframe for a moment, a tired smile on his lips. "I don't know if they'll sleep, considering the newness of the house. But they're down, at least."

The room was dimly lit by the soft glow of the bedside

lamp, its warm light casting gentle shadows that danced across the walls. Boxes were stacked in one corner, half-unpacked, their contents spilling out in the form of books, clothes, and trinkets, the detritus of a life that was still being organized. The bed, large and inviting, was one of the few things that had been properly set up, its fresh linens a stark white against the darkness of the room.

Emma looked up from where she was sitting on the edge of the bed, her feet curled beneath her. She had been flipping through a magazine, though her eyes hadn't really been on the pages. At John's words, she smiled, setting the magazine aside. "It's a lot to take in," she agreed, her voice carrying a note of weariness. "Everything is so new and different. But they'll get used to it. We all will."

John nodded, pushing away from the door and crossing the room to join her. He sat down beside her, the bed dipping slightly under his weight. For a moment, they sat in silence, taking comfort in the quiet, the sense of being alone together. The day had been long, filled with the chaos of moving, the constant motion of boxes and furniture, the noise of unfamiliar sounds. Now, in the stillness of the night, there was a sense of relief, a chance to breathe.

John reached out, taking Emma's hand in his, his thumb gently stroking the back of her hand. "This place already feels different," he said quietly, his eyes meeting hers. "It's like...we can finally start fresh, you know? Leave everything else behind."

Emma leaned against him, resting her head on his shoulder. She let out a soft sigh, her eyes closing for a moment. "I know what you mean," she murmured. "There's something about this house...something peaceful. It's like we're far away from all the noise and rush of before. Just us and the kids. It feels right. I think this will be good."

John smiled, his hand moving to her hair, his fingers combing through the soft strands. He had always loved her hair, the way it caught the light, the way it felt under his fingers. It was one of those small, intimate things that connected them, a touch that spoke of years spent together, of moments both big and small.

"It's what we needed," he said, his voice low and tender. "A chance to slow down, to be together more. I know things haven't been easy lately, but I think…no, I believe this is the right place for us. A place to rebuild, to make new memories."

Emma turned her face up towards his, her eyes shining in the soft light. "I believe that too," she said. "It's been so much, everything all at once, but now, sitting here with you, it feels like we can handle it. Like we can handle anything as long as we're together."

John leaned down, pressing a gentle kiss to her forehead, then her cheek, finally finding her lips. The kiss was slow and unhurried, a gentle meeting of souls that spoke of love and understanding. Emma's hand slid up to rest on the back of his neck, her fingers tangling in his hair. It was a familiar touch, one that carried years of shared history, of nights spent just like this one, finding solace in each other's arms.

As they kissed, the worries of the day seemed to melt away, replaced by the warmth of their connection. They pulled back slightly, their foreheads resting together, breathing in the same air, feeling the steady rhythm of each other's hearts. The room around them, with its half-unpacked boxes and the glow of the bedside lamp, faded into the background, leaving only the two of them, alone in their shared space.

John ran his fingers through Emma's hair, a soft, repetitive motion that brought comfort. He could feel the tension in his shoulders easing, the stress of the move and the uncertainty of the future dissolving under the gentle weight of her presence. Here, in the quiet of their bedroom, there was only peace, a sense of safety that he hadn't felt in a long time.

"I love you," he said softly, the words coming easily, naturally. They were words he had said many times, but tonight they felt new, like a promise renewed. "I love you, and I'm so glad we're here. This is our place, our home."

Emma smiled, her eyes soft and full of love. "I love you too,

John," she replied. "This is our new beginning. I can feel it."

They lay back on the bed, sinking into the comfort of the pillows, their bodies still entwined. The room was filled with the soft sounds of their breathing, the gentle rustle of fabric as they moved closer. John's hand moved to rest on Emma's waist, his fingers tracing slow circles against her skin. Her hand found his, their fingers intertwining, a silent gesture of unity.

As the night deepened, they turned towards each other, their movements slow and unhurried. Their touches grew more intimate, each caress a declaration of love, each kiss a promise of a future together. In the sanctuary of their bedroom, surrounded by the quiet of their new home, they found a moment of pure connection, a moment that spoke of all the things words could not convey.

The house around them, with its silent rooms and the soft hum of night, seemed to hold its breath, as if sharing in the intimacy of the moment. The shadows that danced on the walls, the light that pooled on the floor, all bore witness to the love that was renewed, the bond that was strengthened.

In the quiet of the night, with the stars shining brightly above, Emma and John found each other, found solace in the touch of skin against skin, in the warmth of their shared embrace. It was a moment of new beginnings, a moment where the past was left behind, and only the promise of the future remained.

As the darkness enveloped them, they held each other close, their bodies entwined, their hearts beating as one. The world outside their bedroom faded away, leaving only the two of them, together, in the place that was now their home.

CHAPTER 2

Uneasy Neighbors

T he early morning light streamed through the tall, arched windows of the Millers' kitchen, casting a pale golden hue across the gleaming granite countertops. The faint scent of fresh coffee lingered in the air, mingling with the crisp smell of a new home. The house was unusually quiet, the usual chaos of three children momentarily subdued as they slept. Only the soft ticking of the clock above the stove broke the silence, its steady rhythm marking the start of a new day.

John Miller stood before a mirror hung on the kitchen wall, his reflection staring back at him with a furrowed brow. His hands moved deftly, yet with a hint of uncharacteristic hesitation, as he adjusted his tie, the deep navy silk seeming out of place against the casual atmosphere of the new house. He frowned, tugging at the knot, feeling it constrict around his throat as if it were a noose tightening. He loosened it with a quick, frustrated pull and started over, his fingers trembling slightly.

Emma watched him from the doorway, her head tilted to one side, a concerned expression clouding her features. She was dressed in a simple morning robe, her brown hair falling loosely around her shoulders. Her green eyes, usually bright with morning cheer, were now shadowed with worry. She stepped into the kitchen, her bare feet silent on the cool tile floor, and approached John.

"John, are you alright?" she asked softly, her voice barely breaking the stillness. "You seem... tense."

John's eyes met hers in the mirror. He forced a smile, a poor imitation of his usual confident grin, and turned to face her. He took a deep breath, trying to dispel the sense of unease that had settled in his chest like a weight. "It's nothing," he said, waving a hand dismissively. "Just first-day jitters, I suppose. New job, new expectations. I'm sure it'll pass once I get into the swing of things."

Emma stepped closer, placing a gentle hand on his arm. She could feel the tension in his muscles, taut like a bowstring. "You've started new jobs before, John," she said, her voice low and soothing. "You've never been this nervous. Is something else bothering you?"

John looked away, his gaze drifting to the window, where the leaves of the oak tree in the backyard swayed gently in the morning breeze. He hesitated before speaking, his voice low and subdued. "I... I don't know. I think it's just stress from everything. Maybe just new work jitters, Em. You know how it is, starting over in a new place, trying to make a good impression. I can't help but feel... on edge. I keep waking up at night, my mind racing. It's just so quiet here."

He hesitated, unsure whether to share the rest. The truth was, he'd been having trouble sleeping for the past few nights - the absence of the usual city noise was taking longer to get used to than he'd expected. Now, the only sounds were the wind rustling through the trees and the distant hum from the conservation area, which sometimes seemed to carry faint whispers when he was on the edge of sleep. He knew it was just the lack of rest combined with his vivid imagination. He'd always been good at spotting patterns where others saw nothing, a skill that made him successful at software development. But that ability wasn't helpful when the patterns his mind conjured were irrational. It felt paranoid to even acknowledge the whispers, let alone speak of them. He was sure it was just his mind playing tricks on him, struggling to adjust from the constant noise of the city to the unsettling silence of Briar Vale.

Emma's hand tightened on his arm. She forced a smile and reached up to brush a strand of hair from his forehead. 'It's just the stress of the new job, John. Moving from the city to all this quiet... it's a big change. We just need to give it some time to adjust. I'm sure things will settle down soon. You're strong, and we'll get through this together.' She leaned in and pressed a light kiss to his cheek, her lips warm against his cool skin, hoping her reassurance would ease his visible tension.

John nodded, though his eyes remained distant, his thoughts still elsewhere. He straightened his tie once more, this time more successfully, and adjusted the collar of his shirt. He picked up his phone from the counter, glancing at the screen where a new message had appeared, a reminder about his meeting later that morning. He read it quickly, the familiar routine grounding him momentarily, before slipping the phone back into his pocket.

"I'd better go," he said, his voice steady now, though the hint of worry still lingered in his eyes. He picked up his briefcase, the leather smooth and familiar under his hand, a small comfort in the face of his unease. "I'll call you at lunch," he added, smiling at Emma, the expression not quite reaching his eyes.

Emma nodded, watching as he made his way to the door. "Good luck," she called after him, her voice filled with forced cheer. "You're going to do great."

John paused at the door, turning back to look at her. For a moment, his face softened, the lines of worry easing as he took in the sight of his wife standing in the warm, sunlit kitchen. "Thanks, Em," he said softly. He opened the door, the morning air rushing in with a cool, gentle breeze, and stepped outside. The door closed behind him with a soft click, the sound echoing in the quiet house.

Emma stood alone in the kitchen, the silence pressing in around her. She turned to the window, watching as John's car pulled out of the driveway and disappeared down the street. She wrapped her arms around herself, suddenly feeling the chill of the morning air. A sense of unease settled over her, mirroring the one John had confessed to moments earlier. She shook her head, trying to dispel the feeling.

"It's just the newness," she murmured to herself, echoing her own reassurances. "We'll get used to it. We just need time."

She glanced around the empty kitchen, the light and shadows playing across the walls, and as her eyes moved, something caught her attention. In the mirror above the sideboard, she thought she saw a dark figure standing just behind her, a shape that didn't belong. Her heart skipped a beat, fear surging through her. She turned sharply, eyes wide, but there was nothing - only the soft flutter of the curtains in the breeze and the faint hum of the refrigerator.

She blinked, looking back at the mirror, and saw only her own pale, frightened face staring back at her, wide-eyed and ghostly in the dim light. Her breathing was shallow, her pulse racing. It had been a trick of the light, she told herself, just a shadow cast by the trees outside, or perhaps her own reflection caught at an odd angle.

But doubt gnawed at the edges of her thoughts, whispering that maybe it was something more. Maybe her condition was starting to rear its head again, playing tricks on her, distorting reality. The medication had kept her stable for so long, but she had been off it for a while now. Perhaps she had been too confident in her own strength, too eager to leave that part of her life behind. Maybe the stress of the move, the new environment, could do things - make the lines between reality and imagination blur.

She had convinced herself she didn't need the pills anymore, that she was past those dark days of confusion and fear. John had stood by her through it all, his unwavering love the one thing she could always count on. But now, standing alone in the kitchen of a foreign home with the lingering image of that dark figure in her mind, she couldn't help but wonder if the newness of it all - moving from the city with its hustle and bustle, away from her career, into such a quiet suburban life - was too much a shift. The house was quiet, the silence pressing in on her like a living thing, amplifying every creak, every whisper of the wind outside. Without John by her side in that moment, the stillness felt heavier, and the doubts were harder to ignore.

Emma closed her eyes, taking a deep breath, willing herself to stay calm. "It's nothing," she whispered. "Just my mind playing tricks." She repeated the words like a mantra, trying to push away the lingering sense of unease.

When she opened her eyes again, the kitchen was as it had always been, ordinary and undisturbed, filled with the gentle morning light. But the feeling of being watched, the sense that something was just out of sight, refused to leave her, lingering like a shadow at the edge of her thoughts. She shook her head, turning away from the mirror, telling herself it was all in her head, nothing more.

The morning unfolded slowly in the Miller household. The children were still abed, and the house, for now at least, remained quiet. Emma calmed her nerves and started to take solace in the silence, letting the peace wash over her as she sipped her coffee in the kitchen, the remnants of John's unease lingering in the corners of her mind. She tried to focus on the rhythm of everyday life, the familiar hum of the refrigerator, the occasional creak of the house settling into itself. She was just beginning to relax when a sharp, unexpected knock echoed through the stillness, making her jump and spill a few drops of coffee onto her hand.

Frowning, Emma set her cup down on the counter and wiped her hand with a nearby dish towel. She glanced towards the front door, wondering who could be calling so early in the day. The neighborhood had seemed almost deserted since they'd moved in, the other houses standing silent and empty, like sentinels in the bright Florida sun. Perhaps it was a delivery - she had ordered new curtains online, hoping to add a touch of warmth to the bare windows.

The knocking came again, more insistent this time, rapping sharply against the solid wood of the door. Emma hurried down the hallway, her footsteps muffled by the thick carpet, and peered through the peephole. A distorted image met her gaze: a small figure with a shock of white hair, clutching what appeared to be a round, covered dish.

Emma opened the door cautiously, the bright sunlight flooding in, and found herself face-to-face with an elderly woman. The woman's face was heavily lined, her skin like parchment, and her eyes, a faded blue, were framed by a halo of thin white hair that blew gently in the breeze. She wore a faded floral dress, its colors muted with age, and a pair of sensible shoes. In her hands, she held a pie, covered with a delicate lace cloth.

"Good morning, dear!" the woman exclaimed in a voice that was surprisingly strong, given her frail appearance. Her smile revealed a set of perfectly aligned, gleaming white teeth, stark against her weathered face. "I'm Agatha Cartwright, your neighbor from down the road. I thought I'd drop by to welcome you to Briar Vale."

Emma forced a smile, surprised by the sudden appearance of this neighbor who seemed to materialize out of nowhere. "Oh, thank you!" she said, her voice bright with the politeness she had learned to muster in such situations. "It's so nice to meet you. I'm Emma Miller. We've just moved in, as you can see. Still settling down, really."

Agatha's smile widened, her eyes crinkling at the corners. "I know how it is, dear. Moving can be so overwhelming. I thought you might appreciate a little treat. It's an old family recipe - apple pie. My mother used to make it for all the new neighbors back when I was a girl. A little taste of home to make you feel welcome." She extended the pie towards Emma, the lace cover slipping slightly to reveal a golden-brown crust beneath.

Emma hesitated for a brief moment, taken aback by the sudden hospitality, then reached out to take the pie. As her fingers brushed against the lace, she caught a whiff of its aroma. Instead of the sweet, comforting scent of apples and cinnamon, a strange, sour undertone lingered in the air, like the smell of rotten apples left out in the heat. Emma's smile faltered, but she quickly recovered, masking her unease with a gracious nod.

"That's so kind of you, Mrs. Cartwright," she said, taking the pie into her hands. It was unexpectedly heavy, the warmth of it seeping through the thin cloth. "We haven't had much time to meet the neighbors yet. It's been a whirlwind since we got here."

Agatha waved a hand dismissively. "Oh, don't worry about that, dear. There aren't many of us in this part of the neighborhood. But I'm sure you'll settle in just fine. Briar Vale is a lovely place, truly lovely. And it's always nice to see new faces. You and your family will be a wonderful addition."

As Emma looked up from the pie, she saw Agatha's face soften. The older woman tilted her head, as if recalling something. "Oh, dear, I almost forgot to mention - I'm terribly sorry about all the cats." She gave Emma an apologetic smile, her eyes twinkling with a hint of mischief.

Emma blinked in surprise. "Cats?"

Agatha nodded, chuckling. "Yes, my Pixie - my little outdoor cat - well, she must've found herself a suitor. Now, there's quite a few kittens wandering about. I've been trying to find them homes, but you know how it is. They're quick, and they like to explore. I do hope they haven't been a nuisance."

Emma's thoughts flashed back to the previous morning when she had spotted two little kittens darting through the yard and disappearing into the brush. She shook her head slightly. "No, not at all. I did see a couple yesterday; they ran into the woods. If there's anything we can do to help find them homes, just let me know."

Agatha smiled and waved a hand dismissively. "Oh, I wouldn't want to burden you with that, dear, but it's kind of you to offer. If you hear any meowing at night, though, it's probably one of Pixie's little ones. I do hope they aren't too much trouble - sometimes, they have a mind of their own."

Emma smiled faintly, unsure of what else to say.

Agatha gave a knowing look, her smile faltering just slightly. "But if they start lingering too close to the house, do give me a knock. I wouldn't want Pixie's brood to bother your children. Cats have a funny way of sensing things... places."

Emma's smile tightened, the strange comment heightening her unease. "I'm sure we'll be fine, but thank you for the warning."

Then Agatha took a step back, preparing to leave, her expression turning serious. She paused for a moment, her gaze lingering on Emma with an intensity that was hard to ignore.

"If you ever need anything, anything at all, you just let me know, dear. I live just down across the street, the one with the blue shutters. You can't miss it." Her voice dropped to a conspiratorial whisper. "And do be careful out here, Emma. It can be... lonely sometimes. Not everything is as it seems." With that, Agatha turned and shuffled away, her small frame hunched against the breeze.

Emma watched her go, a frown creasing her forehead. The old woman's words hung in the air, unsettling in their vagueness. She closed the door slowly, the lock clicking into place with a solid sound. She stood in the hallway for a moment, the pie still in her hands, before making her way back to the kitchen.

Setting the pie down on the counter, Emma pulled the lace cover away, revealing the crust beneath. At first glance, it appeared perfectly normal, a well-made pastry with a delicate lattice top. But as she leaned in to take a closer look, the sour odor hit her again, stronger this time, making her stomach churn. She wrinkled her nose, lifting the pie closer to her face, and inhaled cautiously.

The smell was overwhelming - decay mixed with a sickly sweetness, as if the apples inside had rotted, turning the once delectable treat into something vile. Emma gagged, stepping back and holding the pie at arm's length. She glanced around, looking for a place to dispose of it, her eyes settling on the trash can under the sink. She hurried over, lifting the lid and dropping the pie inside with a dull thud. The smell lingered in the air, clinging to the kitchen like a miasma.

Emma closed the trash can lid and opened the windows, letting the fresh air cleanse the space. She leaned against the counter, breathing deeply, trying to shake off the nausea. Her phone buzzed on the counter, a sharp vibration that made her jump. She picked it up, seeing John's name on the screen. A small smile tugged at her lips as she opened the message.

John: How's everything? Settling in?

Emma quickly typed a response, her fingers tapping out a message.

Emma: Good. Just met a neighbor. Old lady named Agatha. Brought us a pie, but it smelled awful. Threw it out.

She hit send, watching as the message was delivered. She stared at the phone for a moment, then set it down, her thoughts drifting back to Agatha's parting words. "Not everything is as it seems." The phrase echoed in her mind, a cryptic warning that seemed to take root, intertwining with her own growing sense of unease.

The phone buzzed again, breaking her reverie.

John: Strange. Maybe she's just old and doesn't notice. I'm sure it's nothing. Don't worry. See you tonight. Love you.

Emma read the message, her heart lifting slightly. She typed a quick reply.

Emma: Love you too. See you tonight.

She set the phone down, the familiar routine of their exchange offering a small comfort.

As the morning approached its peak, the sun hung high in the sky, casting bright, dappled shadows across the streets of Briar Vale. The warmth of the day was already settling in, but the lingering freshness from the early hours still clung to the air. Moisture from the humid night clung to the lawns, sparkling like tiny diamonds in the sunlight. Emma stepped out onto the front porch, tying her shoelaces with deliberate care, feeling the comforting pressure of her familiar routine. Her running shoes, worn and molded to the shape of her feet, were a testament to countless miles spent chasing solace and clarity. The rhythmic thud of her feet against the pavement was her meditation, a way to untangle the threads of her thoughts and let the world slip away, if only for a short while.

She set off at a light jog, her breath syncing with the beat of her steps, her muscles loosening with each stride. The neighborhood was silent, save for the occasional rustle of leaves stirred by the breeze or the distant chirping of birds. It was a different kind of quiet from the city, a stillness that seemed almost too perfect, as though the world was holding its breath. Emma's mind drifted to her conversation with Agatha, the old woman's cryptic words lingering like a shadow at the edges of her consciousness. "Not everything is as it seems." The phrase echoed with each step, mingling with the faint sour smell that had clung to the pie.

As Emma turned the corner onto Sycamore Lane, the front of the Thompson house came into view. It was a modest, single-story home with a neat garden out front, the kind that spoke of quiet, contented lives. A white picket fence bordered the property, flowers spilling over in a riot of color. The house, like most in Briar Vale, was new but built to look charmingly old-fashioned, with a deep porch and a rocking chair swaying gently in the breeze.

To her surprise, Emma saw two figures sitting on the porch. George and Ethel Thompson were side by side, their expressions fixed, their eyes staring blankly at the street. George, a man in his seventies with a thin frame, had a shock of white hair that stood out starkly against his tanned skin. Ethel, equally elderly, sat with her hands folded neatly in her lap, her silver hair pinned back in a neat bun. They did not move or speak, their gazes unfocused as if they were looking at something far beyond the physical world.

Emma slowed her pace, the sight of them jolting her from her thoughts. She considered running past, allowing them their solitude, but a sense of neighborly duty made her hesitate. Mary, the real estate agent, had mentioned the Thompsons as friendly people, always eager to welcome newcomers. Maybe they hadn't heard about the Millers moving in, or perhaps this was just how older folks liked to spend their mornings, soaking in the day's beginnings.

"Good morning!" Emma called, raising her hand in a friendly wave as she approached the gate. Her voice sounded overly cheerful in the quiet street, breaking the stillness. She smiled, trying to project warmth and friendliness, to bridge the distance between strangers.

George's head turned slowly toward her, his movements deliberate and sluggish, as though underwater. His eyes, a dull blue, fixed on Emma, but there was no recognition, no spark of life in them. Ethel's head turned a moment later, her gaze following George's. They looked at Emma with the vacant eyes of sleepwalkers, their expressions devoid of emotion or interest. For a brief, unsettling moment, it was as if they didn't see her at all but were looking straight through her.

Emma's smile faltered. She stood awkwardly, her hand still raised, waiting for some sign of acknowledgment, a nod, a smile, anything. But the Thompsons just stared, their faces as still as masks. A shiver traced its way down her spine, the hairs on the back of her neck prickling. She felt an inexplicable urge to retreat, to turn around and run, to escape those blank, lifeless stares.

"Uh... I'm Emma Miller," she said, her voice wavering slightly. "We just moved in down the street. I just wanted to say hello." The words hung in the air, unanswered. The silence stretched, thick and uncomfortable.

George's mouth twitched, the barest hint of movement, as if he was on the verge of speaking. Emma held her breath, waiting. But no words came. Instead, George's gaze drifted away, back to the street, as if Emma had ceased to exist. Ethel followed suit, her eyes returning to their distant focus, the two of them resuming their silent vigil.

Emma felt a coldness spread through her, a chill that had nothing to do with the morning air. She stood there for a moment longer, uncertain, feeling as though she had stepped into a place where she didn't belong, an intruder in a scene she couldn't comprehend. She forced a smile, though it felt hollow and thin, and gave a small nod, more to herself than to the Thompsons.

"Well, it was nice to meet you," she said, though she wasn't sure they even heard her. With that, she turned and continued her run, quickening her pace as she moved away from the house. Her heart pounded harder, a combination of exertion and unease. The image of the Thompsons' vacant eyes stayed with her, imprinted on her mind like a photograph.

As she jogged down the street, the houses stood silent and empty, their windows dark. The neighborhood felt deserted, the kind of place that looked picture-perfect on the outside but held secrets within. Emma couldn't shake the feeling that she was being watched, that unseen eyes followed her every move. She glanced over her shoulder, half expecting to see George and Ethel still staring after her, but the street was empty. Only the wind whispered through the trees, its voice soft and indistinct.

Emma pulled out her phone as she reached the end of the block, her fingers fumbling to type a message to John. She needed some connection to normalcy, a way to dispel the creeping dread that had settled over her like a shroud.

Emma: Just went for a run. Met the Thompsons. They were... strange. Didn't say anything, just stared at me. Weird vibe.

She hit send and kept jogging, her eyes scanning the quiet houses as she passed. Her phone buzzed a moment later, and she slowed to read John's reply.

John: Odd. Maybe they're just shy or something. Don't worry about it. How's the run? Feeling better?

Emma hesitated before typing back.

Emma: Yeah, feeling fine. Just... something about this place feels off. Can't put my finger on it.

She pocketed the phone, her thoughts swirling with unease. Agatha's voice seemed to echo in her mind, the words resonating with a strange, unsettling clarity: "Not everything is as it seems." As Emma rounded the corner toward home, the image of the Thompsons' blank, unresponsive faces lingered in her thoughts, leaving her with the feeling that something dark and unfathomable might be lurking, just waiting to reveal itself.

Once back home, Emma took a long shower, hoping the warm water would wash away the lingering tension from her run. By the time she finished and cleaned up, the kids had woken up and settled into their daily routines, enjoying the freedom of summer vacation in their new home. The ordinary sounds of their laughter and footsteps brought a sense of normalcy that Emma clung to, even as her mind replayed the morning's events.

The sun now hung high in the sky, bathing Briar Vale in a blanket of warmth. The Miller's backyard, with its neatly trimmed lawn and the edge of the conservation area beyond, seemed the very picture of suburban tranquility. The air was thick with the hum of cicadas, blending with the faint, sweet scent of blooming jasmine, their white petals stark against the lush green of the hedges. The conservatory stood at the property's edge, a dense thicket of ancient trees and tangled underbrush stretching as far as the eye could see, casting long shadows that crept slowly over the manicured lawn, as if reaching out to touch the Miller's world.

Emma stood on the back patio, a glass of iced tea in her hand, watching Owen play in the yard. He moved with the carefree energy of childhood, darting from one spot to another, his brown hair glinting in the sunlight. A cluster of Gravitrax tracks lay sprawled on the grass, evidence of a morning spent building and rebuilding with his usual enthusiasm. But now, his focus seemed to have shifted. He stood near a large oak tree at the edge of the backyard, where the manicured lawn blended into the untamed growth of the conservatory. His small figure was half-obscured by the shadows of the trees, as if drawn to something hidden in their depths.

At first, Emma thought he was simply lost in his own world, as he often was, his mind captivated by some elaborate fantasy. But as she watched, she noticed his lips moving, his head tilting as if in response to a voice only he could hear. His hands gestured animatedly, pointing into the darkened woods, then gesturing back towards the house. It was a conversation, one-sided but intense, with pauses as if he were listening to some unseen companion before offering his own replies.

Curiosity piqued, Emma set her glass down on the patio table and walked toward Owen, her footsteps soft on the grass. The closer she got, the more clearly she could hear his voice, a soft, high-pitched murmur interspersed with laughter. She couldn't make out the words, but the tone was one of animated excitement. Her heart gave a small lurch at the sight - her son, her youngest, always so full of life and wonder. Yet there was something about his manner that sent a flicker of unease through her.

"Owen, honey," Emma called softly as she approached, not wanting to startle him. "Who are you talking to?"

Owen turned, his face lighting up at the sight of his mother. He bounded over to her, his smile wide and innocent, his eyes shining with a brightness that was almost feverish. "My new friends, Mommy!" he exclaimed, pointing back towards the trees. "They live in the woods. They want to come out and play with me."

Emma felt a chill creep up her spine. Her eyes flicked to the conservatory, to the shadows that seemed to stretch out like dark fingers toward her son. She could see nothing beyond the thick curtain of leaves and the occasional shaft of sunlight that pierced the gloom. The trees stood silent and still, the shadows beneath them deep and impenetrable.

"Your friends?" she echoed, keeping her voice light, though her stomach had begun to twist with unease. "What kind of friends, Owen?"

Owen giggled, a sound so bright and carefree it was almost jarring against the backdrop of the darkened trees. "My tree friends," he said simply, as if that explained everything. "They don't have names, but they're really nice. They talk to me and tell me stories about the woods. They say they like it here because it's quiet."

Emma's unease deepened. She knew it was normal for children to have imaginary friends, especially at Owen's age. Jack had had a few when he was little, invisible companions that faded with time. But something about the way Owen spoke, the intense focus in his eyes when he looked toward the woods, sent a ripple of fear through her. It was as if he truly believed these friends were real, more than just figments of his imagination. And the fact that they supposedly came from the woods - a place that had always seemed slightly foreboding to Emma - only heightened her concern.

"Owen, sweetie, why don't you come play closer to the house?" Emma suggested gently, reaching out to take his hand.

"It's nicer here in the sun, don't you think? And your toys are out here. You can show me how your Gravitrax works. I'd love to see what you've built."

Owen hesitated, casting a longing glance back at the line of trees, as if reluctant to leave his unseen companions. Then he nodded, his smile returning. "Okay, Mommy. But my friends said they'll wait for me. They like watching from the trees. They can see everything from there."

Emma squeezed his hand, leading him back towards the patio, her mind racing with questions she didn't dare voice. As they walked, she noticed the shadows of the trees seemed to shift, as if moving in response to their departure, a trick of the light that sent another shiver down her spine.

They were barely halfway across the yard when Emily's voice cut through the stillness, sharp and mocking. "Owen, you're such a weirdo, talking to yourself like that," she called from the doorway. Her arms were crossed over her chest, her expression a mixture of disdain and amusement. She had her long brown hair pulled back into a ponytail, and she wore a T-shirt with some anime character on it, her face framed by a fringe of bangs.

Owen's face fell, the light in his eyes dimming. He scowled at his sister, his small hands clenching into fists. "I'm not weird!" he shot back, his voice quivering with indignation. "You're the weird one! My friends are real, even if you can't see them!"

Emma felt a flicker of irritation at Emily's teasing. She released Owen's hand and walked over to her daughter, giving her a gentle but firm look. "Emily, that's enough," she said quietly. "Owen's allowed to have his imaginary friends. It's perfectly normal."

Emily rolled her eyes, huffing in exasperation. "Whatever, Mom. It's still weird. He's almost twelve. Shouldn't he be over the whole imaginary friend thing by now?"

Emma put a hand on Emily's shoulder, her touch light but grounding. "He's just playing, Emily. There's no harm in it. Besides, we're all adjusting to the new house in our own ways.

Try to be more understanding, okay?"

Emily shrugged, still unconvinced but unwilling to argue further. "Fine," she muttered, turning back into the house. "But if he starts talking to the tv or something, don't say I didn't warn you."

Emma watched her daughter disappear into the house, the door swinging shut behind her with a soft click. She turned back to Owen, who had already dropped to his knees on the patio, his focus now on his Gravitrax set, the earlier conversation seemingly forgotten.

Yet, as Emma stood there, watching her son play, the unease that had been building all morning refused to dissipate. She could still feel the weight of the trees' shadows pressing against her, and in her mind, she heard Agatha's voice once more, a whisper on the wind: "Not everything is as it seems."

She reached for her phone, feeling the need to connect, to hear John's voice. She typed out a quick message, her fingers moving faster than her thoughts.

Emma: Owen's been talking to imaginary friends in the woods. Emily says it's weird. I don't know... it just feels strange.

She sent the message, watching the screen as if it might hold some answers. A moment later, the phone buzzed with John's reply.

John: Imaginary friends are normal, Em. He's just adjusting to the move. I think you are reading to much into it.

Emma read the message, letting out a slow breath. John's reassurance was a small comfort, but it did little to quell the knot of anxiety tightening in her chest. She slipped the phone back into her pocket, her gaze drifting back to the edge of the conservatory, to the shadows that lay beneath the trees. For a moment, she thought she saw something move, a flicker of darkness within darkness, like a figure slipping away between the trunks.

Her heart skipped a beat, but when she looked again, there was nothing. Only the trees, swaying gently in the afternoon breeze, and the whisper of the leaves as they rustled against one another, like voices just out of earshot.

The rest of the week unfolded in much the same way, each day blending into the next with an unsettling monotony. The demands of John's job had become increasingly stressful, leaving him feeling inadequate and overwhelmed. He had taken a position in a field of software development he wasn't as familiar with, hoping it would make the move worthwhile. "Fake it till you make it," he had told himself. "How much different can it be?" But that mantra had begun to dissolve into self-doubt, worry that he was in over his head among those more competent. His frustration seeped into his mood, with his temper flaring over the smallest things. Emma, too, found herself increasingly on edge, her eyes constantly flickering to the shadows at the edges of her vision. Even the children seemed to pick up on the growing tension, their laughter quieter and their footsteps more subdued as they moved through the house.

Emma kept up her morning runs, hoping to shake off the feeling of unease that clung to her like a second skin. Each time she passed the Thompsons' house, she glanced up at the porch where George and Ethel sat, always in the same positions, their faces still and expressionless. It reminded her of The Stepford Wives - too perfect, too synchronized, as if something unnatural lurked beneath the surface. Each time she waved, their response was the same - a slow, synchronized turn of their heads, with their blank eyes meeting hers for a moment before drifting away.

Emma had since asked Owen to stay away from the conservatory and the large oak tree at the edge of the yard, warning him that snakes could be lurking in the thick brush.

Living in Florida, near a swamp, meant some of those snakes could be dangerous - not to mention whatever else might reside beyond the border of the yard. Despite her caution, Owen continued his daily adventures, wandering closer to the tree than Emma liked, carrying on animated conversations with an unseen friend. He'd talk and laugh, as if someone - something - was keeping him company in the shadows.

Meanwhile, Emily kept mostly to herself, either chatting with her friends on her phone or playing Genshin Impact on her computer in her room, distancing herself from the family as usual. Jack, similarly, had retreated deeper into his own world, spending nearly all his time in isolation. The faint sounds of his latest horror game seeped through the walls, punctuated by his occasional shouts and the eerie, muffled voices of his online friends. His room had become his sanctuary, a place where he could lose himself in dark, virtual worlds, seemingly unfazed by the tension that was slowly enveloping the rest of the house.

Emma tried to fill the days with normal activities - cleaning, organizing, preparing meals - but the stillness allowed her mind to wander, stirring feelings of aloneness that weighed on her. It felt as though the walls were gradually closing in, and something unseen lingered nearby, hidden in the shadows, waiting for the right moment to emerge.

As for John, his temperament had deteriorated. Each day, he became noticeably more irritable. Emma wasn't sure if it was due to work, but John refused to discuss it. His daytime replies to her texts had become noticeably shorter to her, and sometimes he didn't respond at all. What began as minor mood swings had steadily escalated. By Friday, the strain was evident in everything he did. He snapped at Emily for leaving her shoes by the front door, his voice rising to a sharp bark that startled everyone. When Owen accidentally spilled his juice at breakfast, John's face flushed with anger, his fists clenching at his sides. "Can't you be more careful?" he shouted, his tone harsher than Emma had ever heard. The look on Owen's face - wide-eyed and fearful - seemed to snap John back to reality, and he quickly muttered an apology, rubbing a hand over his face as if trying to wipe away the outburst. But his apologies, however sincere, did little to dispel the tension that now clung to him like a second skin.

John's once meticulous appearance had also begun to slip - his shirts wrinkled, his hair unkempt, the dark circles under his eyes deepening. He moved through the house like a shadow of his former self, his usual easy-going demeanor replaced by a growing restlessness. Small things set him off - a misplaced remote, a glass left unwashed in the sink. After each outburst, he would retreat into silence, his face drawn with regret, but his apologies were growing less frequent and more perfunctory, as though even he was beginning to accept this new version of himself.

As the week came to an end, the light outside had softened, fading into the warm, golden hues of late afternoon. Long shadows stretched across the Miller's backyard, creeping slowly towards the house as if seeking entry. Inside, the atmosphere was quiet, but not the peaceful quiet that Emma had cherished in the mornings. It was a tense, heavy silence, broken only by the faint ticking of the clock on the mantle and the low murmur of a television program drifting from the living room.

Emma stood in the doorway of the kitchen, wiping her hands on a dish towel, her eyes fixed on John as he sat in the living room. He was hunched over in his armchair, elbows resting on his knees, his hands clenched together. His once meticulously styled hair now hung limply, and the dark circles under his eyes were more pronounced than she had ever seen. He stared at the TV, but Emma could tell he wasn't really watching. His eyes were unfocused, distant, as if his thoughts were miles away.

She took a deep breath, steeling herself, and walked into the living room. She sat down on the sofa, her hands folding in her lap, and studied John's profile in the fading light. The lines around his mouth were deep, his jaw clenched. She could see the muscle ticking in his cheek, a sure sign of his inner turmoil. He looked up briefly as she entered, giving her a half-hearted smile that didn't reach his eyes.

"Long day?" she asked gently, trying to sound casual, though her heart was heavy with concern.

John nodded, running a hand through his hair. "Yeah. Just... a lot going on at work. New projects, tight deadlines. You know how it is." His voice was flat, lacking its usual warmth, and Emma noticed the way his fingers drummed restlessly on the arm of the chair.

She hesitated, choosing her words carefully. "You've seemed... different lately. Distant. Is everything okay? You can talk to me, John. You know that, right?"

John's face tightened, his eyes narrowing slightly. He let out a short, humorless laugh. "It's just stress, Emma. That's all. I'm handling it." His tone was dismissive, a clear signal that he didn't want to pursue the conversation. He turned back to the TV, his eyes glazing over once more.

Emma's heart sank. She knew him well enough to recognize when he was putting up a wall, shutting her out. She felt a surge of frustration, the words bubbling up inside her before she could stop them. "John, snapping at the kids isn't handling it. I know you're under a lot of pressure, but we're your family. You can't keep pushing us away."

John's head whipped around, his eyes flashing with irritation. "I'm not pushing anyone away!" he snapped, his voice louder than he intended. He saw the flicker of hurt cross Emma's face, and his own expression softened immediately, guilt replacing the anger. He rubbed a hand over his face, sighing deeply. "I'm sorry, Em. I didn't mean to... It's just..."

He trailed off, his shoulders slumping. Emma reached out, placing a hand on his arm. "I'm worried about you, John," she said quietly. "This isn't like you. Ever since we moved here, you've been... different. I don't know how to help if you won't let me in."

John stared at her, his eyes dark and unreadable. For a moment, Emma thought he would finally open up, share whatever burden he was carrying. But then he shook his head, his lips pressing into a thin line. "There's nothing to tell," he said, his voice resigned. "It's just this place, this job... It's all so new. I'm still trying to adjust, that's all. I'll be fine. We'll all be fine."

Emma wanted to believe him, wanted to take his words at face value and put her fears to rest. But the nagging feeling in her gut wouldn't let her. There was something he wasn't telling her, something gnawing at him from the inside. She squeezed his arm gently, offering a small smile. "Okay," she said softly. "But I'm here, John. Whatever it is, you don't have to go through it alone."

He nodded, though his eyes remained distant, his thoughts still far away. Emma sat back, watching him for a moment longer before turning her gaze to the TV. The news was on, the anchor's voice a steady drone, but she couldn't focus on the words. Her mind was too occupied with the man beside her, and the creeping sense of unease that seemed to have settled over their home like a dark cloud since moving here.

Her phone buzzed on the coffee table, breaking the silence. She reached for it, grateful for the distraction. A message from Mary, the real estate agent, flashed on the screen.

Mary: Hi Emma, just checking in to see how you and the family are settling in. If you need anything or have any questions about the house or the neighborhood, don't hesitate to reach out.

Emma read the message, her fingers hovering over the screen. She thought of the Thompsons, of Owen's imaginary friends, of the sour-smelling pie Agatha had brought. She thought of John, sitting next to her, his jaw clenched and his mind miles away. The words "not everything is as it seems" echoed in her head once more, refusing to be silenced.

Emma: Thanks, Mary. We're getting there, still settling in. The neighborhood seems... quiet. A bit different from what we're used to.

She sent the message, setting the phone back on the table. John glanced at her, one eyebrow raised. "Mary checking in?" he asked.

Emma nodded. "Just seeing how we're doing. I mentioned that things seem a bit... strange around here." She gave him a sideways look, gauging his reaction.

John shrugged, a noncommittal gesture. "It's a new place, Em. Of course it feels strange. We'll get used to it. Give it time. And hey, remember - this is Florida. Weird is basically part of the package."

Emma forced a smile, nodding as if in agreement. But as the evening wore on, and the shadows deepened in the corners of the room, she couldn't shake the feeling that time was the one thing they didn't have.

As the night settled in, casting long shadows across the quiet rooms, the rest of the family retired to their beds, seeking solace in sleep. Jack, however, remained in his room, the glow of his computer screen flickering like a lone beacon in the darkness. His door was closed, sealing him in his private world, where the only sounds were the rapid clicks of his keyboard and the distant, disembodied voices of his online friends. Oblivious to the stillness that enveloped the house, Jack was completely absorbed in his late-night gaming, the eerie light from the screen casting strange, shifting patterns on his face, making his eyes seem hollow and his features ghostly in the dim room.

The digital clock on Jack's desk read 11:58 PM, its red numbers glowing ominously. The only other light came from his computer screen, its eerie blue glow casting long, angular shadows that seemed to stretch toward the walls. Jack's room was a typical teenage haven, a mix of chaos and obsession.

Posters of horror icons like Freddy Krueger and Michael Myers stared down from the walls, their eyes following you no matter where you stood. Interspersed between them were game characters like Pyramid Head from Silent Hill and the haunting visage of Phasmophobia's ghostly entities, frozen mid-scream.

Piles of laundry lay in disarray across the floor, and a stack of horror novels - ranging from Stephen King classics to obscure, spine-chilling paperbacks - teetered precariously on his bedside table, threatening to collapse at any moment. His prized possession, a limited-edition figurine of Nemesis from Resident Evil, stood menacingly on his desk, its grotesque features highlighted by the soft glow of his monitor, adding to the room's unsettling vibe.

Hunched over his keyboard, Jack's fingers moved rapidly, his eyes fixed intently on the screen, where a grotesque creature lurked in the shadows of a virtual haunted house. His headset buzzed with the voices of his online friends, their banter a comforting murmur that added a sense of camaraderie to the otherwise tense atmosphere of the game. Jack's heart pounded with adrenaline, his senses heightened, attuned to the slightest movement or faintest whisper of sound. His character moved cautiously down a darkened hallway, the beam of a flashlight bobbing in the murky gloom.

Suddenly, a noise - a subtle, scuttling sound - cut through the quiet, emanating from somewhere within the game's shadows. Jack jumped, his body reacting instinctively, his fingers freezing over the keys. His eyes widened, straining to see through the pixelated darkness, searching for the source of the sound. The voices in his headset faded into the background, drowned out by the pounding of his own heart.

"Did you hear that?" he whispered into the microphone, his voice tinged with excitement and fear.

"Probably just the wind," a friend replied, his tone dismissive. "Keep moving. We're almost to the exit."

Jack nodded, more to himself than to his friends, and continued, his character creeping forward. The house on the screen was a maze of narrow corridors and darkened rooms, each turn holding the promise of something sinister. Jack's breathing slowed, his focus narrowing, shutting out everything except the game. He lived for these moments - the thrill of the unknown, the rush of fear that made his skin prickle.

Then, without warning, the screen went black. The game stuttered, froze, and Jack's headset went silent. He blinked, confusion turning to irritation as he clicked the mouse, tapped the keyboard, but nothing happened. The Wi-Fi had gone out, the connection severed. He let out a frustrated groan, pulling off his headset and tossing it onto the desk.

"Damn it," he muttered, leaning back in his chair. The house was eerily silent, the only sound the faint hum of his computer's cooling fan. He glanced at the clock: 12:03 AM.

With a resigned sigh, Jack pushed himself away from the desk and stood up, stretching his arms over his head. His muscles ached from hours spent hunched over, his eyes gritty from staring at the screen. Maybe it was a sign he should call it a night, get some sleep.

He flicked off the computer, the screen going dark, and the room was plunged into near darkness. The only light now came from the faint glow of the streetlamp outside, filtering through the slats of his window blinds. Jack moved to his bed, pulling back the covers, when a soft sound reached his ears - a faint, almost inaudible shuffling coming from the hallway outside his room.

Jack froze, his hand tightening on the edge of his bedspread. He listened carefully, trying to focus past the rapid thudding of his heartbeat. Footsteps. Soft, slow, deliberate, moving just beyond his door. His first thought was Emily - his sister, always sneaking around late at night, usually to raid the kitchen, despite her constant portrayal of being the smallest of eaters. She thought no one knew about it. He knew.

But she also loved to mess with him, bragging to her friends about how easily she could spook him. Annoyance flickered through Jack, and he almost called her out, but something stopped him. The footsteps didn't sound quite right. They were too slow, too measured, like someone trying to move without being heard. A chill crept up Jack's spine, the hairs on his arms standing on end. He strained his ears, catching the faintest whisper of movement, a soft creak of the floorboards just outside his door.

Swallowing his unease, Jack crossed the room and reached for the door handle, his fingers trembling slightly. He hesitated, his mind racing with possibilities. Maybe it was his dad checking the house, or his mom. But the images from his earlier game flashed in his mind, and his heart skipped a beat. I probably did this to myself, he thought.

Gathering his courage, Jack twisted the handle and pulled the door open, peering into the dimly lit hallway. The corridor stretched before him, bathed in the pale, sickly light from a nightlight plugged into the wall. The shadows were deep, swallowing the corners and leaving the middle of the hall in a thin strip of light.

"Emily?" Jack whispered, his voice sounding too loud in the silence. "Mom? Dad?"

There was no reply, only the faint creak of the house settling, the distant hum of the refrigerator downstairs. Jack stepped out into the hallway, his bare feet silent on the carpet. He looked to the left, toward his sister's room, the door shut, the faint outline of light visible beneath. To the right, the hallway stretched toward the staircase, ending in a darkened corner.

Just as he was about to turn back, dismissing it as his imagination, something flickered at the edge of his vision. A shadow, darker than the rest, moved at the far end of the hall, near the staircase. It was a fleeting glimpse, a shape that seemed to blend with the darkness, gone almost before he registered it.

Jack's breath caught in his throat, his pulse quickening. He blinked, his eyes straining to see in the gloom, but there was nothing there now, only the deep shadows and the faint glow of the nightlight. He stood frozen, staring into the darkness, his heart pounding in his chest.

Suddenly, the darkness seemed to press in around him, the shadows taking on a life of their own, twisting and writhing. The air felt heavy, thick with a presence that was both unseen and oppressive. Jack's skin prickled with a sensation of being watched, of eyes hidden in the dark, observing his every move.

He retreated slowly towards his bedroom door, his gaze never leaving the end of the hall. As he reached the threshold, he turned with a swift, silent motion, slipping back into the sanctuary of his room. He shut the door behind him with a deliberate, quiet firmness and turned the lock with trembling fingers. His hand lingered on the handle, as if seeking reassurance from the cold, unyielding metal, while his breath came in shallow, rapid bursts, each exhale a whisper of the fear that now gripped his heart.

For a long moment, Jack stood in the darkened room, listening, waiting. The silence was thick, almost tangible, broken only by the faint thud of his own heartbeat. He leaned against the door, closing his eyes, trying to convince himself it was nothing, just his mind playing tricks on him.

He heard his phone buzz from the desk, the sound startling in the silence. He walked over and picked it up, a message from one of his friends, probably wondering why he'd gone offline.

Dylan: Dude, what happened? You just disappeared. We were so close to beating that level!

Jack stared at the message, his mind still wrapped around the shadow he'd seen. He typed out a quick reply.

Jack: Wifi went out. Catch you tomorrow.

He set the phone down, his fingers still shaking slightly. He climbed into bed, pulling the covers up to his chin, his eyes fixed on the door. The shadows in his room seemed deeper now, more alive, as if they held secrets he was not meant to know.

Jack then laid down, burying himself under the covers as the house settled around him. The footsteps still echoed in his mind, a soft shuffling that seemed to grow louder in the silence of his thoughts. The image of the shadow lingered, a dark smudge at the edge of his vision, always just out of reach. He whispered reassurances to himself, insisting it was nothing - just the remnants of the game playing tricks on his mind. Yet, despite his rationalizations, a cold chill coursed through his bones, a silent testament to a fear his conscious mind couldn't fully dispel.

As the night stretched on and the minutes ticked by, Jack's eyes finally grew heavy. Sleep began to creep in, pulling him under, but the noises from earlier seemed to follow him into his dreams. A faint whisper, like a breath against his ear, and the soft sound of footsteps just beyond his door. As his consciousness faded, the sounds grew louder, more insistent, until they seemed to echo in the depths of his mind.

CHAPTER 3

Voices in the Woods

Emma Miller slipped into her running shoes, tightened the laces, and quietly opened the front door. The early morning sun began to cast long, golden fingers across the streets of Briar Vale, dappling the neat rows of newly planted trees and pristine lawns. The air held a stillness, broken only by the occasional chirp of a bird, as if the day itself were reluctant to stir. Emma paused on the threshold, taking in a deep breath of the cool, fresh air. She cherished this time of day - the tranquility, the sense of a world yet untouched by the burdens and noise of daily life. This was her sanctuary, her moment of peace before the demands of family and home crowded in.

She set off at a gentle jog, the rhythmic sound of her feet on the pavement a steady beat against the silence. As she ran, Emma's thoughts drifted, touching on mundane worries - grocery lists, the children's constant bickering, John's recent distant behavior. She glanced down the empty street, noting the lack of movement behind the curtained windows of the neighboring houses. Briar Vale was still waking up, its inhabitants hidden away in their suburban shells, cloaked in the early morning shadows.

The neighborhood was in a state of transition, much like the lives of those who inhabited it. Only a handful of the houses were occupied; the rest stood empty, skeletal frames of wood and metal scaffolding, waiting for the breath of life that would transform them into homes. Emma often passed by these unfinished structures, their exposed beams and yawning windows giving them an eerie, hollow look, like giant, unblinking eyes. The scent of fresh lumber and sawdust filled the air, mingling with the faint odor of paint and wet concrete. It was a place on the verge, caught between the promise of new beginnings and the silence of what was yet to come.

Approaching the Thompson house, Emma slowed her pace. George and Ethel Thompson, an elderly couple, had moved in a few months before the Millers. She had tried to give a polite greeting on occasion, but both had always seemed withdrawn, never offering a response. They were like phantoms in their own home, silent figures that slipped into and out of their lives with scarcely a whisper.

Today, something was different. Emma's eyes narrowed as she caught sight of George sitting alone on the porch. His hunched figure was a dark silhouette against the pale siding of the house. As Emma drew closer, she saw that his clothes were streaked with dirt, his usually neat appearance disheveled. He sat with his head bowed, shoulders slumped forward, his hands covering his face. The soft sound of his sobs reached Emma's ears, a low, mournful keening that cut through the morning stillness.

Emma slowed to a stop at the edge of the Thompson's yard, hesitant to intrude yet compelled by concern. "George?" she called softly. Her voice seemed to shatter the quiet, hanging in the air like a fragile whisper. George did not respond. His sobs continued, uninterrupted, as if he hadn't heard her at all.

"George, are you alright?" Emma tried again, taking a tentative step closer, her skin prickling with unease. There was no sign of Ethel - no movement from inside the house, no rustling curtains to suggest she was nearby. The porch was in disarray, flowerpots overturned and soil scattered across the wooden boards. A shovel lay on the ground, its blade caked with mud. Emma's gaze flickered to the dark smudges on George's shirt, her mind racing. What had happened? And why was he crying?

For a moment, Emma stood frozen, the dread coiling tighter in her stomach. She thought of reaching out, of crossing the threshold and laying a hand on George's shoulder, but something held her back. There was a darkness about him, a sense of something profoundly wrong, as if some unseen malady had hollowed him out from within. He still did not even acknowledge her presence. The image of his tear-streaked face, hidden behind dirt-stained hands, rooted her in place.

Realizing she would get no response, Emma took a step back, her heart pounding. She turned and resumed her run, glancing back over her shoulder as she did. George remained on the porch, a forlorn figure, his grief unacknowledged, his eyes never lifting to meet hers. The sight sent a chill through Emma, one that lingered as she continued down the street.

Her mind was a whirl of thoughts, trying to piece together what she had seen. She fumbled for her phone, pulling it from her pocket as she ran. Her fingers trembled slightly as she tapped out a message to John:

Emma: Saw George Thompson on the porch, crying. Looks really upset. Ethel wasn't there. Something's not right. I'm worried.

She hit send and waited, glancing down at the screen as she ran. The seconds ticked by, the phone silent in her hand. She sent another message:

Emma: John? Did you see my text?

Still no response.

Emma slipped her phone back into her pocket, unable to shake the growing sense of unease that clung to her. She came to a house with blue shutters, where numerous cats lounged in the yard like silent sentinels. Casting a wary glance toward it - Agatha's house - she noted that the old woman was nowhere to be seen. For that, Emma exhaled in quiet relief, though a cold shiver still ran through her. There was something about Agatha, some indefinable quality that unsettled her deeply.

Beyond Agatha's house the streets of Briar Vale became emptier, hollow and lifeless. As she passed one of the unfinished houses, its bare framework stood stark against the fading sky, casting long, jagged shadows across the road. The wind threaded through the exposed beams, its whistle low and mournful, like the distant cry of something unseen. The skeletal structure creaked and groaned, as if the house itself were alive.

As Emma approached yet another vacant lot, the stillness of the morning air carried a faint rustling from within the framework of a house yet unfinished. She halted looking to the source of the sound, her keen eyes narrowing as they sought to pierce the dim recesses of the structure. A shadow shifted, or so it seemed - a figure weaving through the skeletal beams. Her breath caught in her throat, a primal instinct stirring within her as the fine hairs on the back of her neck rose in silent alarm.

For a moment, she stood, her gaze transfixed by the stirring darkness. Then, almost as if a spell had been broken, she exhaled slowly, her tension giving way to relief as her reason prevailed. A piece of plastic sheeting, snagged on the wooden frame, fluttered in the morning breeze, harmless and mundane. She allowed herself a soft, humorless smile, but her body remained taut, as though the air itself clung to her with unseen fingers.

Just as she turned to depart, the plastic snapped violently, the sound sharp and sudden. Emma's eyes darted back to the shadowed interior, and before she could fully comprehend what she was seeing, a figure - no, a creature - burst forth from behind the beams. A white buck, sleek and spectral, shot from the depths of the half-constructed walls. Its coat, unnaturally pale, shimmered in the morning light, as though the sun itself feared to touch its form.

Emma's heart leapt to her throat, her breath frozen as she watched the creature move with unearthly grace. Its eyes - blood-red and gleaming like embers - met hers in a moment so brief yet so profound. The beast moved as though it were a whisper of the wind itself, fleeing the structure and vanishing into the tree line beyond, swallowed by the shadows of the woods.

She stood motionless, her pulse pounding in her ears, the silence of the morning now a palpable weight pressing against her chest. The plastic sheeting flapped once more, yet it no longer seemed benign. The wind felt a little colder now. Emma's hand drifted to her throat as she forced herself to breathe, her mind reeling at the unnatural sight she had just beheld.

Meanwhile, inside the Miller household, Emily lounged on the sofa, her phone held close to her ear, her voice a low murmur as she gossiped with a friend. She was half-listening, her eyes lazily drifting to the window where she could see her younger brother, Owen, playing outside. She had been tasked with watching him while their mother was out, but her attention was only half there. Owen was playing with his imaginary friends again, talking animatedly to himself as he wandered toward the conservation area at the edge of their yard.

Emily twirled a strand of hair around her finger, giggling at something her friend said on the other end of the line. "I know, right?" she said, her voice full of mock exasperation. "There's literally nothing to do here. Just trees and, like, empty houses. It's so boring."

Outside, Owen had moved closer to the large oak tree that stood at the boundary of their yard, its massive branches stretching toward the sky. The tree marked the edge of the conservation area, where the grass grew wild and untamed, mingling with the ferns and creeping vines. Beyond lay a swamp, its still waters shimmering darkly in the late afternoon light. Owen paused at the base of the tree, looking up into the dark canopy of leaves, his small body bathed in the dappled light that filtered through. His eyes were wide with fascination, and he tilted his head as if listening to a voice only he could hear. The breeze carried with it the faint scent of stagnant water, and the air was thick, almost suffocating, with humidity.

"Really?" Emily laughed again, still unaware of her brother's activities. "No way! That's so crazy..."

Owen took a step toward the tree, placing one small hand on the rough bark. He hesitated, his fingers trailing along the grooves as if tracing invisible patterns. The tree seemed to hum under his touch, a low, resonant sound that vibrated through the air. Owen nodded to himself, his face serious. "Okay, I'll do it," he whispered, responding to the invisible voice. "I'll go up and see."

He began to climb, his feet finding the familiar holds in the tree's trunk, his hands grasping the low-hanging branches. As he climbed higher, the sounds of the swamp grew louder - the croak of frogs, the rustle of unseen creatures moving through the underbrush. The tree's ancient wood creaked and groaned under his weight, the sound like the protest of a door long sealed. Owen didn't seem to notice, his face set with determination as he ascended higher, his small figure disappearing into the dense foliage. A crow cawed loudly from a nearby branch, its cry echoing in the stillness.

Inside the house, the front door swung open, and Emma stepped in, wiping the sweat from her brow. Her run had not done much to dispel the unease that had settled in her stomach that morning after seeing George Thompson. She glanced toward the living room and saw Emily on the sofa, her phone now resting on her chest, eyes closed as if she were lost in thought.

"Emily, where's Owen?" Emma asked, her voice edged with concern.

Emily's eyes snapped open, and she sat up, startled. "Uh, outside, I think," she replied, glancing toward the window. "He was just playing around."

Emma's gaze followed her daughter's, and her eyes widened in alarm as she caught sight of a small figure high up in the oak tree, silhouetted against the sky. "Oh my God, Owen!" she cried, rushing toward the back door. Panic surged through her veins as she threw the door open, the screen door slamming against the frame, and sprinted across the yard, her feet pounding against the grass, the world narrowing to the sight of her son teetering precariously above.

The creaking of branches reached her ears, followed by a loud, splintering crack. Owen's foot slipped, and he let out a yelp of fear, his hands scrambling to find a hold. The tree swayed under his weight, its branches groaning as if in protest, as if trying to shake off an unwelcome guest. Emma's heart lurched, her breath catching in her throat. She reached the base of the tree just as Owen's fingers slipped from the branch. His body pitched forward, arms flailing, and he fell, his small form a blur of motion against the green and brown of the tree.

"Owen!" Emma screamed, arms outstretched. She caught him, the impact nearly knocking her to the ground. She staggered backward, clutching him tightly, her heart racing. For a moment, neither of them moved, caught in the shock of what had just happened.

Owen's breath came in short, terrified gasps. His eyes were wide with fear, his face pale. Emma pulled him close, her body trembling. Relief washed over her, followed quickly by a surge of anger. She held him at arm's length, her eyes blazing.

"Owen, what were you thinking?" she demanded, her voice shaking. "You could have been seriously hurt! Why would you do something so reckless?"

Owen's lower lip quivered, and tears welled up in his eyes. "They told me to," he whispered, his voice small and frightened. "They said there was something special up there, something I had to see."

Emma's anger faltered, replaced by a cold chill that settled in her bones. "Who told you?" she asked, her voice dropping to a whisper. "Who's been talking to you?"

Owen looked down at his feet, his small hands twisting together. "My friends," he said quietly. "The ones who live in the trees. They told me it was safe."

Emma's grip tightened on his shoulders, a wave of fear and frustration crashing over her. Her mind raced, trying to make sense of it all. She pulled Owen into a tight hug, her heart aching with the need to protect him.

"From now on, you don't listen to them," she said firmly, her voice trembling. "Do you understand me? You don't go near that tree, and you don't climb it ever again."

Owen nodded, tears spilling down his cheeks. "Okay," he mumbled. "I'm sorry, Mom."

Emma hugged him close, her heart still pounding in her chest. She looked up and saw Emily standing in the doorway, her expression a mix of guilt and annoyance. Anger flared again, sharp and hot.

"Emily!" Emma called, her voice cracking like a whip. "Why weren't you watching him? I asked you to keep an eye on your brother!"

Emily's eyes flashed with defiance, and she crossed her arms over her chest. "I did! He was just playing. I didn't know he'd do something stupid like that!" she snapped.

Emma's eyes narrowed. "This isn't a joke, Emily! He could have been seriously hurt. You need to take this seriously."

Emily rolled her eyes, her face twisting into a scowl. "Whatever," she muttered, turning on her heel. "I'm going to my room." She stomped off, the door slamming shut behind her.

Emma watched her go, her heart heavy with frustration and fear. She looked down at Owen, who was still clinging to her, his small body trembling. The shadows around them seemed to deepen, the sun dipping lower in the sky, casting the yard in a dusky light. The oak tree loomed above, its branches swaying gently in the breeze, whispering secrets that only Owen seemed to hear.

As the day wore on, the late afternoon sun dipped below the tree line, casting long, jagged shadows across the Miller's living room. The room was filled with the golden haze of twilight, making the air seem thick and almost dreamlike.

Emma stood in the kitchen, her hands shaking slightly as she prepared dinner. Her mind replayed the events of the afternoon: Owen's fall, his insistence on talking to invisible friends, the sound of that branch snapping beneath his weight. The knot of anxiety in her chest had not loosened, and the house seemed unusually quiet, save for the faint hum of the refrigerator and the ticking of the wall clock.

She glanced at her phone on the counter, her earlier text to John still unanswered. She picked it up and read the message again:

Emma: Saw George Thompson on the porch, crying. Looks really upset. Ethel wasn't there. Something's not right. I'm worried.

And another one:

Emma: John? Did you see my text?

Emma frowned, her concern deepening. John had never been this unresponsive before. Unable to settle, she opened the "Find Friends" app and checked his location. Relief washed over her - he was almost home. But the feeling was fleeting, quickly replaced by a familiar tension as the unsettling events of the day replayed in her mind.

The sound of the front door opening broke her thoughts. Emma's heart leaped in relief. She heard John's footsteps as he entered the hallway, his heavy gait unmistakable. The rustling of his coat being hung on the rack, the thud of his briefcase being set down - familiar sounds that brought a brief sense of normalcy.

"John?" Emma called, stepping out of the kitchen. She met him in the hallway, her face a mixture of relief and tension. "Why didn't you return my texts? I've been trying to reach you all day."

John looked at her, his brow furrowing. He was a tall man, his dark hair flecked with the first signs of gray. He had a tired, distracted look about him, his shoulders slightly slumped as if carrying an unseen weight. "I was busy, Emma," he replied curtly, brushing past her toward the living room. "Work's been insane. You know that."

Emma followed him, her voice edged with frustration. "Busy? You couldn't spare two seconds to reply? John, it was important. Something happened with Owen today. He was climbing the oak tree by the swamp. He could have been seriously hurt!"

John paused in the doorway to the living room, his expression shifting to annoyance. He turned to face her, his eyes narrowing. "And where were you?" he asked sharply. "I thought you were supposed to be watching him. I'm out all day working to pay for this place, and you can't even keep an eye on the kids?"

Emma recoiled, his words hitting her like a slap. She opened her mouth to respond, but no words came out. John's gaze was hard, unyielding, and she felt her own anger rising. "I was out for a run," she managed to say, her voice trembling. "When I got back realized he was up there. He was talking to his imaginary friends again, John. He's not safe."

John shook his head, a derisive snort escaping his lips. "Imaginary friends? He's a kid, Emma. Kids have imaginary friends. You're blowing this way out of proportion." He moved into the living room, dropping onto the couch and grabbing the TV remote. "One of us has to work, and one of us has to watch the kids. I can't do both."

Emma felt a surge of frustration. She wanted to argue, to make him see the seriousness of the situation, but the look on his face told her it would be futile. She stood in the doorway, watching as John turned on the television, the blue light casting an eerie glow across his features. He leaned back, his expression one of irritation more than concern.

A sense of helplessness washed over her. She wanted to

scream, to shake him out of his complacency, but instead, she turned back to the kitchen, her hands trembling as she resumed chopping vegetables for dinner. The rhythmic sound of the knife against the cutting board was the only thing that kept her from losing her composure.

A few minutes later, Jack entered the living room, his face pale, his movements hesitant. He was tall for his age, with dark hair like his father's, and a serious demeanor that often made him seem older than his fourteen years. He hovered by the door, shifting from one foot to the other.

"Dad?" he said quietly.

John didn't look up from the TV. "What is it, Jack?" he replied, his voice tinged with irritation.

Jack swallowed, glancing over his shoulder toward the kitchen where he could see his mother's silhouette. He stepped closer to his father, lowering his voice. "I heard something last night," he said. "Footsteps, outside my room. And I saw... I think I saw a shadow at the end of the hall. It freaked me out."

John sighed heavily, his eyes still on the screen. "Jack, how many times have I told you not to play those horror games late at night? They're messing with your head. You're imagining things."

Jack shifted uncomfortably. "I know, but this felt real. It wasn't the game. And I didn't imagine it, Dad. I heard the footsteps, and the shadow... it was there."

John turned to his son, his face tight with frustration. "Listen, you need to drop this nonsense, okay? I don't want to hear another word about it. And don't even think about running to your mother with this - she's barely holding it together as it is. The last thing we need is her getting more paranoid." His voice hardened as he leaned in. "You need to grow up, Jack, and stop acting like a scared little kid. Take a break from the games. Do you understand me?"

Jack nodded, his eyes downcast. "Yes, sir," he murmured, backing away. He turned and left the room, his footsteps soft against the carpet.

As Jack disappeared down the hallway, Emma appeared in the doorway, wiping her hands on a towel. "What was that about?" she asked, her voice tight with suspicion.

"Nothing," John said dismissively, waving a hand. "Just Jack being Jack. He needs to lay off those games. They're making him jumpy."

Emma watched him for a moment, her expression skeptical. She walked over to the couch, positioning herself in front of the television, forcing John to meet her eyes. "John, I need to talk to you. I think something's wrong with the Thompsons. They've always acted a bit strangely, but..." She hesitated, her voice tightening with concern. "This morning, George was on the porch - crying. Ethel wasn't there, and he was... covered in dirt. It was so strange. I'm really worried. What if something's happened? Should we go check on them? Call the police? They're both old, and I never see anyone else with them. I think they're alone."

John rolled his eyes, sitting up and leaning forward. "Emma, you're overreacting. George is probably just having a bad day. People cry, okay? It's not the end of the world."

"But, John, it's not just that," Emma insisted, her voice tightening. "I've been seeing things too - shadows, out of the corner of my eye. And today, with Owen... I don't know. I feel like something's not right here. I can't shake it."

John's expression darkened, his patience clearly wearing thin. He sighed heavily, setting down the remote with a deliberate thud. "Emma, we've been over this before. You're off your meds, and I'm worried you're starting to slip into your old habits. You know how you get. Seeing things that aren't there, imagining problems where there aren't any. You need to take care of yourself, for everyone's sake. I can't handle this constant overreacting every time something small happens. We can't afford to make mountains out of molehills. We can't repeat what happened before."

Emma stared at him, the words cutting into her like a knife. A cold sensation spread through her chest, making it hard to breathe. "You think I'm making this up? You think I'm crazy?" Her voice wavered, a mixture of hurt and anger.

John didn't even look up to meet her gaze, his focus already drifting back to the flickering screen. He paused, then replied, "No, but I think you're stressed, Emma. When you get stressed, you start seeing things that aren't there. You've done it before - you know how you can be. You're letting your imagination run wild, and it's affecting the whole family. You need to get a grip and stop jumping at shadows. We've got enough real problems without you chasing ghosts."

Emma felt her resolve crumble, her anger deflating into a painful mix of self-doubt and shame. The uncertainty she had been trying to fight off all day crept back in, gnawing at her. Maybe he was right. Maybe she was just overreacting, her mind playing tricks on her. She looked away, unable to face him, her hands clenched into fists at her sides, knuckles white.

"Maybe you're right," she said quietly, more to herself than to him. "Maybe it's just me."

John nodded, a look of grim satisfaction crossing his face, and picked up the remote again, turning his attention back to the television. He didn't offer any further comfort or reassurance, simply let the topic drop as if it were of no importance. The flickering light of the TV reflected off his face, casting sharp shadows that seemed to accentuate his indifference.

Emma stood there for a moment longer, feeling hollow and defeated, her mind a whirl of doubts and fears. She turned and left the room, her footsteps soft on the carpet, the sound of the television fading behind her. She felt as though she were sinking, the walls of the house closing in around her, making it hard to breathe.

Down the hall, Jack stood just out of sight, his heart pounding in his chest. He had heard every word, his parents' voices cutting through the stillness of the house like a knife. The tension between them was palpable, a suffocating presence that seemed to fill every corner of the room. Jack felt a knot of fear tighten in his stomach, twisting with each passing second. This was not the dad he knew - the father who had always been steady and reassuring, the one who had taught him how to ride a bike, catch a baseball, or just weeks ago, shoot a BB gun. There was a harshness in John's voice now, a coldness that was unfamiliar and unsettling.

The next morning dawned with a pale, wan light, the sun struggling to break through the heavy cloud cover that had settled over Briar Vale. The air was thick with humidity, and the lingering scent of last night's rain hung like a veil over the neighborhood. Emma stood at the kitchen counter, pouring herself a cup of coffee, her movements slow and deliberate. She hadn't slept well, the events of the previous day replaying in her mind like a broken record. The tension with John, the fear for Owen, the unsettling sense that something was terribly wrong - all of it pressed heavily on her, making her feel weighed down and exhausted.

She turned to look out the window, her gaze drifting over the backyard. The grass was still wet, glistening with tiny droplets of moisture. Beyond the lawn, the oak tree stood tall and imposing, its branches stretching wide, their shadows cast long and dark over the ground. The swampy conservation area beyond was cloaked in a mist that clung to the underbrush, making the edges of their yard seem almost otherworldly, as if it were a gateway to some hidden, darker place.

John was already up, though his appearance was noticeably unkempt. His shirt was wrinkled, his tie crooked, and the stubble on his face hinted at a missed shave. He stood by the kitchen door, staring out at the same view, his eyes fixed on some distant point. His face was set, his expression hard and unreadable. He held his coffee cup with a rigid stillness, as though he were afraid that the slightest movement might shatter the fragile calm.

Emma watched him for a moment, her heart aching with the desire to reach out, to bridge the growing chasm between them. She approached him, her own coffee cup clutched in her hands. "Morning," she said softly, trying to catch his eye.

John didn't turn to look at her. "Morning," he replied, his voice flat, devoid of warmth. He continued to stare out the window, his jaw clenched tight.

Emma hesitated, feeling the silence stretch out between them like a physical barrier. "You're up early," she said, trying to sound casual, to invite conversation. "Is something on your mind?"

John's eyes remained fixed on the backyard, his face emotionless. "I'm going to start a garden," he said abruptly, as if stating a fact rather than making a decision.

Emma blinked in surprise. "A garden?" she echoed. "That's... a good idea. It might be a great way for you to relax, to take your mind off things."

John gave a small nod, still not looking at her. "Yes," he said curtly. "That's the idea."

Emma felt a flicker of hope, a chance to connect. She took a step closer, trying to engage him. "What do you plan to plant? Maybe we could pick some things out together. Flowers, vegetables, maybe some herbs?"

John's face remained impassive, his eyes never leaving the view outside. "I haven't decided," he said, his tone clipped. "I'll figure it out. I don't need any help."

The cold detachment in his voice sent a chill through Emma. She tried to mask her hurt, keeping her tone light. "I just thought it might be something nice we could do together. You know, a project."

John finally turned to look at her, his eyes flat and unfeeling. "I don't need a project," he said sharply. "I need you to stay out of it and let me have my own thing. Can you do that?"

Emma felt the sting of his words like a slap. She took a step back, her hope faltering. "I was just trying to be supportive," she murmured, her voice barely above a whisper.

John shrugged and turned away from her, his gaze drifting back to the backyard. "If you really want to be supportive, then stop creating problems for me to fix and focus on the kids," he said, his voice cold. "I've got enough to handle without constantly dealing with your need for drama."

Emma recoiled, the accusation piercing through her. She felt her chest tighten, a lump forming in her throat. "John, that's not fair," she said, her voice shaking. "I'm just trying to help…"

John cut her off with a dismissive wave of his hand. "Just leave it, Emma. I don't have time for this," he said, his tone final, leaving no room for argument.

He drained the last of his coffee and set the cup down on the counter with a sharp clink. He adjusted his tie, straightening it with a jerk, and picked up his briefcase. "I've got to go," he said, not looking at her. "Don't wait up."

With that, he walked out of the kitchen, leaving Emma standing there, stunned and hurt. The screen door banged shut behind him, the sound echoing through the house like a finality. Emma listened to the car start in the driveway, the rumble of the engine as it pulled away, leaving her alone in the silence.

She turned back to the window, staring out at the backyard. The oak tree loomed dark and foreboding, its branches swaying slightly in the morning breeze. The mist still clung to the ground, swirling in the underbrush, making the edges of their yard seem distant, unreachable.

Emma's hands shook as she set her cup down on the counter. She wrapped her arms around herself, feeling the cold seep into her bones. The warmth of the morning sun did nothing to chase away the chill that had settled over her heart.

After John left, the house felt emptier than ever, the silence oppressive, pressing in from all sides. Emma stood in the kitchen, her arms wrapped around herself, as if trying to hold the pieces of her world together. The light outside was bright, but it did little to dispel the darkness she felt creeping in around her. She let out a long, shaky breath and made her way to the kitchen table, her hands trembling as she picked up her cup of coffee.

Owen sat at the table, crayons scattered around him, his small fingers clutching a blue crayon as he worked diligently on his latest drawing. His face was a mask of concentration, his brow furrowed, tongue sticking out slightly from the corner of his mouth. Emma watched him for a moment, a pang of love mixed with worry stabbing at her heart. He was so young, so innocent. She had to protect him, even if she wasn't entirely sure what she was protecting him from.

She sat down across from him, taking a sip of her coffee, the warmth doing little to chase away the chill that had settled in her bones. "What are you drawing, sweetie?" she asked gently, trying to keep her voice light, masking the worry that had taken root inside her.

Owen looked up, his eyes bright with excitement. "It's the tree, Mommy," he said, pointing to the paper. His voice was innocent, unaffected by the shadows that loomed over their family. "The big tree in the backyard."

Emma leaned forward, peering at the drawing. The large oak tree was there, its branches spreading wide, reaching toward the sky. Beneath it, Owen had drawn small figures - himself, with his tousled brown hair and big eyes. But there were other figures, too. Dark shapes, looming around him, their bodies elongated and strange, each with piercing red eyes that seemed to burn from the page. They stood among crude representations of flowers, stark and menacing against the bright colors of the scene.

A chill ran down Emma's spine, her stomach twisting. "Owen," she said slowly, pointing to the dark figures. "What are these?"

Owen's face lit up with the innocent delight of a child sharing a secret. "Those are my friends," he said proudly. "They live in the tree and come out to play with me. They said the tree is their home."

Emma's breath caught in her throat, unease spreading through her like ice. "Your friends?" she repeated, trying to keep her voice steady.

Owen nodded, his eyes wide with sincerity. "Uh-huh. They're always around. They like to watch us and show me things. Special things."

Emma's hands shook as she reached for the paper, her fingers grazing the dark, ominous shapes that stood among the bright flowers. "Owen, what do they show you? What kind of things?"

Owen's once bright eyes seemed to darken as he stared at the figures. He traced one of the red eyes with his crayon, a small frown creasing his forehead. "They show me where to find the coolest bugs," he whispered. "And... they showed me where the trees grow, and where it's really dark. They said that's where they came from, and it's where they take things when they want to keep them safe."

Emma's heart pounded in her chest, a cold dread settling over her. She forced herself to keep her voice calm. "Owen, do your friends talk about anything else? Did they tell you why they wanted you to climb the tree?"

Owen's expression darkened, his small body stiffening. He looked up at Emma, his eyes serious, holding a glimmer of something ancient, something unsettling. "They don't like you, Mommy," he said softly, as if sharing a forbidden secret. "They said you try to stop them from talking to me. And that you won't listen."

Emma's blood ran cold at his words. "Listen to them?" she asked, fighting to keep the panic out of her voice. "What do they want?"

Owen glanced back down at his drawing, his fingers tracing over the red eyes. "They think we took something from them, something they want back," he murmured.

Emma's grip tightened on the table, her knuckles white. "Owen, what do you mean? What did we take?"

Owen shrugged, his focus returning to his drawing. "I don't know. They just don't like it when you're around. They said they don't want you near the tree. They said if you come too close, they'll have to show you, like they showed the others. They don't like it when people don't listen."

Emma swallowed the lump in her throat, her heart hammering against her ribs. "Owen, what others?"

Owen's eyes flickered up to hers for a brief moment, a shadow passing over his face. "They don't want me to talk about it," he whispered. "They said if I tell you, you'll try to stop them, and then they'll get mad."

Emma's breath caught, her mind racing. The weight of his words settled over her like a heavy shroud, each one sinking in like a stone. She looked at her son, so small and innocent, yet speaking of things far beyond his understanding. The shadows on his paper seemed to throb with life, their red eyes burning into her, and she felt as though they were watching her, waiting.

"Owen," she said softly, reaching out to touch his hand. "Please, you have to tell me more. I need to know what's happening. I need to keep you safe."

Owen pulled his hand away, his face closing off, his small shoulders hunching. "I can't, Mommy," he said, his voice almost a whisper. "They said if I tell, they'll be angry. They said they'll come for you. They said they'll take you into the dark and make you stay there."

Emma felt a wave of nausea wash over her, the room seeming to tilt. The image of the dark figures, of the tree, of the shadows that seemed to be encroaching on every corner of their lives, filled her mind. She stood up, her legs unsteady, the ground beneath her feeling like it might give way.

She knew she couldn't ignore this. The signs, the warnings, the feelings that had been gnawing at her - all pointed to something real, something malevolent that was closing in. She had to protect her son, to understand what these spirits wanted and how to keep them at bay.

"Owen, why don't we go see the doctor today?" she

suggested gently, her voice trembling. "Just for a check-up. And afterward, we can get some ice cream, just you and me."

Owen looked up at her, his eyes shadowed and wary. He nodded reluctantly. "Okay," he said, setting down his crayon. "But I don't want to talk to the doctor about my friends. They said I shouldn't tell anyone else."

Emma nodded, a tight smile on her face. "That's fine, sweetheart. We'll just make sure everything is alright."

Emma watched him, her heart aching. She wanted to reach out, to hold him, to tell him everything would be alright. But the words caught in her throat, tangled with her fear. The shadows on the paper seemed to grow darker, their red eyes burning into her, and she felt the weight of the unknown pressing down on her.

She sat back, taking a shaky breath, her mind racing. The dark figures, the red eyes, the way Owen spoke of them as if they were real - it all felt too real, too dangerous to ignore. She couldn't brush it aside, couldn't pretend that it was all just the product of a child's imagination. Something was wrong, something that she didn't understand, and it was growing in the shadows of their lives.

Her thoughts turned to John. He'd likely brush this off, just like every other time she tried to bring up her worries. He'd probably roll his eyes, chalking it up to her imagination running wild again. She could almost hear his voice - calm, dismissive - telling her she was overreacting, that Owen was just a child, that children have imaginary friends. But this time felt different. It felt dark. There was something lurking behind Owen's words, something unsettling that clung to her no matter how hard she tried to shake it. This wasn't just a phase, or a harmless game - it felt like a warning.

She needed John to understand. He needed to know what she was dealing with, whether he believed her or not. After calling the doctor and scheduling an appointment for the afternoon, she picked up her phone again. Her fingers hovered over the screen for a moment, shaking as she tried to find the right words.

Emma: I made a doctor's appointment for Owen. Something's not right. I am sending you the appointment time and address if you want to come.

She hesitated before pressing send, her pulse quickening. She hoped this time, he would listen.

The doctor's office was cool and sterile, the faint scent of antiseptic lingering in the air. The walls were painted a soft, calming blue, adorned with framed posters of smiling children and cheerful animals. Emma sat in one of the waiting room chairs, her fingers tapping nervously on her knee. Owen sat beside her, swinging his legs back and forth, his eyes wandering around the room with the innocent curiosity of a child.

John had arrived separately, coming straight from work after receiving a text from Emma. He stood by the door, his shoulders stiff, his face lined with frustration. His eyes darted to his watch every few minutes, his impatience growing. It was clear to anyone who looked that he was irritated at being pulled away from his responsibilities. His business-casual attire was immaculate, but there was a tightness in the set of his jaw and the way he held his phone, as if he were bracing himself against the intrusion into his day.

When the nurse called their names, Emma stood, taking Owen's hand as they followed her down a short hallway to a small, brightly lit examination room. John followed, his footsteps heavy with irritation, his expression a mix of annoyance and exasperation. The doctor, a middle-aged man with thinning hair and a kind face, looked up from his notes and smiled warmly as they entered.

"Good morning," he said, his voice calm and reassuring. "I'm Dr. Patterson. What seems to be the concern today?"

Emma hesitated for a moment, then took a deep breath, trying to steady herself. "It's Owen," she began, her voice tinged with worry. "He's been... saying things, seeing things. He talks about these friends of his, imaginary friends, I guess, who live in the tree in our backyard. And yesterday, he climbed up into the tree and nearly fell. He said his friends told him to do it, that they wanted to show him something. He draws these pictures of them, dark figures with red eyes, and... and he says they don't like me. That they think we don't belong here."

Dr. Patterson listened intently, his expression serious but not alarmed. He glanced at Owen, who was sitting quietly, clutching his drawing, and then back at Emma. "I see," he said thoughtfully. "Children at Owen's age often have very vivid imaginations. It's not uncommon for them to create imaginary friends, especially when they're adjusting to a new environment. You mentioned you've recently moved?"

Emma nodded. "Yes, about a month ago. We're still settling in."

The doctor looked over at John. "Where did you move from?"

John straightened in his chair. "Atlanta, Georgia. We used to live downtown."

Dr. Patterson raised his eyebrows slightly. "Wow, that's a big shift - from the city to here. A lot quieter, I imagine."

John nodded. "Yeah, it's definitely different. We thought it would be a good change, more space, less noise. Near the beach."

The doctor smiled gently. "That could explain quite a bit. Moving to a new place can be a huge adjustment for a child. Sometimes, they create imaginary friends as a way to cope, to have something familiar in an unfamiliar setting. It helps them explore their feelings and make sense of their world."

Emma felt a flicker of doubt. "But these friends... they sound so... dark. It's like he's afraid of them, but he still listens to them. Shouldn't I be worried?"

Dr. Patterson leaned back in his chair, his hands resting on his knees. "From what you've told me, it sounds like Owen is using his imagination to process the move and maybe some of the emotions he's feeling. The important thing is to keep an open line of communication with him. Encourage him to talk about his friends, but also to understand the difference between what's real and what's imaginary. If his behavior becomes more concerning - if he starts having trouble distinguishing between reality and imagination, or if his friends start telling him to do harmful things - then it might be worth consulting a child psychologist. But for now, I'd advise not to be overly concerned. Give it some time, and keep an eye on how things develop."

John, who had been standing by the door, let out an exasperated sigh. "So, you feel it's just kid stuff, then?" he asked, his voice sharp and edged with frustration. "No reason to panic?"

Dr. Patterson nodded. "Yes, that's right. It's quite normal for children to have imaginary friends and to express themselves through drawings and stories. It's part of their development."

John's eyes flicked to Emma, frustration clear in his gaze. "See? This is what I've been saying all along," he said, his voice rising slightly, the irritation spilling over. "You're overreacting, Emma. If you'd been paying more attention instead of getting worked up over nothing, we wouldn't even be here. I had to leave work for this, and you know how much I have on my plate. This is a waste of time, and I can't keep dropping everything because you're panicking."

Emma felt her face flush with a mix of anger and embarrassment. She opened her mouth to respond but caught herself, biting back the retort that was on the tip of her tongue. She didn't want to argue in front of Owen, didn't want to make things worse. She turned back to Dr. Patterson, her voice tight. "Thank you, Doctor. I appreciate your time."

Dr. Patterson nodded, standing up. "Of course. If you have any more concerns, don't hesitate to call. And remember, it's normal for kids to have active imaginations. Just keep talking to him, and try to understand what he's feeling."

Emma managed a small smile, though it felt hollow. "We will," she said quietly.

As they left the office, John walked ahead, his phone already in his hand, typing out a message as they headed back to the parking lot. Emma followed with Owen, her thoughts still swirling, the doctor's words doing little to calm her fears. The man she once turned to for comfort and support seemed like a stranger now, his cold detachment a barrier she couldn't cross.

By the time they reached the cars, John had already started the engine of his own vehicle, barely glancing up. "I've got to get back to the office," he said abruptly. "You can take Owen home. I can't afford to be late. We've wasted enough time here."

Emma nodded, feeling a sting of hurt at his dismissiveness. "Fine," she replied, trying to keep her voice even. She buckled Owen into his seat in her car, then turned to face John. "You could at least try to understand how worried I am."

John looked up from his phone, his expression hard. "I understand perfectly, Emma. I understand that you're blowing this out of proportion. You won't listen to me, so listen to the doctor. The doctor said it's normal. Stop looking for problems that aren't there." Without waiting for a response, he pulled out of the parking lot, his car disappearing around the corner.

Emma stood there for a moment, watching him go, a mixture of anger and despair tightening in her chest. She climbed into her own car, her movements slow, her mind heavy with doubts. In the backseat, Owen hummed softly to himself, still clutching his drawing, his eyes distant.

As she drove home, the shadows of his drawing haunted her, the figures with their red eyes a constant reminder that something was wrong. She glanced at Owen in the rearview mirror, her heart aching with a mix of love and worry.

John might dismiss her concerns, but Emma knew she couldn't ignore her instincts. She had to protect her son, even if it meant standing alone. She would keep watch, keep listening, and keep Owen safe. No matter what it took.

Emma pulled into the driveway, glancing to the back at the house. The oak tree loomed in the yard, its branches swaying gently in the breeze, casting long, dark shadows over the lawn. As they stepped out of the car, Emma felt the weight of those shadows pressing down on her, a silent reminder that the darkness surrounding them was far from gone.

As the afternoon gave way to evening, the house settled into an uneasy quiet. Emma moved through the rooms, her thoughts clouded with the doctor's reassurances and John's harsh words. She tried to distract herself with mundane tasks - sorting laundry, tidying up Owen's toys - but the sense of dread lingered, a constant companion. Outside, the shadows lengthened, creeping across the yard as the sun dipped below the horizon. By the time she prepared dinner, the darkness had fully settled, draping the house in a thick, suffocating blanket. The conversations at dinner were sparse and stilted, each family member seemingly lost in their own thoughts, their voices low and careful. John did not speak, his mind clearly elsewhere, and Emily chose to stay in her room, her absence an unspoken protest, sounds of The Pool movie playing from within. When bedtime came, Emma went through the motions, tucking the children in, checking the locks, turning off the lights, all the while feeling the weight of the house pressing down on her. John had already gone to bed without her, without even saying goodnight to the kids, his silent withdrawal a cold reminder of the growing chasm between them.

That night was thick with silence, the kind that seemed to press in from all sides, wrapping the house in a suffocating embrace. The only sound was the soft ticking of the clock on the nightstand, its rhythmic beat marking the slow passage of time.

Emma laid in bed, her eyes wide open, staring at the

ceiling above her. The darkness felt alive, as if it were breathing around her, whispering secrets she couldn't quite hear.

Beside her, John lay on his side, his back turned to her. His breathing was deep and even, the peaceful slumber of someone unburdened by the worries that plagued Emma's mind. She turned her head slightly, watching the rise and fall of his shoulders, the familiar silhouette of his figure in the dim light. He seemed so far away, an island of calm in the storm of her thoughts.

It hadn't always been like this. Emma remembered a time, not so long ago, when John would hold her close as they fell asleep, his arm draped protectively over her, his presence a comfort. But lately, that intimacy had faded, replaced by a cold distance that made Emma's heart ache. She couldn't remember the last time he had kissed her goodnight or taken her hand in his. Every night, he turned away from her, lost in his own world, as if a wall had sprung up between them.

He insists it's her, Emma thought, her eyes tracing the outline of his figure. He insists I'm the one pulling away. But it doesn't feel that way. It feels like he's slipping further and further from my grasp, like he's already half-gone. She turned onto her side, facing his back, the feeling of isolation settling over her like a shroud. What if it's all in my head? What if he's right?

Restless, Emma threw back the covers and slipped out of bed, careful not to wake John. The cool floorboards beneath her feet sent a shiver through her, and she wrapped her arms around herself as she moved toward the window. She parted the curtains slightly, peering out into the quiet street below.

The neighborhood was still, bathed in the soft glow of the streetlights. The houses stood in neat rows, their windows dark and empty, the trees casting long shadows over the lawns. Emma scanned the street, her eyes drifting from one vacant house to the next, the silence pressing in on her.

Then she saw them. At first, she thought her eyes were playing tricks on her. But there they were, faint but unmistakable - faces. Pale, ghostly faces, peering out from the windows of the neighboring houses. The vacant neighboring houses. They seemed to glow faintly in the dark, their eyes a reddish hue that sent a chill down Emma's spine. The faces were staring straight at her, their expressions seemingly twisted into eerie smiles that sent a wave of nausea through her. Emma's breath caught in her throat, her heart beginning to race.

She blinked, trying to clear her vision, hoping the images would vanish. But they remained, each one more menacing than the last, all eyes fixed on her house. She took a step back, her hand flying to her mouth, stifling a gasp. The faces didn't move, didn't waver, their gazes locked onto her like predators stalking their prey.

Emma stumbled backward, her heart hammering in her chest. She looked again, and the faces were gone, replaced by the empty, dark windows of the sleeping houses. Her breath came in ragged gasps, her skin clammy with fear. As she stood there, frozen, she caught sight of a few cats slinking through the shadows near the edge of the yard, their eyes gleaming in the dim light. For a moment, she hesitated - had she imagined it? Were the faces just tricks of the light, confused with the cats moving through the night? Her mind felt muddled, unsure if what she had seen was real or if it was her imagination running wild.

A cold sweat broke out on her forehead, her hands trembling as she clutched the edge of the windowsill. The silence of the night pressed in around her, heavy and oppressive. She felt the darkness closing in, whispering to her, filling her mind with shadows. It was as if a lingering presence hovered in the air, unseen but felt.

Emma turned away from the window, her heart still racing. She had to calm down. She had to believe that it was nothing more than a trick of her mind, a fleeting illusion brought on by stress and exhaustion. But the fear gnawed at her, digging its claws into her thoughts.

She crossed the room, her footsteps silent on the

floorboards, and entered the bathroom. The light flickered on, casting a harsh glow over the small space. Emma opened the medicine cabinet, her eyes scanning the shelves until they landed on the familiar bottle. Her fingers shook as she reached for it, her reflection in the mirror pale and drawn.

For a moment, she hesitated, her hand hovering over the bottle. She didn't want to rely on the medication again. She had worked so hard to wean herself off, to find balance and control. But the fear was too great, the images too vivid. She needed something to calm her mind, to push the shadows back.

Emma unscrewed the cap and shook out a pill, swallowing it with a sip of water. The cool liquid soothed her throat, and she closed the cabinet, her reflection staring back at her with hollow eyes. A sense of guilt washed over her, mingling with the relief as she waited for the medication to take effect.

She turned off the light and made her way back to the bedroom, the darkness greeting her like an old friend. John was still asleep, oblivious to the turmoil that raged inside her. Emma slipped back under the covers, the cool sheets brushing against her skin. She lay on her back, staring up at the ceiling, waiting for the calm to come.

Slowly, she felt the edges of her fear begin to dull, the pounding of her heart slowing to a more regular rhythm. Her breathing evened out, and the shadows that had seemed so threatening began to recede. The faces, the red eyes, the silent smiles - they faded into the background, becoming a distant memory, a faint whisper.

But even as the medication soothed her, Emma couldn't shake the feeling that something was watching her, lurking in the darkness just beyond her sight. She closed her eyes, forcing herself to breathe deeply, to let the calm wash over her. She had to believe that it was all in her head, that the faces were nothing more than a figment of her imagination.

For Jack, the heavy stillness of the night settled over everything like a shroud. In his bedroom, Jack lay in bed, his eyes also fixed on the ceiling, albeit for much different reasons. He could feel the darkness pressing in around him, thick and oppressive, as if the night itself were a living thing, creeping closer with each passing moment. He tried to close his eyes, to push away the thoughts that crowded his mind, but the memory of the footsteps from before echoed in his ears, a ghostly whisper that refused to fade.

Jack turned onto his side, his eyes scanning the room, every shadow seeming to shift and twist in the faint light from his nightstand lamp. He pulled the covers up to his chin, his heart beating a little faster. The house felt different at night, as if it held secrets that were hidden during the day. He could feel the weight of those secrets pressing down on him, filling the space with an unseen presence that set his nerves on edge.

He tried to tell himself it was nothing, just his imagination playing tricks on him. But deep down, Jack knew that something was wrong. There was a darkness in the house, something lurking just beyond his sight, waiting. He felt it in the way the shadows seemed to move when no one was looking, in the way the silence was never truly silent, always filled with the faintest of whispers.

Jack's eyes drifted to the door, the memory of the footsteps haunting him. They had been so real, so deliberate, stopping just outside his room. He had almost convinced himself it was a dream, a figment of his imagination. But now, lying in the dark, he wasn't so sure. The sound had been too clear, too purposeful, like someone or something was out there, waiting.

As if in answer to his thoughts, a soft sound reached his ears - footsteps, faint but unmistakable, padding quietly down the hallway. Jack's heart leaped into his throat, his body freezing in fear. The footsteps grew closer, each one a deliberate, measured tread, coming straight toward his door. He held his breath, his eyes wide, his heart pounding so hard he thought it might burst from his chest.

The footsteps stopped, just outside his door. Jack lay there, every muscle in his body tensed, waiting. The silence stretched out, thick and heavy, until it was almost unbearable. Then, there was a knock - so soft it was barely audible, a light tap-tap that sent a shiver down his spine.

Jack's breath came in short, ragged gasps, his eyes locked on the door. For a moment, he thought about calling out, asking who was there, but the words stuck in his throat. His instincts screamed at him to stay silent, to not make a sound. He could feel the presence on the other side of the door, a cold, malevolent force that sent a wave of terror through him.

Gathering his courage, Jack slowly sat up, the covers slipping off his shoulders. He reached out, his hand trembling as he flicked on the bedside lamp. The soft glow filled the room, casting long shadows that danced across the walls.

Jack slid out of bed, his bare feet touching the cold floor. He crept toward the door, every step a battle against the fear that gripped him. His hand shook as he reached for the lock, turning it with a quiet click. The sound seemed to echo through the room, loud in the stillness of the night. Jack listened, his ear pressed to the door, but the silence was unbroken, the footsteps gone.

He hesitated, then slowly turned away from the door, his eyes drifting to the window. The curtains were open, the darkness beyond a solid wall of black. He approached the window, his steps slow and cautious. He reached out, his fingers trembling as they gripped the edge of the curtain, ready to close. Glancing outside, he could see the backyard stretched out, a sea of shadows, the oak tree looming in the distance, its branches swaying gently in the night breeze.

At first, he saw nothing, just the familiar outline of the yard, the faint glimmer of moonlight filtering through the leaves. Then, out of the corner of his eye, he caught a flicker of movement. Jack's breath caught, his eyes narrowing as he peered into the darkness.

There, in the shadows near the tree line, he saw them - two

red eyes, glowing faintly in the dark, staring back at him. They were set low to the ground, unblinking, watching. Jack felt a cold wave of fear wash over him, his blood turning to ice. The eyes seemed to burn with an inner light, piercing the night, their gaze locked onto him.

Jack blinked, his heart pounding in his chest. The eyes were gone. The shadows shifted, the darkness swallowing them up, leaving no trace. He stumbled back from the window, his breath coming in ragged gasps, his mind reeling. Had he imagined it? Was it a trick of the light? But the memory of those eyes was burned into his mind, vivid and real.

Just then, the door rattled with a furious force, as if something on the other side was clawing and shoving to get in. Jack's entire body tensed as the door shook violently in its frame. His heart pounded in his chest, and he jumped back, eyes wide with terror. The handle twisted, and the door creaked as if it would burst open at any moment. Jack's breath caught in his throat, frozen in fear. He held his gaze on the door, praying it would hold.

And then, as suddenly as it had started, the shaking stopped. The handle went still. The room fell silent once more. The only sound left was the blood rushing in Jack's ears. For a brief moment, he wondered if it had given up, but the tension in the air told him otherwise. Whatever it was, it wasn't gone - it was waiting, watching.

And that's when he heard it. Distant laughter, faint and eerie, hidden in the white noise of the air conditioning vent. It was so brief, so subtle, but Jack swore it was there, a chilling sound that sent a cold shiver down his spine. It felt like something was toying with him - mocking his fear. Like his worst nightmare had leapt out of his video game and into real life. This wasn't just scary - it was personal, and it wasn't over.

Jack's chest rose and fell with ragged breaths as he desperately scanned the room, looking for some kind of defense, anything that would protect him. But what was he even up against? His trembling hands fumbled across his nightstand, finally landing on his phone. Without thinking, he unlocked it and opened a live-streaming app.

His thumb hovered over the "Start Stream" button. He knew this wouldn't protect him physically, but the thought of broadcasting his fear made him feel less alone. If something was coming for him, maybe having an audience - people who could see it - would force the thing to reveal itself. Or maybe it wouldn't want to be seen. Jack hoped, prayed, that it feared exposure.

He started streaming, his phone screen glowing softly in the dim room. The familiar chat box appeared at the bottom of the screen, but it was empty - no one watching yet. He swallowed hard, feeling the weight of his decision. This wasn't really a plan, but it felt better than doing nothing.

"Hey," he whispered, his voice shaky, barely above a breath. "Something's outside my room." His fingers tightened around the phone. "I... I don't know what it is, but it's been... it's been knocking. Rattling the door." He paused, listening again to the silence. "And there's something in the yard. I saw its eyes... red eyes."

As soon as the words left his lips, a fresh wave of fear hit him. He hated saying it out loud - it made everything feel more real, more immediate. His thoughts flashed to the Blair Witch Project. Dammit, he thought. This is exactly like that... just a camera and nothing else.

Shaking off the creeping dread, Jack glanced at the phone. A few viewers had joined the stream, and the chat started coming to life.

"Bro, you okay?" "What's happening??" "Red eyes? Are you messing with us?"

Jack's fingers hovered over the keyboard, but his heart wasn't in it. He wasn't trying to scare anyone for fun. The feeling of being hunted - of something watching him from the shadows - was far too real. He needed help.

The phone's screen cast an eerie glow in the room, a small lifeline in the suffocating darkness. Jack turned back to the bed, his legs shaking as he climbed in, pulling the covers up to his chin, phone still clutched in his hands. The soft light from the screen illuminated his face, casting long shadows across the walls that seemed to pulse with every small flicker of the lamp.

He kept streaming, eyes darting around the room. Every creak of the house, every whisper of the wind outside sent fresh jolts of fear through him. The phone buzzed again as more viewers joined, asking questions, throwing out suggestions, but Jack barely glanced at the chat. All he could focus on was the silence that felt too heavy, too alive.

The footsteps, the knock, the shaking door, the red eyes - Jack knew he hadn't imagined any of it. Whatever was outside was real. It was there, lurking, waiting. And it was patient. He could feel it, a cold, malevolent presence pressing in around him, creeping through the cracks in the door, filling the room with an oppressive weight.

He clutched the phone tighter, the chat buzzing with concerned messages.

"Lock your windows, bro!" "Get your parents, this is crazy!" "You've gotta show us the red eyes, dude. Go to the window!"

The last message made Jack's stomach turn. Go to the window? He couldn't. Not after what he'd seen. His mind replayed the image of those glowing eyes staring at him from the shadows. What if they were still out there, waiting for him to look again?

"No," Jack whispered to himself, his voice trembling. He wasn't going near that window again. Not tonight.

His eyes darted back to the door, as though expecting it to tremble again. A small part of him wanted to barricade it, to drag his dresser or chair in front of it, but he knew whatever had shaken the door with such force wouldn't be stopped by something so simple. The rattling wasn't just an attempt to enter - it was a message. It could get in anytime it wanted. And that thought made his blood run cold.

The shadows in his room seemed to thicken, like the very

darkness was pressing in around him. The phone screen became his anchor, a small island of light in the oppressive gloom. He pulled the covers tighter around him, his body trembling as he lay there, phone in hand, its light barely holding back the darkness. For Jack, sleep would not come that night. Instead, he would lie awake, listening to the silence that seemed to whisper, to the darkness that seemed to pulse with life.

The shadows in his room felt alive, moving in time with his heartbeat, as though the unseen threat was lurking just beyond the door, watching him through the thin veil of the night. Even the air felt thicker, colder, as though something in the room had shifted, become denser, waiting to see what Jack would do next.

A message popped up in the chat, "Check the hallway. Show us what's out there."

Jack's breath caught in his throat. He couldn't ignore the chat forever. His audience was growing; more people were joining, watching, waiting for something to happen. Jack didn't want to open the door. Every fiber of his being screamed at him to stay where he was, to leave the door closed, but the chat wouldn't let up.

"Open the door."

"We wanna see!"

"Dude, you've gotta check. What if it's gone?"

Jack's hand shook as he typed, "No way. You didn't hear the door rattle." He stared at the door, the soft glow from the phone casting just enough light to show the faint outline of the frame. But his audience wasn't satisfied.

"Do it. Open the door."

"Prove it's real."

"Just a peek."

Jack's heart raced, his breathing shallow. A horrible thought crossed his mind - what if he didn't open the door, and whatever was out there did it for him? What if the handle started to turn again, and this time, it didn't stop?

He took a deep breath, gripping the phone tighter, his

fingers slick with sweat. He had to do something. Slowly, trembling, Jack sat up in bed. His bare feet hit the cold floor, and the sensation sent a jolt of dread through him. He stood, legs shaking beneath him, eyes fixed on the door.

"I'm only gonna look," he whispered into the stream, his voice barely audible. He took a shaky step toward the door, then another. Each step felt like he was marching toward the edge of a cliff. His hand reached out toward the doorknob, hovering inches away, the cold air around it biting at his fingertips.

"Open it!"

"Do it!"

"Don't chicken out now!"

Jack swallowed hard, his heart pounding in his chest so loudly he was sure it would echo through the room. His hand trembled as he grasped the doorknob, the cool metal feeling foreign and wrong against his skin. For a moment, he hesitated, frozen in place.

Then, with a shaky breath, he twisted the knob.

The door creaked open an inch.

Silence.

Jack peered through the small gap, heart hammering in his chest. The hallway stretched out in front of him, dimly lit by the moonlight filtering through the window at the end. It was empty. No movement, no shadows. Just the long stretch of silence.

He exhaled, a small, shaky laugh escaping his lips. "There's nothing - "

The door slammed shut with a violent crash, sending Jack stumbling backward, his phone tumbling from his hands as the sound reverberated through the room. His breath came in ragged gasps, the echo of the slam still ringing in his ears.

The door didn't move again. The rattling had stopped, but the air felt wrong - heavy, thick with something unseen.

And then, a new anonymous message appeared in the chat. As Jack's eyes skimmed the words, a chill crept up his spine, the cold seeping into his skin, enveloping him like a shroud.

It simply read: "We see you."

CHAPTER 4

Signs Of Trouble

The early morning sun streamed through the sheer curtains of Emily's bedroom, casting delicate patterns of light across her walls. The faint hum of the air conditioner provided a comforting drone, a soft backdrop to the world outside. Emily lay sprawled across her bed, eyes fixed on her phone, scrolling through an endless feed of social media posts. Her room was a sanctuary, filled with plush pillows, posters of her favorite anime characters, and the faint scent of vanilla from the candles on her dresser.

Outside, the rest of the house began to stir. Emma had left for her morning run, and Owen was in his room, watching a YouTube video. John had already gone to work, his usual gruff goodbye barely audible. The normalcy of the day stood in stark contrast to the suffocating fear Jack had felt just hours before.

A soft knock broke Emily's solitude. She sighed, irritation flickering across her features. Before she could respond, Jack pushed the door open. His disheveled appearance startled her - dark circles under his eyes, his body tense, as though he'd been through a nightmare. There was something in his eyes, a wild unease that didn't sit well with her. He glanced around her room before finally fixing his gaze on her.

"Emily," Jack began, his voice low and trembling. "I need to talk to you."

Emily didn't look up from her phone, her fingers

continuing their rhythmic scroll. "What is it, Jack? Can't you see I'm busy?" Her tone was dismissive, the same tone she always used when dealing with her younger brother. It was the tone that said she had more important things to worry about than whatever was troubling him.

"I think there's something wrong with the house," Jack whispered, stepping closer. His voice was shaky, each word carrying the weight of something terrible. "Last night, I heard footsteps outside my door. And I - I saw something... red eyes, staring at me from the woods."

Emily's fingers stilled on her phone, her eyes narrowing as she finally looked up at him. For a brief moment, concern flickered in her expression, but it was quickly replaced by a smirk of amusement. "Red eyes? Really, Jack? You sound like a five-year-old scared of the dark." She rolled her eyes and sat up, crossing her arms over her chest.

Jack's face flushed with frustration. "I know it sounds crazy," he said, his voice rising, more desperate now. "But I swear, I saw them. And the footsteps - they were real. And something knocked on my door. Then it rattled, Emily! It was like something was trying to get in."

"Come on, Jack," Emily scoffed, her annoyance clear. "This isn't some horror movie. There's no such thing as ghosts. This isn't Poltergeist, or Amityville Horror, or whatever other movie you have been watching. No one died here, and there's no ancient burial ground under the house. This place is brand new!" She gestured around her room, emphasizing the pristine walls, the freshly painted trim. "The only thing that haunts this house is your absolute dorkness. Now get out of my room."

Jack's hands clenched into fists at his sides. His pulse quickened as he recalled the door slamming shut, the eerie laughter in the air vent, and the final message on his stream: "We see you."

"It's not nothing, Emily," he insisted, his voice trembling. "Something is wrong here. You didn't hear the footsteps or see those eyes. I'm telling you, there's something here - watching us."

Emily let out a heavy sigh, shaking her head. "You've really got to stop watching scary stuff before bed," she muttered. "Next thing I know, you'll be telling me our parents have been replaced by pod people."

Her words stung, cutting through the fear Jack had been carrying since last night. "You don't believe me," he said, his voice barely above a whisper.

"Nope," Emily replied casually, her fingers already back on her phone. "Now leave me alone."

Jack stood there for a long moment, his body tense, his eyes still wide with the terror that gripped him. When Emily didn't look up again, he turned and left her room, closing the door with a soft click.

As soon as the door closed, Emily shook her head. "What a baby," she muttered, sending a message to her friends.

Emily: My brother is acting so weird. He swears he saw red eyes outside his window and heard footsteps in the hall last night. Seriously, what a freak.

A few moments later, her phone buzzed with replies.

Mia: LOL, is he five? Maybe he needs a nightlight!

Jules: Sounds like he's trying to get attention. Classic.

Emily: Right? He's so dramatic. Maybe I'll get him a big teddy bear for his next birthday.

As Emily typed, Jack trudged back to his room, every step heavier than the last. He felt a growing sense of isolation as his sister's laughter echoed faintly behind him. Reaching his room, he leaned against the door and stared into the shadows. The memory of those red eyes burned in his mind, and the tension in the house felt heavier than before.

He pulled out his phone and sent a message to Emily.

Jack: I'm not making it up. There's something here. Just... be careful.

Her reply came almost immediately.
Emily: Stop being paranoid, Jack. You're fine.

Jack tossed his phone onto the bed, frustration boiling inside him. He sat down, staring at the spot where the door had rattled so violently the night before. The room felt smaller now, the shadows longer and darker than before. In his mind, he could still hear the faint echo of the laughter from the vent.

As the morning wore on, Emma watched her husband with a growing sense of dread that gnawed at her insides. The change in John had been gradual, so subtle at first that she had barely noticed it. But now it was impossible to ignore.

Only a few days after John casually mentioned his plan to build a garden in the farthest corner of the yard, he had already begun tearing up the sod. What had initially seemed like a harmless hobby quickly morphed into something much darker - a relentless obsession. And neither the size of the garden nor his fixation on it seemed to have any boundaries.

One of his first projects had been assembling a large wooden shed from a kit - something much more substantial than Emma had expected, complete with shelving, hooks, and ample storage space for tools. It had seemed innocent at first, but John became consumed by it, spending late evenings outside, sawing and hammering long after the sun had set.

He had taken the week off for the Fourth of July, a time she had hoped would be filled with family barbecues, fireworks, and the kind of carefree joy that summer vacations should bring. Instead, John had retreated into a strange isolation that left her feeling more alone than ever. He had taken to sleeping on a makeshift bed in the garage on nights he planned to work late, a sparse arrangement of old blankets and a worn pillow thrown haphazardly on a camp cot. He explained it away, saying he didn't want to disturb her by coming in late at night or waking early in the mornings. But the sight of that makeshift bed in the garage made her heart ache. It felt like he was building a wall between them, a physical embodiment of the emotional distance that had slowly grown over the past few weeks.

In the morning, before the sun had fully risen, Emma would hear the soft click of the garage door opening and closing, signaling John's start of the day. He moved through the house like a ghost, barely acknowledging her presence. He no longer joined her for breakfast or even bothered to greet the kids, who largely spent their mornings in their own rooms. His interactions had dwindled to mere grunts and nods, a far cry from the lively man who used to fill the house with laughter and warmth.

Emma found herself standing in the doorway to the garage more often, staring at the empty cot, the truck pushed aside to make room for John's new bed. The space smelled of soil and fertilizer, mingling with the musty scent of dust and gasoline. It was a smell she was beginning to associate with John, a constant reminder of his absence from the house. He would come inside only to grab a quick bite, his clothes stained with dirt, his hair matted with sweat. She could tell he hadn't showered in days, and the sight of him so disheveled, so unlike himself, filled her with a quiet despair.

The kids had also settled into their own routines. Jack could be found wandering aimlessly through the house, sometimes with his skateboard tucked under one arm, other times outside in the driveway, or playing on his Gameboy in the living room - anything to avoid the solitude of his room. Owen spent most of his time glued to the television or playing quietly in his own space, blissfully unaware of the tension that surrounded them. Meanwhile, Emily stayed in her room, sprawled on her bed with her phone in hand, chatting with her friends, seemingly untouched by the unease that had taken hold of the house.

For Emma, the nights were the worst. Lying in their bed, she would stare at the ceiling, listening to the faint sounds coming from the garden. The rustle of leaves, the soft thud of a shovel hitting the earth, the hammering of wood. John was out there, in the darkness, long after the sun had set, his silhouette barely visible through the curtains. She would hear the garage door creak open in the early hours of the morning, signaling his return.

As the days passed in their father's absence, the children began to notice John's growing obsession as well. Jack, with eyes far too old for his age, would sometimes stand beside Emma, gazing out at the newly formed garden, his face reflecting the same worry she felt. Owen had stopped asking to play with his father, instinctively sensing the widening gap between them. And Emily, always perceptive, watched John with a blend of curiosity and caution, as if trying to piece together the changes she was witnessing in him.

Emma felt helpless. She didn't know how to reach him, how to pull him back from whatever dark place he had gone. She had thought about confronting him, demanding that he talk to her, tell her what was going on. But every time she tried, the words stuck in her throat. The few times she had pushed, he had brushed her off with such irritation, his eyes flashing with anger, that she had backed down, afraid of pushing him further away.

So she watched and waited, her heart aching with the growing sense of loss. The house, once filled with laughter and life, now felt empty, the silence pressing down on her like a weight. The garden flourished, each bloom a stark contrast to the withering connection between her and John. The beauty of it mocked her, a silent reminder of the husband she was losing to its depths.

Emma stood at the window, her eyes fixed on John's distant figure. The sun was setting, casting long shadows across the yard, but he remained in the garden, digging, planting, his movements tireless. A lump formed in her throat, and she turned away, wiping at the tears that had begun to fall. She didn't know how much longer she could watch him slip away, how much longer she could pretend that everything was okay.

As the afternoon sun hung low in the sky, it cast long shadows across the quiet neighborhood of Briar Vale. The air was still thick with the heat of the day, pressing down upon the earth with a suffocating intensity. Inside the Miller house, the oppressive warmth had seeped through the windows into every corner, filling the rooms with a stifling stillness. The only sound was the distant hum of a lawnmower from a neighboring yard, a monotonous drone that seemed to amplify the eerie quiet within.

Owen sat alone in his bedroom, perched on the wide windowsill that overlooked the backyard. His small figure was silhouetted against the fading light, his face pressed against the cool glass. Below, in the sprawling expanse of the backyard, John was hard at work, his movements methodical and deliberate as he tended to the garden that had become his obsession.

The garden, once a simple patch of grass, had transformed under John's relentless efforts. Now, it was a barren expanse of raw earth, its surface scarred by deep trenches where John had torn up the sod with a fervor that bordered on mania. The flower beds, carefully lined with freshly cut boards, stood in stark contrast to the surrounding desolation, their edges sharp and precise, like the lines of a graveyard.

Owen watched his father with wide, unblinking eyes, his small hands pressed against the window. There was something about the scene that held him captive, a mixture of fascination and dread that he couldn't quite understand. John worked with an intensity that Owen had never seen before, his focus unwavering as he shoveled dirt from one bed to the next. The garden seemed to be all that mattered to him now; he barely looked up, barely acknowledged anything beyond the task at hand.

Owen's breath fogged the glass as he leaned closer, his heart pounding with a rhythm that matched the steady thud of his father's shovel. The scene below felt surreal, like something out of a dream - or a nightmare. The once vibrant backyard had taken on an ominous quality, the shadows lengthening into strange, twisting shapes that seemed to dance at the edges of Owen's vision.

And yet, despite the unease that gnawed at him, Owen couldn't tear his eyes away. He watched as John paused for a moment, wiping sweat from his brow with the back of his hand, his face set in a grim, determined expression. There was no joy in his work, only a grim purpose that Owen couldn't fathom.

Owen shivered, even though the room was warm. A strange feeling had settled over him, a heavy, suffocating weight that pressed down on his chest. It was as if he could feel the earth's pulse beneath the ground, a slow, steady beat that resonated through the very air. His small body trembled with a sensation he didn't have words for, a deep, instinctual understanding that something was terribly wrong.

Tears welled up in Owen's eyes, blurring his vision as he continued to watch his father. The tears came unbidden, a silent stream that ran down his cheeks and dripped onto the windowsill. He didn't know why he was crying, only that the feeling inside him was too much to bear. It was as if he were witnessing something he wasn't meant to see, something that frightened him in a way he couldn't explain.

"Owen, honey, what's wrong?"

The soft voice of his mother startled him, and he turned quickly, wiping at his tears with the back of his hand. Emma stood in the doorway, her expression a mixture of concern and confusion as she took in the sight of her son crying. She crossed the room swiftly and knelt beside him, brushing a strand of hair away from his damp cheek.

"Owen, why are you crying?" she asked gently, her eyes

searching his face for an answer. "What's the matter?"

Owen sniffled, his gaze darting back to the window. "Its Dad," he whispered, his voice trembling. "He's... he's been out there all day. He doesn't stop. He doesn't come inside anymore." His words came out in a rush, the fear and confusion bubbling up to the surface.

Emma glanced out the window, her eyes narrowing as she watched John work in the garden below. She had noticed his strange behavior over the past few days, the way he seemed to lose himself in his tasks, but seeing it now through Owen's eyes made it all the more unsettling. A familiar unease curled in her stomach, a feeling she had tried to dismiss as her own irrational anxiety.

"He's just working on the garden, sweetheart," Emma said softly, though her own unease crept into her voice. "He's been really focused on it lately. I'm sure he'll come in soon." She wanted to sound reassuring, but the words felt weak, as if saying them out loud might make them real.

Owen shook his head, fresh tears spilling over. "No, Mom," he insisted, his voice rising with a child's earnest conviction. "I don't think he will. I think he is going to the dark place."

Emma felt a chill run down her spine. Her heart skipped a beat, her breath catching in her throat. She had grown accustomed to Owen's talk of his imaginary friends, had brushed it off as harmless child's play. But now, hearing him say these things, her mind reeled. She had been fighting to keep herself grounded, to not let her past fears resurface. But this - this was something else.

"What do you mean, honey?" Emma's voice was soft, almost a whisper. She struggled to keep her tone light, not wanting to alarm Owen, or herself. The way her voice wavered made her want to scream.

Owen's gaze dropped to his hands, which were clenched tightly in his lap. "I don't know mom," he admitted, his voice quivering. "My friends said... he has been bad." His tears flowed freely now, his small body shaking with the effort to hold back sobs.

Emma's mind raced, her thoughts a chaotic jumble of fear and confusion. What could Owen's imaginary friends possibly know about John's work in the garden? And why did the mention of wrongdoing send a pang of dread through her chest? Was this just Owen's imagination, or was there something darker at play? A flash of John's recent behavior flickered in her mind - his harsh words, his growing distance, his obsession with the garden. How much of this was her own paranoia?

She pulled Owen into her arms, holding him close as she stroked his hair. "Shh, it's okay," she murmured, though her own words felt hollow. "Everything's going to be okay. Daddy's just been busy, that's all. You know how he gets with his projects."

But even as she said it, Emma felt the weight of doubt pressing down on her, crushing the fragile calm she was trying to maintain. There was something terribly wrong, something that had taken hold of her family and wouldn't let go. As she held her son close, his small body trembling against hers, Emma couldn't shake the feeling that whatever it was, it was only just beginning. And she was powerless to stop it.

Emma looked out the window one last time, her eyes following the rhythm of John's digging. She could see the strain in his movements, the lines of tension etched into his face. Whatever he was burying in that garden, it wasn't just seeds. And whatever was growing there, it wasn't just flowers.

She closed her eyes, a single tear slipping down her cheek. As much as she wanted to believe this was all in her head, she couldn't shake the gnawing certainty that something sinister was unfolding right in front of her. The ground beneath her feet felt unsteady, as if the very foundation of her life was shifting, and she was helpless to stop it.

"Everything's going to be okay," she whispered again, this time more to herself than to Owen. But the words hung in the air, empty and meaningless, as the darkness outside crept closer.

The next couple days brought stunning weather, the kind that seemed almost too perfect, as if the world outside had decided to put on a show. Each morning, the sky was a flawless expanse of deep blue, unmarred by a single cloud, and the air was warm and fragrant with the scent of blooming flowers. The sun hung high in the sky, its golden rays streaming down with a relentless intensity that made the air shimmer with heat, casting everything in a soft, almost dreamlike glow.

Emily emerged from the cool interior of the house, slipping out through the sliding glass door that led to the backyard. Her long brown hair was tied back in a ponytail, with loose strands catching the sunlight as she moved. At sixteen, Emily's figure was fully developed, her curves lending her a maturity that often caused people to mistake her for someone older. Her serious green eyes, sharp and focused, only added to that impression. She wore a bikini that accentuated her athletic, filled-out frame, the fabric clinging to her skin as she walked across the patio with an effortless air of confidence.

She squinted against the bright light, her eyes adjusting to the sunlit expanse that stretched out before her. It was the perfect summer day - the kind that beckoned for cool water and lazy afternoons, where the weight of the world felt distant, even if only for a little while.

The backyard pool sparkled like a sapphire gem, its surface rippling gently with the breeze. Emily walked to the edge, her bare feet warm against the stone tiles, and dipped a toe into the water. It was refreshingly cool, a perfect contrast to the oppressive heat of the day. Without hesitation, she slid into the pool, letting the water envelop her in a soothing embrace.

For a moment, the world fell away. The clear blue water muffled all sound, cocooning her in silence. Emily floated on her back, staring up at the cloudless sky. She felt her muscles relax, the tension that had coiled in her body over the past few days slowly unwinding. Here, in the water, she could forget about the strange behavior of her family, the eerie stories of her younger brother, and the mounting unease that seemed to linger in every corner of their new home.

As she floated, she closed her eyes, letting her mind drift. The cool water was a balm against her worries, each lap a soothing distraction from the unsettling changes she'd noticed around the house. Her father's obsession with his garden, Owen's imaginary friends, and her mom's increasing jumpiness - all of it felt so far away here, under the bright glare of the Florida sun.

Time slipped by unnoticed. After a while, Emily swam to the edge of the pool and climbed out, water streaming from her body as she reached for a towel. She wrapped it around herself, the soft cotton soaking up the water from her skin. With a contented sigh, she settled onto a sunbathing chair, leaning back and closing her eyes. The warmth of the sun on her face, combined with the lingering coolness of the water, was blissfully calming. Emily let her thoughts drift, enjoying the rare moment of peace.

She thought of her friends back in the city, of the bustling energy of streets filled with people, the chatter of voices, the hum of life that seemed to pulse through every alley and avenue. Here, in Briar Vale, everything was so quiet, so still. It was a different kind of peace, but one that sometimes felt unsettling rather than soothing.

Time seemed to stretch, the rhythmic rustling of the palm leaves above her mingling with the distant chirping of cicadas. She could almost imagine she was back in the city, where everything was predictable and familiar. The strange happenings in her home feeling like a distant dream, fading away under the gentle caress of the sun.

But as she lay there, her eyelids growing heavy with the drowsiness of mid-morning, a flicker of movement caught her attention. Emily opened her eyes, blinking against the brightness, and turned her head slightly. For a moment, she saw nothing, her eyes skimming over the familiar outline of the house next door, the low wooden fence that separated their properties.

And then she saw him.

Standing in the doorway of the neighboring house, partially hidden by the shadows, was George Thompson. His elderly frame was stooped, his posture unnaturally still. His eyes were fixed on her, staring with an intensity that made Emily's skin crawl. There was something unsettling about the way he watched her, his gaze unwavering and predatory, like a bird of prey eyeing its next meal.

Emily's heart skipped a beat, a chill racing down her spine. The way he stood there, motionless and silent, was deeply unnerving. It wasn't the casual glance of a neighbor passing by - it was something more deliberate, more invasive. She suddenly felt exposed, as if his gaze could strip away her defenses and see into her very soul.

Emily forced herself to look away, pretending not to notice. She turned her head to the other side, letting her hair fall across her face like a curtain. Her fingers tightened around the edges of her towel, pulling it closer around her body. She felt a prickling sensation on the back of her neck, the kind of instinctual reaction that warned of danger. The moment stretched, the seconds dragging into minutes, each one more agonizing than the last.

Unable to resist, she glanced back towards George's house. He was still there, still watching. This time he raised his hand and gave her a big, unsettling smile. His face was twisted with a look of lustful wanting, his eyes roaming over her body in a way that made her skin crawl. His mouth was slightly open, as if he were about to speak, but no words came. It was as if he were drinking in the sight of her, absorbing every detail with an intensity that made her feel sick.

Quickly, Emily sat up, her movements abrupt. She wrapped her towel tighter around her body, a flimsy barrier against the scrutiny of his eyes. Her breath came faster, her sense of relaxation evaporating like the droplets of water on her skin. She forced herself to meet his gaze for a brief moment, hoping to convey a message of discomfort, but George didn't move. His expression was inscrutable, his eyes dark and cold.

A car drove by in the distance, the sound momentarily breaking the eerie silence. Emily flinched at the noise, her heart hammering in her chest. George didn't even blink. The world around him seemed to fade into the background, leaving only his unsettling stare. She felt a wave of nausea rising, her stomach twisting into knots.

Feeling a surge of panic, Emily gathered her things, snatching up her phone and sunglasses. She moved quickly, almost stumbling as she made her way back to the house. She slid the glass door open with more force than necessary and slipped inside, the cool air of the interior hitting her like a wall. She locked the door behind her, her hands trembling slightly as she fumbled with the latch.

For a moment, she stood there, back pressed against the glass, her heart thudding in her chest. She peeked through the curtains, her eyes scanning the backyard. George was still there, still watching, his figure now a dark silhouette against the bright daylight. A shiver of revulsion rippled through her, and she pulled the curtain closed, shutting him out.

The minutes dragged by, each second stretching into an eternity as Emily sat in the living room, anxiously watching the clock. Her thoughts whirled, replaying the unsettling encounter with George Thompson over and over again in her mind. She needed to tell her father, to make him understand how wrong it felt, but a nagging voice at the back of her head kept questioning whether he would believe her, or worse, if he would care. The sound of the garage door opening snapped her from her thoughts.

Emily wandered outside again, this time with a sense of purpose. She headed straight to the garden, which had become her father's new obsession, consuming his every waking moment. The garden had changed remarkably in the past few days, transforming from a barren patch of dirt to a vibrant tapestry of green and color. The transformation was almost surreal, as if the garden itself was alive with an unnatural energy. John had been working tirelessly, his focus almost manic, and the results were strikingly beautiful yet strangely unsettling.

Lush Florida wildflowers, vivid and bright, seemed to bloom out of nowhere, their colors so intense they almost hurt to look at. Their petals caught the light in a brilliant display, shimmering like jewels under the sun. The garden buzzed with life, insects flitting from flower to flower, each bloom swaying gently in the breeze. The air was filled with the faint scent of earth and blossoms, a heady aroma that was almost intoxicating, wrapping around Emily like a seductive whisper. It was a sight that should have been calming, a small paradise in their backyard, yet it only made Emily's skin prickle with unease in an almost indescribable way.

Emily couldn't deny that the garden was impressive, but its sudden flourishing seemed almost unnatural. It's just she never envisioned her father as someone with a green thumb. She stepped carefully around the flower beds, the dark soil soft under her feet, looking for her father. She found him near the back of the yard, kneeling on the ground, his hands caked with dirt as he planted another row of flowers.

"Dad," she called out, trying to keep her voice steady. John didn't look up immediately, his focus entirely on his work. It took a moment before he acknowledged her, wiping his brow with the back of his hand and turning his head to glance at her.

"What is it, Emily?" he asked, his tone flat, as if he were being interrupted from something far more important.

She hesitated, suddenly unsure how to bring up what she'd seen earlier. "I... I saw George Thompson watching me while I was by the pool," she began, her voice wavering slightly. "It was really weird, Dad. He was just... staring. It made me uncomfortable."

John's head snapped up at that, his eyes narrowing. He set down his trowel with an exaggerated sigh, standing up slowly. His expression darkened, and Emily could see the muscles in his jaw tightening. He wiped his hands on his jeans, leaving dark smears of dirt, and turned to face her fully.

"Let me get this straight," John said, his voice low and sharp. "You were out here prancing around in your little bikini, and now you're complaining because an old man looked at you? Maybe you should think about what kind of attention you're attracting, Emily." His words were like a slap, cold and stinging.

Emily recoiled, shock spreading across her face. "What? No, Dad, that's not what I - "

"Enough," he cut her off, his voice rising. "I don't need you making up stories and causing trouble. George is our neighbor, for God's sake. He's harmless. You're the one who needs to be careful. And I don't want to hear any more of your whining about it. Got it?"

Emily felt tears prickling at the corners of her eyes, a mixture of humiliation and anger bubbling inside her. She opened her mouth to protest, but the look on her father's face stopped her. His eyes were cold, his expression set in a hard, unyielding line. There was no point in arguing. He had already made up his mind, and nothing she could say would change it.

"Fine," she muttered, her voice barely more than a whisper. She turned on her heel and walked away, her head bowed to hide the tears that now streamed freely down her cheeks. As she moved toward the house, her father's words echoed in her mind, each one a painful barb. She felt utterly alone, her father's dismissal cutting deeper than any stare from the neighbor ever could.

Inside, she slammed the door shut, the sound reverberating through the silent house. She leaned against it, her body shaking with silent sobs. Emily felt the crushing weight of isolation, a growing sense that she was adrift in a sea of indifference. Her father didn't believe her. He didn't even care.

Pulling out her phone, Emily typed out a frantic message to her friends, needing some semblance of validation.

Emily: Mia, Jules, my dad's being such a jerk. I caught our neighbor staring at me at the pool. A real creep. I told my dad and he basically blamed me for it. Said I'm just trying to get attention.

The responses came quickly, a flurry of concerned messages that did little to ease the ache in Emily's chest.

Mia: OMG, what the hell? That's so messed up!

Jules: Seriously, what's his problem? You don't deserve that, Ems. Maybe you should just ignore him for a while. Like, totally ghost him.

Mia: Yeah, just stay in your room and chill. You don't need that negativity.

Emily stared at her screen, her friends' words offering a small comfort, but the ache inside her remained. She wanted to believe it was just her dad being stressed, that everything would go back to normal if she just stayed out of his way. But deep down, she knew that wasn't true. Something was wrong with him. And it wasn't just her father's dismissive attitude or the neighbors' unsettling behavior. It was something darker, something that crept into the corners of her mind, whispering that things would never be the same again.

The sun had dipped below the horizon, leaving the sky a deep shade of indigo as the shadows lengthened across the Miller's living room. The house, once filled with the laughter of children and the comforting hum of daily life, now seemed cloaked in an unsettling quiet. The only sound was the ticking of the old clock on the mantle, its steady rhythm marking the passage of time with a somber inevitability.

Emma stood by the window, peering out into the darkening backyard where John's figure moved like a restless specter. His silhouette was faint against the gathering night, the soft glow of the garden lights casting eerie shadows on his face. He was kneeling by the flowerbeds, hands working furiously, oblivious to the fading light. The backyard, which had once been a sanctuary for their family, now felt like something else entirely - a place that consumed him, swallowing his time and energy with a hunger that Emma couldn't understand.

"John," she called softly, her voice barely cutting through the thick air. She watched as he paused, his back to her, his hands still buried in the soil. For a moment, she thought he hadn't heard her. Then he turned his head slightly, just enough for her to see the tension in his shoulders.

He didn't respond, didn't look up, just resumed his digging. Emma's heart ached as she watched him. This was not the man she knew, the man who had once taken joy in the simple pleasures of family life. This was someone consumed, driven by an obsession she couldn't comprehend.

She turned away from the window, feeling the weight of his absence pressing down on her, and moved to the couch. Her phone lay on the coffee table, screen glowing with a recent message from Emily. She picked it up, her fingers hesitating over the screen as she read the text again.

Emily: Dad's been out there all day again. What's wrong with him?

Emma's fingers trembled as she typed a response.

Emma: I don't know, sweetie. I wish I did. He's just... really focused on this garden right now.

The truth felt inadequate, like a flimsy shield against the growing storm. Emma sent the message and set the phone down, her mind racing. She had to do something, had to try to bring him back.

Gathering her resolve, she headed toward the back door, her steps purposeful. The air was thick with the scent of earth and the sweet fragrance of the wildflowers that now blanketed the garden. She could see John's figure more clearly as she stepped outside, his hands moving with a rhythmic precision that seemed almost mechanical.

"John," she called again, her voice firmer this time. He didn't respond, his focus unbroken, as if he were in a trance. The sight of him, so absorbed, so disconnected from everything else, sent a shiver down her spine.

"John," she repeated, louder now, stepping closer. "It's getting late. Why don't you come inside? You've been out here for hours."

Finally, he looked up, his face illuminated by the soft glow of the garden lights. His eyes were shadowed, dark circles underscoring his exhaustion, yet they held a strange intensity that Emma hadn't seen before. He stared at her for a moment, as if trying to recognize who she was.

"I can't," he said finally, his voice rough. "The garden isn't finished. I need to get it right."

Emma took a step closer, her heart aching with the need to reach him. "John, it's just a garden. You've done so much already. It's beautiful. But you need to take a break. Come inside, eat something, rest."

His expression tightened, irritation flickering across his features. "You don't understand," he snapped, turning back to his work. "It's not just a garden. It's important. This is a piece of me. It has to be perfect. You wouldn't get it."

The harshness of his tone stung, like a slap across the face. Emma recoiled slightly, her mouth opening in surprise and confusion. "John, I'm just worried about you," she said softly, trying to keep her voice calm. "You've been out here all the time. You barely talk to us. The kids miss you. I miss you. I miss us."

He paused again, his back rigid, hands motionless over the soil. For a brief moment, she thought he might turn around, that he might see the pain in her eyes and come back to her. But then he shook his head, a dismissive gesture that sent a fresh wave of hurt washing over her.

"No, Emma," he said, his voice dripping with frustration.

"The problem isn't me. It's you. You're not seeing things clearly because you were off your meds for so long. I think you're just confused. You're making this into something it's not."

Emma felt a cold shiver run down her spine. "My meds? John, I've been taking them. I'm not confused. I see what's happening. You've been out here for days, barely speaking to any of us."

John's eyes narrowed, and he stood up, the motion sudden and angry. "You're being paranoid, Emma. There is nothing wrong. You are just imagining things, seeing problems where there aren't any. Out here... what I am doing.... I'm doing this for us. I'm trying to make our home better, a sanctuary, and all you do is criticize and complain."

The accusation hung in the air, heavy and oppressive. Emma opened her mouth to respond, but no words came. She watched as he turned away from her, resuming his work with a renewed intensity, as if the conversation had never happened.

Inside the dimly lit living room, Emma slumped onto the couch, her shoulders sagging under the weight of her frustration. Her mind raced with thoughts of John, of the man he used to be. She glanced at her phone again, considering whether to reach out to someone for advice, but she hesitated. Who could she talk to about this? Who would even understand?

Emma stared at her phone, her vision blurred by tears that she refused to let fall. The weight of John's words hung heavily in the air, filling the room with an oppressive silence. She felt as if she were drowning, each breath a struggle against the overwhelming tide of confusion and doubt that threatened to pull her under. She needed someone to talk to, someone who could make sense of the chaos that her life had become, but the thought of reaching out made her feel even more vulnerable. Who could possibly understand the fear gnawing at her, the sense that she was losing everything she held dear?

She glanced back out the window at John, his figure now barely visible in the dim light, and felt a wave of hopelessness crash over her. He had always been her person. The one she turned to. Without him, his companionship, she felt lost. With a heavy sigh, she curled up on the couch, pulling a blanket around her shoulders as if it could shield her from the growing darkness. As the night deepened around her, Emma felt more alone than she had ever felt in her life.

Eventually, exhaustion overtook her. She lay in bed, her body sinking into the mattress as the weight of her emotions pressed down on her, heavy and unrelenting. At last, sleep crept in, soft and insistent, pulling her under. Her dreams were fragmented, filled with fleeting glimpses of John - his face hovering at the edges of her vision, always just beyond her grasp. His figure seemed to flicker in and out of the haze, distant and unreachable, like a shadow lost in mist. Even in the depths of sleep, she clung to him, sensing that he was her last connection to a world that was slowly unraveling, though she couldn't be sure if he was real, or merely a fading memory.

John knelt upon the yielding earth, his fingers burrowing into the soil with a frantic urgency, as though the very pulse of his life depended upon it. The cool dampness pressed against his skin, a grounding sensation in a world that had begun to unravel. He worked with a feverish precision, each movement deliberate, as if the weight of existence rested upon his ability to make this garden whole. No longer was it a mere patch of land - it had grown into something far beyond that. It had become sacred, demanding his every breath, his every thought.

His chest rose and fell in shallow bursts, his eyes flickering toward the darkening horizon. The shadows crept across the ground, long and skeletal, though he scarcely registered them. The world beyond the garden had shrunk into insignificance. The wind whispered through the trees, the leaves rustling like a distant memory, yet these were sounds of another life. All that mattered now was what lay beneath the surface.

He wiped his brow with the back of a trembling hand, smearing dirt across his face in a careless gesture. His hands quivered - not from weariness, but from something deeper, something gnawing at his very soul. Try as he might to focus on the task before him, a darker pull was at work, growing stronger with each passing hour. There was a presence in the soil, something alive, something breathing beneath his fingers. A force he could neither name nor escape, yet it called to him with an unrelenting insistence.

The garden was not merely a garden - it had become everything. His mind drifted, unbidden, to what he had done - the act that had marked him. He could still feel the weight of that moment, the way his hands had moved with a quiet, eerie certainty. Fear had no place in it. No, it had been necessary - inevitable. There had been no other choice. The whispers that now inhabited his mind had told him so, their quiet voices weaving through his thoughts like a serpentine hiss, insistent, relentless.

For a moment, John straightened, his gaze lifting toward the heavens. The stars had begun to punctuate the night, distant pinpricks of light in the vast, consuming darkness. He felt the weight of their presence, as though the cosmos itself watched his every move, waiting for him to finish what he had started. He swallowed, the taste of earth lingering on his tongue, a bitter reminder of how far he had descended. He no longer remembered when the garden had ceased to be a mere project - when it had begun to claim him. But now, it was all that mattered.

He knew Emma was watching from the house. He could feel her eyes upon him, her concern pressing against him like an unwanted shroud. But she didn't understand - none of them did. They could not hear the whispers, could not feel the pulse of life beneath the soil. He was doing this for them. For her. For all of them.

His fists clenched at the memory of their last conversation. Emma had tried to reason with him, her voice soft but insistent, speaking of trivialities that no longer held meaning. The neighbor, the children - none of it mattered anymore. Only the garden mattered. Only the truth that lay beneath the surface, waiting to be uncovered. Emma, Emily, Owen - they were blind to it, but John could see. He alone understood the garden's call, the deep, thrumming pulse that beckoned him closer.

For years, John had carried the weight of failure - of being not enough. Not enough of a father, not enough of a husband. The pressure had worn him down, day after day, until the garden had offered him salvation. Out here, amidst the earth and the whispers, his mind was clear. The doubts had fallen away, silenced by the dark certainty that now guided his every step. He was enough. More than enough. The garden had shown him that.

The wind shifted, bringing with it a voice, soft and insidious, barely more than a breath upon the air. Yet it spoke to him, drawing him in, urging him to dig deeper, to uncover the garden's hidden need. His eyes darkened, his heart quickening, not with fear, but with a grim anticipation.

"Yes," John murmured, his voice low and rough, barely more than a whisper. "It will be over soon."

He dropped to his knees once more, his hands plunging into the earth with renewed fervor. The whispers grew louder, the shadows seemed to move with a life of their own, twisting and writhing around him. Red eyes flickered in the dark, watching him with a malevolent gaze, and soft laughter echoed on the wind. But John no longer felt fear. He knew what had to be done. The voices had made it clear. The garden was nearly complete. And when it was finished, everything would be right again.

As the night deepened and the stars wheeled overhead, John worked in silence, his hands moving with an eerie precision, guided by the unseen force that had claimed him.

Each stroke of the trowel, each handful of earth, brought him closer to something - something vast, something powerful. Though he could not name it, he understood its purpose. It had chosen him.

The garden was no longer a mere patch of soil. It had become a sanctuary. A shrine. A terrible offering. And soon, it would be complete.

It waited, silent and dark, for the final stroke.

CHAPTER 5

Drowning in Secrets

The morning air was thick and still, carrying with it the scent of freshly cut grass and the faint tang of chlorine from the pool. The sun had just begun to cast its early light, streaking the sky with hues of orange and pink. Emma jogged along the familiar paths of Briar Vale, her feet hitting the pavement in a steady rhythm that usually brought her solace. But today, there was no comfort to be found in the ritual of her morning run. Her thoughts were as heavy as the humid Florida air, swirling with unease as she tried to make sense of the changes in her life and her family.

As she approached the Thompson house, Emma's eyes were instinctively drawn to the front porch. There sat George, slumped in his usual chair. His figure was hunched, his face a mask of despair. Dirt streaked his clothes, and his eyes were vacant, staring off into the distance. He looked more like a man who had lost everything than one simply enjoying the morning sun. Ethel's absence hung in the air like a question that refused to be answered. Emma hadn't seen her in weeks. She had tried to convince herself that Ethel had gone to visit family or was staying with friends, but George's haunted expression made her doubt her own reassurances.

Emma slowed her pace, considering calling out to George, but something about his demeanor stopped her. His shoulders sagged under an invisible weight, and his eyes seemed to see nothing but the void in front of him. The image of him sitting there, alone and unresponsive, sent a shiver down her spine. She had seen him like this before, the day she'd noticed the dirt on his clothes and the streaks of dried tears on his cheeks. Whatever had happened to Ethel, George was clearly in no state to talk about it. Emma picked up her pace again, feeling the chill of unease settle deeper into her bones.

Just past the Thompson house, Emma caught a glimpse of Agatha Cartwright through her kitchen window. The older woman's silhouette was barely visible behind the sheer curtains, but there was no mistaking her frail frame, the distinctive cane she always kept close, and the cats that constantly lounged around her yard. Emma hadn't seen much of Agatha lately, not since the unsettling pie incident, which she had tried - and failed - to forget. There was something about the woman's reclusiveness that amplified the strange, uneasy feeling in the neighborhood. As if sensing Emma's gaze, Agatha turned suddenly, her head jerking in her direction. A spike of fear shot through Emma, triggering a primitive urge to flee. She quickened her pace, her feet pounding against the pavement as she hurried away from the Cartwright house, eager to avoid any interaction with the odd woman.

She continued her run through the winding streets, past rows of houses that still stood empty, their dark windows staring out like the hollow eyes of the dead. The newest phase of Briar Vale was still incomplete. The half-built skeletons of future homes loomed around her, their wooden frames jutting into the sky like bones picked clean. As Emma ran past, she thought she heard a low whisper, the sound of wood creaking in the breeze. She told herself it was just the wind, just the natural settling of timber, exposed to the gentle breeze.

As she continued to run, the heat became oppressive, clinging to her skin like a second layer. Emma wiped a bead of sweat from her brow, her thoughts drifting back to the recent weeks. John had been off work, but instead of spending time with the family, he had thrown himself into his garden project with an intensity that bordered on obsession. He had cleared the backside of the backyard, turning it into a landscape of perfectly arranged wildflower beds and neatly pruned bushes. At first, Emma had been hopeful. John had always talked about wanting a garden even while in the city, a place to relax and unwind. But this was different. The garden had become his whole world, consuming his every thought and action. He spent hours outside, long after the sun had set, moving about in the dark as if guided by some unseen hand.

And now, there were his nighttime walks. Something new. He would leave the house late, sometimes past midnight, with the excuse that he needed to clear his head. Emma would watch him from their bedroom window, the glow of his phone lighting up his face as he texted and scrolled through messages before heading out into the night. At first, she had dismissed it, thinking he just needed space. But the more she watched, the more she sensed something was wrong. He would return in the early hours, looking disheveled and distant, as if he had been wandering for hours in a daze.

"Where do you go?" Jack asked one evening, his voice cutting through the thick tension at the dinner table. He was fourteen now, no longer the little kid who could be brushed off without a thought.

John looked up from his plate, his eyes narrowing in clear irritation. He held Jack's gaze for a long moment, as if debating whether to respond. Finally, he let out a short, dismissive sigh.

"Nowhere you need to worry about," John said flatly, pushing his plate away. He stood up abruptly, the chair scraping against the floor. "Mind your own business, Jack."

Without waiting for a response, he turned and walked out of the room, leaving an uncomfortable silence in his wake. Emma glanced at her son, wanting to say something, but the cold, distant look on John's face had silenced her, too.

Still deep in thought, Emma rounded the corner and slowed her pace, her breath coming in ragged, uneven gasps, the cool night air doing little to soothe the fire in her chest.

Her thoughts were consumed by John, his presence a shadow that loomed over her even in his absence. It was as though he had become an echo of himself, distant and unknowable. She could not shake the dreadful certainty that she was losing him - losing the man she had once loved to some dark, unseen force that drew him away, into places where her heart could no longer follow.

Every time she reached for him, it felt as if he slipped further from her grasp, retreating behind a wall of coldness and silence. But a more sinister thought had begun to take root in her mind, a poisonous seed planted by John himself: Was it just her imagination? Had she, in her growing desperation, begun to weave these fears from nothing more than shadows and half-formed doubts? He had warned her - more than once - that she had a tendency to make mountains of molehills, to see danger where none existed, just as she had before.

The memory of his words stung, a sharp prick of accusation, feeding the ever-creeping doubts that had begun to gnaw at the edges of her sanity. Was it all in her head? she wondered, her pulse quickening. Was she, once again, falling victim to the specters of her own mind? The question burned within her, a cruel reminder of the dark times she had fought so hard to leave behind. Could it be that her illness - dormant for so long - had returned to haunt her, distorting reality into nightmare?

At home, the faint light of dawn filtered through the blinds of Emily's bedroom, casting soft, pale shadows across the floor. The house was quiet, the silence broken only by the distant hum of the air conditioner and the soft chirping of early morning birds outside. Emily lay tangled in her sheets, the remnants of a restless sleep weighing heavily on her. She had stayed up late, lost in the comforting glow of her laptop screen, her favorite anime, Oran High School Host Club, playing quietly in the background, a distraction from the dull monotony of Briar Vale. Moving here had been a drag. Nothing ever happened in this sleepy suburb, and the few friends she had managed to keep up with online were miles away.

Suddenly, the sound of the front door closing hard reverberated through the house, followed by the familiar, fading rhythm of her mother's running shoes against the pavement. Emily stirred, her eyes blinking open to the dim light, and she groaned softly, her body still tired. She glanced at the clock on her nightstand; it was earlier than she would have liked to be awake. She sighed, resigning herself to the fact that sleep would not come easily now.

Pushing herself up, she swung her legs over the side of the bed and rubbed her eyes. She felt a dull heaviness behind them, the lingering fog of dreams that had faded into the murky recesses of her mind. She stood and stretched, feeling the stiffness in her limbs, and then made her way to the bathroom, her feet padding softly on the cool hardwood floor.

In the bathroom, she closed the door behind her and turned on the light, squinting at the sudden brightness. She caught a glimpse of herself in the mirror: her long brown hair disheveled, her eyes puffy with sleep. She reached for her hairbrush and ran it through her tangled locks, wincing as the bristles caught on knots. She felt a little better once her hair was smoothed, but the heaviness in her head remained.

Emily turned on the shower, waiting for the water to heat up before stepping in. She pulled the translucent shower curtain shut, the sound of the water cascading down around her providing a soothing, familiar rhythm. She stood under the spray, letting the warm water wash over her, easing the tension in her muscles. She closed her eyes, trying to let the monotony of the past few weeks wash away with the water. Her thoughts drifted to her brother Jack and his insistence that something was wrong in the house. He had talked about hearing footsteps in the hallway at night and seeing shadows outside his window. She had brushed him off, thinking it was just his overactive imagination, fueled by all those horror games he played.

As she reached for the shampoo, she noticed a subtle shift in the light beyond the shower curtain. Emily froze, her hand hovering over the bottle, her heart suddenly pounding in her chest. She opened her eyes and looked toward the curtain. The light outside was dim, filtered through the blinds, but she could see the outline of a figure, a dark silhouette standing just beyond the translucent plastic. Her breath caught in her throat, her body tensing. It was tall, the outline faint but unmistakable, the vague shape of a head and shoulders, motionless.

"Jack!" she shouted, her voice cutting through the silence, laced with a sharp edge of irritation, and beneath it, the faint tremor of fear. "If you're trying to scare me, it's not funny! You creep!" Her words hung in the air, defiant yet trembling, as the stillness around her seemed to close in tighter.

The figure did not move. It stood there, silent and still, the indistinct features blurred by the curtain. Emily's mind raced, her pulse quickening. She waited for a response, but the only sound was the rush of the water around her. The figure remained motionless, a silent sentinel watching from the other side.

"Jack, I'm serious!" she shouted, her voice cracking slightly. "Get out you fucking psycho!"

Silence. The figure did not move.

Emily's fear spiked, adrenaline flooding her veins. Her hand trembled as she reached for the curtain, her fingers grasping the edge. She hesitated, her breath coming in short, shallow gasps. She yanked the curtain aside, the rings clattering against the metal rod, her eyes wide with anticipation.

There was no one there. The bathroom was empty, the door still closed. The dim light filtered through the blinds, casting long shadows on the tiled floor. Emily's heart pounded in her chest, her breathing shallow. She glanced around the small room, her eyes darting to every corner, but there was no sign of Jack, or anyone else. She was alone.

She stepped out of the shower, her body trembling

slightly, and wrapped a towel around herself. Her mind was a whirlwind of thoughts, each more unsettling than the last. She glanced at the mirror, half expecting to see something behind her reflection, but there was nothing. Just her own wide-eyed gaze staring back at her. She tried to steady her breathing, telling herself it was nothing, just a trick of the light, her imagination playing tricks on her. The memory of Jack's earlier stories was causing her own imagination to run wild.

But she couldn't shake the image of the silhouette, standing silently outside the curtain, watching her. She knew Jack liked to scare her sometimes, but this felt different. It felt wrong. She thought again about what Jack had said, about the shadow and the red eyes outside his window. She had dismissed him at the time, calling him silly and telling him to lay off the horror games. But now, a sliver of doubt crept in. What if he wasn't imagining things? What if there was something more?

She shut off the water, her hands shaking slightly as she did. She wrapped herself more tightly in the towel and opened the bathroom door, peering out into the hallway. The house was silent, the morning light casting long shadows on the floor. She listened, straining to hear any sound, but there was nothing. Just the quiet hum of the air conditioner and the faint chirping of birds outside.

Emily stepped out into the hallway, her eyes scanning the shadows. She moved cautiously, her feet soft on the hardwood, her senses alert to any sign of movement. She reached Jack's room and paused, her hand hovering over the doorknob. She took a deep breath and knocked, the sound echoing in the silent hallway. There was no answer.

"Jack?" she called softly, her voice wavering. She pushed the door open and peered inside.

Jack was still asleep, his form buried under a pile of blankets, his breathing deep and even. Emily sighed, a mixture of relief and lingering unease washing over her. She stepped back and closed the door quietly, not wanting to wake him. She turned and headed back to her room, her mind still reeling from the experience.

As she entered her room, she caught sight of her phone on the bedside table. She picked it up, her thumb hovering over the screen. She thought about texting her mother, telling her what had happened, but she hesitated. What could she say? That she had seen a shadow in the bathroom? That she felt like she was being watched? She knew how it would sound, like the overactive imagination of a teenager, nothing more. And what if it really was nothing? Just a trick of the light, a shadow cast by the early morning sun? She didn't want to worry her mother over nothing.

Emily put the phone down and sat on the edge of her bed, the towel still wrapped around her. She stared at the floor, her mind racing. Briar Vale was boring, that much was true, but this? This felt like something out of one of Jack's creepy stories, and she didn't know whether to be scared or just annoyed. She thought of her father again, his distant stares, the nights he disappeared into the darkness. Whatever was going on, it was more than just boredom. She felt like their family was unraveling, and she didn't know how to stop it.

She lay back on the bed, her eyes fixed on the ceiling, the shadows shifting in the morning light. The house was quiet, but the silence felt heavy. Emily closed her eyes, trying to push the thoughts away, but the image of the silhouette lingered, burned into her mind. She took a deep breath, telling herself it was nothing, just her imagination. The sense of unease clung to her, a shadow that refused to fade. Deciding she needed to do something to shake off the feeling, she sat up, glancing out the window toward the backyard. The pool. Maybe a swim would help clear her head, wash away the remnants of fear still clinging to her. The idea of cool water and sunlight felt like a balm. She stood up, determined, and headed for the door, hoping the water would soothe her restless thoughts.

The sun hung high in the sky, its rays bearing down with an intensity that shimmered off the blue water of the pool. The air was thick and heavy, laden with the scent of chlorine mingling with the floral notes of the garden. Emily stood by the edge of the pool, staring into the clear depths, her thoughts still buzzing with the morning's unsettling encounter in the bathroom. She needed a distraction, something to clear her mind and rid herself of the lingering sense of unease. Swimming had always been a way to escape, to lose herself in the rhythm of the water.

She set up her pill speaker on a nearby table, the small device blasting her favorite songs into the still afternoon air. The upbeat tunes offered a sense of normalcy, filling the space with a semblance of life that the silent house lacked. Emily glanced toward the Thompson house, her eyes narrowing as she searched for any sign of George. The memory of him standing at his doorway, watching her last week, sent a shiver down her spine. She could still see his eyes, cold and empty, fixed on her like she was some object of fascination.

Seeing no one, she relaxed slightly, letting out a breath she hadn't realized she was holding. The backyard was empty, just the garden with its neatly pruned bushes and the open space of the pool. "We really need a taller fence" she muttered to herself.

Emily felt a momentary sense of relief as she kicked off her sandals and slipped out of her t-shirt and shorts, leaving them in a pile on the poolside chair. She stood there for a moment, basking in the warmth of the sun on her skin, before diving into the water with a fluid grace.

The cool water enveloped her, washing over her skin and bringing an instant sense of relief. She moved through the pool with long, smooth strokes, relishing the feel of the water gliding against her. The world above seemed to fade away, the music from the speaker muffled, leaving only the sound of her own heartbeat and the rhythmic movement of her limbs. For a few precious moments, Emily felt at peace, her mind clear, her body free.

She swam toward the deep end of the pool, luxuriating in the rare moment of calm as she floated on her back, her eyes shielded from the glaring sun. The water's gentle embrace soothed her, allowing her thoughts to drift as easily as her body. But then, a sinister chill pierced her serenity. An icy grip, cold and unrelenting, clamped around her ankle. Her eyes flew open, her heart pounding with sudden fear, but the vastness of the pool swallowed her gasp.

Peering down, her breath caught in her throat. A dark, undulating shape lurked beneath her, a shadowy blur swirling ominously in the otherwise clear water. For a heart-stopping moment, she thought she glimpsed red, glowing eyes, glaring up from the abyss with a predatory malice. Panic surged through her like a shockwave, sharp and paralyzing.

Desperation fueled her movements as she began to flail wildly, her legs kicking and her arms thrashing in a frantic bid for freedom. The icy grip around her ankle tightened, dragging her downward with a nightmarish force. Her head dipped below the water's surface, and she fought against the mounting pressure, her body convulsing as she struggled to stay afloat. Each gasp for air was met with bubbles and silence, her cries swallowed by the encroaching pool.

Emily's fight grew increasingly frantic. Her hands clawed desperately at the water's surface, her legs propelling her with wild energy, but the darkness seemed to pull her down with relentless determination. The pressure in her chest built painfully as she struggled to keep her head above water, her movements growing more erratic and desperate.

The red eyes appeared to follow her every move, their malevolent gaze piercing through the murk. The darkness around her deepened, spreading like ink and turning the once-familiar pool into a churning abyss. Her vision blurred, the world becoming a dizzying swirl of shadows and light. Her strength waned with each passing moment, but she fought with every ounce of energy she had, splashing and kicking, determined to escape the icy grip that threatened to drag her under.

As the struggle intensified, the sensation of being pulled down persisted, but Emily managed to keep herself partially above the water. The cold, dark tendrils of the pool seemed to recede slightly, giving her a fleeting respite. Her lungs burned for air, and she gasped with each desperate breath. She continued to splash and fight, her body wracked with the effort to stay afloat, as she fought against the encroaching darkness and the unseen force that sought to pull her into the depths.

Inside the house, Jack stumbled down the creaky stairs, his hair a wild tangle from another late night. Bleary-eyed and disoriented, he shuffled into the kitchen and surveyed the cluttered pantry, searching for something to quell his hunger. The faint strains of music from the backyard had interrupted his sleep; Emily's parties were always a bane to those who needed rest, especially him. With a weary sigh, he grabbed a yogurt topped with M&Ms and sank into a chair at the table, his Game Boy in hand.

As he played, the upbeat tunes from outside were suddenly pierced by an unsettling cry. The music was now punctuated by splashes and muffled thrashing that seemed out of place. Jack's heart began to race, and the game controller slipped from his fingers as he strained to decipher the disturbance. The noises grew louder and more frantic, igniting a deep sense of alarm. He sprang from his chair, burst through the back door, and his feet pounded against the deck as he sprinted toward the pool, a cold wave of dread washing over him with every step.

"Emily!" he shouted, his voice cracking with fear. He saw her flailing in the water, her head bobbing below the surface, her arms reaching out in desperation. Without thinking, he dove into the pool, the cold water shocking his system as he swam toward her. He grabbed her arm, pulling with all his strength, the water churning around them as he fought to bring her up. Her eyes were wide with terror, her mouth open in a silent scream.

With a final heave, he dragged her to the edge of the pool, her head breaking the surface as she gasped for air, coughing and sputtering. He pulled her out of the water, his arms shaking with the effort, and laid her down on the warm tiles. Emily lay there, gasping, her chest heaving, water streaming from her hair and her eyes wild with panic.

"Emily, what happened?" Jack asked, his voice tight with fear. He knelt beside her, his hands on her shoulders, his eyes searching hers.

Emily coughed, struggling to catch her breath. "Something... something was pulling me down," she managed to gasp. "There was something in the water... I saw eyes... red eyes."

Jack's face paled, his own fear mirrored in his sister's eyes. He glanced around the pool, half expecting to see something emerging from the water, but there was nothing. The surface was calm, the water clear. He looked back at Emily, her expression one of terror and confusion.

He stood up and grabbed his phone, his fingers fumbling as he dialed their father's number. The phone rang, and Jack's heart pounded in his chest. Finally, John answered, his voice gruff and annoyed.

"What is it, Jack?" John snapped, his tone edged with irritation.

"It's Emily," Jack said, his voice shaking. "Something happened... in the pool. She says something tried to pull her under."

There was a pause on the other end, and then John's voice came through, tinged with frustration. "Where's your mother?"

"She's out running, I think." Jack replied. "Dad, you need to come now!"

John sighed, the sound heavy with exasperation. "I'm in the garden. I'll be there in a minute." The line went dead, and Jack lowered the phone, his hands trembling.

A moment later, John appeared, his face set in a frown, dirt smudging his hands. He looked down at Emily, who was still lying on the tiles, her face pale, her eyes wide. He glanced at Jack, his expression hardening.

"What's going on?" John asked, his voice flat.

"I told you," Jack said, his voice rising with frustration. "Emily says something tried to drown her!"

John knelt beside Emily, his eyes narrowing as he studied her. "Are you sure you're not just imagining things?" he asked, his tone dismissive. "Maybe you were daydreaming, and you slipped under. Or is this some kind of stunt for attention?"

Emily stared at him, her eyes filling with tears. "I know what I felt," she said, her voice shaking. "There was something... it grabbed me."

John shook his head, a look of irritation crossing his face. "This is ridiculous," he muttered. "You're just trying to scare yourself. There's nothing in the water. You need to stop this nonsense, Emily."

Jack felt anger rise within him, his fists clenching. "Dad, she's telling the truth! I heard her... I saw her struggling!"

John stood up, brushing the dirt from his hands. "I don't have time for this," he said coldly. "If your mother were here, she'd be all over this, turning it into something it's not. But she's not, and I won't entertain these fantasies. Now, both of you, calm down and stop causing a scene."

He glanced down at the pool, his eyes narrowing as he noticed some leaves and debris swirling around the intake at the bottom. It looked like the filter might be clogged, creating a stronger pull than usual. John frowned, stepping closer to the pool's edge. "Maybe the suction is too strong," he muttered, half to himself. "You must have gotten too close, Emily. That's all it was. I'll check the filter and see if it needs adjusting. Until then, stay out of the pool. Both of you. We don't need any more incidents like this."

Emily opened her mouth to protest, but John cut her off with a sharp wave of his hand. "I mean it. No more talk of things grabbing you or red eyes or whatever nonsense you think you saw. Stop entertaining these fantasies. They're not helping anyone." His voice was firm and final, leaving no room for argument.

With that, he turned and walked back toward the garden, his shoulders tense, as if carrying an unseen weight. He didn't look back, didn't see the way Emily's face fell, her fear and confusion deepening, leaving her fealing isolated and alone.

Without another word, Emily pushed herself up from the edge of the pool. She wrapped her arms around herself, a shiver running through her despite the warmth of the sun. Her eyes were downcast, avoiding Jack's concerned gaze. She turned and walked away, her footsteps light on the patio, her wet hair dripping water onto the tiles. She moved quickly, slipping back into the house and up the stairs, retreating to the sanctuary of her room.

Jack watched her go, his expression tightening with frustration and anger. He could see the way she had hunched her shoulders, the way she kept her head down to hide her face. He knew she was upset, her fear and hurt turning inward, festering. He wanted to call after her, to say something to make it better, but the words stuck in his throat. He glanced toward the garden, where John had disappeared among the flowers and bushes, his figure hunched over his work, oblivious to the impact of his dismissive words.

Jack remained standing by the pool, the water now calm and silent, reflecting the clear blue sky above. The cheerful music from Emily's pill speaker continued to play, a stark contrast to the tension that had settled over the backyard. He felt the weight of the unspoken words between them, the rift growing wider. Beneath the surface, Jack sensed the presence of something dark and unseen, waiting. He took a deep breath, steeling himself. Whatever was happening, he was determined to find out the truth, to protect his sister, even if it meant confronting his father.

The sun beat down on him, but Jack felt a chill, a sense of foreboding that had nothing to do with the water. He stood there for a long moment, his thoughts churning like the water had moments before, before finally turning and walking back toward the house, following the path Emily had taken.

The afternoon sunlight streamed through the windows, casting bright, warm rays across the floor as Jack ascended the stairs. Each step felt like a heavy burden, the weight of the day pressing down on him. The house was eerily quiet, the stillness amplifying the rhythmic sound of his own breathing. At the top of the stairs, he paused, his gaze drifting toward his sister's room. The door stood slightly ajar, a sliver of light slicing through the encroaching shadows of the hallway.

From within, the faint, muffled sound of sobbing reached his ears. His heart tightened at the sound, and he moved with deliberate softness, trying not to disturb the delicate silence that hung in the air. The contrast between the bright, cheerful daylight and the sorrowful noise from the room felt stark and unsettling. With each cautious step, he drew closer, the quiet intensity of the moment weighing heavily on him.

He pushed the door open a little wider and peered inside. Emily was sitting on her bed, her knees drawn up to her chest, her face buried in her hands. Her shoulders shook with each silent sob, her body curling in on itself as if trying to become as small as possible. The sight of his sister like this - so vulnerable, so alone - sent a wave of protectiveness surging through him. He stepped into the room, the floorboards creaking softly under his weight.

"Emily?" Jack's voice was gentle, barely above a whisper. He didn't want to startle her, but he needed her to know he was there.

Emily looked up, her eyes red and swollen from crying, her cheeks streaked with tears. For a moment, she just stared at him, her expression a mix of anger, fear, and a desperate kind of relief. She wiped at her eyes with the back of her hand, sniffing loudly, but said nothing.

Jack hesitated by the door, then walked over to the bed and sat down beside her. He didn't know what to say, how to make her feel better, but he knew he had to try. He reached out and put a hand on her shoulder, squeezing gently.

"I'm sorry, Em," Jack began softly. "I'm sorry about what Dad said. He had no right to dismiss you like that." He paused, searching for the right words. "I was there. I know you're telling the truth. I saw how scared you were. I just... I didn't see anything myself."

Emily's lip trembled, and she shook her head, fresh tears spilling down her cheeks. "He thinks I'm lying," she said bitterly, her voice cracking. "He thinks I made it up for attention. But Jack, I felt it. There was something in the water, something pulling me down. I saw... I saw these eyes. They were red. I'm not imagining it. I know what I felt!"

Jack nodded, his face serious. He didn't doubt her for a second. The fear in her voice was too real, too raw to be a fabrication. He had seen the terror in her eyes when he pulled her out of the pool, the way she had clung to him, her body shaking. He had felt the strange pull himself, the way the water had seemed almost alive, its grip unnatural.

"I believe you," he said quietly. "I've been feeling it too, ever since we moved here. The shadows, the noises... the feeling of being watched. I told you about it before, remember? You laughed at me. But I knew something was off." He looked at her, his eyes earnest. "And now you've seen it too. There's something here, something in this house or in this neighborhood. I don't know what it is, but I know it's real."

Emily bit her lip, guilt flickering in her eyes. "I'm sorry, Jack," she whispered. "I didn't believe you. I thought you were just being paranoid, playing too many horror games. I made fun of you... but you were right. I see that now. I'm scared, Jack. I don't know what's happening, but it's like... like there's something evil here, something we can't see."

Jack's grip on her shoulder tightened. "It's okay," he said firmly. "You didn't know. But now we both do. And we're going to figure this out, together. We have to. We can't just ignore it and hope it goes away."

Emily looked at him, her eyes wide with fear but also with a glimmer of hope. "What do we do?" she asked. "How do we figure it out? It's not like we can just go around asking people if they've seen ghosts."

Jack leaned back, propping himself up on his hands. "I've been thinking," he said after a moment. "Maybe we start by looking into the history of this place. I know Briar Vale is new, but that doesn't mean there wasn't something here before. Maybe there's a reason why all this is happening now. Something to do with the land or the houses. We need to find out if there's any record of strange things happening here before."

Emily nodded slowly, considering his suggestion. "Yeah," she said thoughtfully. "Maybe we can find something online. Old news articles, local history sites, that kind of stuff. If there's anything weird, it might be documented somewhere."

Jack's eyes lit up with determination. "Exactly. We start there. And maybe we talk to some of the neighbors, the ones who've been here the longest. They might have noticed something strange, even if they don't realize it."

He thought quietly about his father. We need to figure out what's going on with him too. He's been acting strangely. I wonder where he's going at night?

Emily's mouth curved into a small, tentative smile. "You're a nerd, you know that?" she said, a hint of teasing in her voice. "But I think you're right. We need to do something. I'm tired of feeling scared and alone. If there's a reason for all this, we need to find it."

Jack smiled back, relieved to see some of the color returning to her cheeks. "We're not alone, Em," he said. "We've got each other. We're going to figure this out. I promise."

They sat in silence for a moment, the quiet settling around them like a blanket, warm and reassuring. The dim light of the bedside lamp cast a soft, comforting glow, and the shadows on the walls seemed less threatening with Jack there. Emily's tears had stopped, and her breathing had evened out, each inhale and exhale slowing as the tension in her body unwound. The storm of emotions that had gripped her was subsiding, leaving behind a heavy calm, as if she were floating in a sea of stillness. Jack's hand on her shoulder felt like an anchor, grounding her in the present, reminding her that she wasn't alone.

The sense of dread that had weighed on them all day seemed to lift slightly in the shared silence, a fragile truce against the darkness that surrounded them. Jack watched his sister, her eyes closed, her face softened by the fading light, and he felt a surge of protectiveness. Whatever was happening, whatever malevolent force was creeping into their lives, he would face it with her.

As the sun dipped below the tree line, night enveloped Briar Vale like a velvet shroud, thick and impenetrable. Jack kept his distance as he followed his father, John, through the quiet, dimly lit streets. Their footsteps were swallowed by the dense Florida air, leaving only the whisper of the breeze rustling the leaves. Jack's heart pounded in his chest, a steady drumbeat that echoed in his ears. He had never done anything like this before - spying on his own father - but with everything else happening and the strangeness of John's recent behavior, he had no choice. He needed to find out what was going on.

John walked briskly, his shoulders hunched slightly as if under an invisible weight. He rounded a corner, disappearing from Jack's sight for a moment. Jack hurried to catch up, careful to stay hidden in the shadows. He reached the corner and peered around it, just in time to see John come to a stop in front of one of the older houses, its dark façade looming like a silent sentinel against the night sky.

Jack recognized the house immediately. It was Mr. Thompson's, the older neighbor next door. Despite being part of the newer developments in Briar Vale, it looked out of place.

The paint, though new, was an unusual, dark color, and the porch had a worn appearance that contrasted sharply with the pristine condition of the surrounding homes. The windows were dark, giving the house a foreboding look, as if it were hiding something beneath its surface. John stood on the cracked pathway leading up to the front door, his posture rigid and his hands clenched into fists at his sides.

Jack stayed as close as he dared, slipping into the deeper shadows cast by a tall hedge, his heart pounding in his chest. The night was still, the silence almost tangible, wrapping around him like a second skin. He watched as Mr. Thompson emerged from the darkness of his porch, stepping into the dim pool of light cast by the single bulb hanging overhead. His expression was cautious, his eyes narrowed as he took in the sight of John standing on his walkway.

For a moment, the two men simply stared at each other, the tension between them thick and palpable. Jack strained to hear, but the words that passed between them were muffled, carried away by the breeze. He could see their faces, though, and the emotions written plainly across them. John's face was twisted in anger, his mouth moving rapidly, while Mr. Thompson's eyes widened in what could only be described as fear. Whatever John was saying, it was having a profound effect on the older man.

Jack inched closer, his movements slow and deliberate, his breath shallow. He couldn't hear the exact words, but he could see the way John's hands balled into fists, the way his posture became more aggressive, almost threatening. Mr. Thompson raised his hands defensively, his mouth opening in what looked like a plea. Jack's mind raced, trying to piece together what was happening. What could his father be so angry about? Why was Mr. Thompson so afraid?

The argument escalated, their voices rising in intensity even if Jack couldn't make out the specifics. John's face was a mask of rage, his eyes dark and flashing. He took a step closer to Mr. Thompson, his body language rigid and unyielding. The older man took a step back, his hands still raised, his face pale and drawn. Jack felt a chill run down his spine. He had never seen his father like this before - so full of anger, so ready to lash out. It was as if something had taken hold of him, something dark and uncontrollable.

Jack's breath caught in his throat as he saw John raise a finger, jabbing it toward Mr. Thompson's chest. The gesture was aggressive, a clear warning, and it sent a spike of fear through Jack's heart. He could sense the danger in the air, the potential for violence simmering just beneath the surface. He had to do something, say something to diffuse the situation. But he couldn't move, couldn't speak. Fear had rooted him to the spot, his limbs frozen in place.

Suddenly, as if sensing another presence, John turned his head sharply, his eyes scanning the darkness. Jack's heart lurched as his father's gaze swept over the hedge where he was hiding. For a moment, he was sure John could see him, his figure outlined in the shadows. He held his breath, his body tensed, willing himself to be invisible. John's eyes lingered on the spot for what felt like an eternity, the silence stretching out like a taut string, ready to snap.

Then, without a word, John turned back to Mr. Thompson, his voice dropping to a low, menacing tone that Jack couldn't quite hear. Whatever he said, it had an immediate effect on Mr. Thompson, who flinched as if struck. The older man nodded quickly, his mouth moving in what looked like a hurried agreement, his eyes wide with fear. Jack watched as John turned away abruptly, striding back down the walkway with a purposeful gait, leaving Mr. Thompson standing there, pale and shaken.

Jack didn't wait to see what happened next. As soon as his father disappeared around the corner, he slipped back into the deeper shadows, his heart racing. He moved quickly, silently, his feet barely touching the ground as he made his way back to the house. The shadows seemed to close in around him, the darkness alive with the echoes of his father's anger, the tension that had crackled in the air.

His mind was a whirl of confusion and fear as he reached the front door of his house. He slipped inside, closing the door softly behind him, his breaths coming in short, sharp gasps. The house was dark and silent, the ticking of the hallway clock the only sound.

He stood for a moment in the entryway, his back against the door, his mind racing. The image of his father, angry and threatening, loomed large in his mind. The way John had looked, the way he had spoken - it was all so unlike the man Jack had known. What was happening to his father? What had driven him to confront Mr. Thompson with such rage?

Jack made his way to his room, his thoughts a tangled mess. He needed to talk to Emily, to tell her what he had seen. But not tonight. Tonight, he needed to think, to make sense of what had just happened. As he lay down on his bed, the darkness of the room seemed to close in around him, the shadows shifting and moving like living things. He closed his eyes, but sleep did not come easily. The image of his father's face, twisted with anger, haunted him, and the night stretched on, long and dark.

CHAPTER 6

Weapons of Influence

T he early morning sun drenched Briar Vale in a soft, golden radiance, casting elongated shadows that danced across the freshly paved streets. The air hung heavy with the promise of yet another sweltering Floridian day, yet a lingering coolness in the morning invigorated Emma's senses. The rhythmic thud of her sneakers on the pavement and the steady beat of her heart provided a rare sanctuary from the storm clouds of tension that had taken root within her home.

Emma drew in a deep breath, relishing the crispness that filled her lungs and momentarily soothed her troubled mind. Her morning runs had always been her refuge - a time of solitude where the burdens of daily life could be momentarily cast aside. Her feet pounded the pavement as she turned the corner, heading past the Thompson residence.

It was customary for George Thompson to be ensconced on his front porch at this early hour, a familiar figure in the neighborhood's serene tableau. But today, as Emma approached, she found the porch conspicuously vacant. The wicker chair, typically occupied by George's stooped form, stood deserted, swaying gently in the morning breeze. A frown of concern etched itself on Emma's face. The absence of George, compounded by Ethel's recent disappearance, struck a discordant note. She slowed her pace, scanning her surroundings as though expecting him to materialize from the shadows.

It was then that Emma's gaze fell upon a disturbing sight - a glimmer of broken glass catching the sunlight. Her steps faltered as she took in the disquieting scene. One of the Thompson's front windows was marred by a jagged, gaping hole, the glass shattered in a sinister pattern like a spider's web. Shards lay scattered on the porch, glittering menacingly in the golden light. The house, once the epitome of quaint charm, now exuded an air of foreboding, the broken window a dark, accusing eye watching the world outside.

A chill, incongruous with the morning warmth, crept across Emma's skin. She approached with trepidation, her steps muted on the lush lawn. Hesitation gripped her as she neared the porch, her gaze darting for any sign of movement within. The house loomed ominously, its silence oppressive. Swallowing the uneasy knot in her stomach, she edged closer, her heart pounding with growing trepidation.

"George?" she called, her voice quavering in the heavy stillness. No response emerged from the silent house. The only sounds were the rustling of leaves stirred by the breeze and the distant hum of an air conditioner. Emma's hand trembled as she raised it to knock on the door, the sound hollow and forlorn. Still, no answer came. The house remained a mute, lifeless sentinel.

As Emma leaned in closer to the broken window, a sense of dread intensified. The interior of the house was cloaked in shadow, but then, from within, there emerged a faint, unsettling creak - a rhythmic sound as though someone were moving slowly across the floorboards. Emma's heart leapt in her chest, and a cold shiver snaked down her spine. The sound seemed incongruous with the emptiness she had observed through the window. She called out once more, her voice trembling with fear, but received no reply. The eerie creaking persisted, a spectral presence haunting the darkened rooms. Overwhelmed by the sinister atmosphere, Emma retreated hastily, her breath coming in ragged gasps. The ominous creaking, coupled with the

130

suffocating silence, was unbearable. With one last apprehensive glance at the house, she fled, her steps quickening as she distanced herself from the source of her growing dread.

Emma cast a final, lingering look at the Thompson residence. The broken window seemed to glare back at her, a mute witness to an unknown disturbance. Her nerves were frayed, and a tightening knot settled in her stomach. She briefly contemplated calling the police from the sidewalk, her finger hovering over her phone with an urgency that nearly overcame her hesitation.

Yet doubt gnawed at her. Was she merely overreacting? Could there be a mundane explanation for the Thompsons' absence, and was the broken window merely the result of a minor accident? The last thing she wished was to attract unwarranted attention or involve the authorities without cause. She envisioned John's inevitable reaction - his dismissive sigh, his shake of the head as if she were being overly dramatic.

No, she resolved. She would wait until she returned home. Within the comfort of her own space, she could think more clearly. If her unease persisted, she would make the call from there.

With a final, reluctant sigh, she turned away and resumed her run, quickening her pace as though she might outrun the disquiet that trailed her. Emma tried to banish the image of the empty porch and the broken window, but it clung to her like a shadow, darkening the bright morning. Her thoughts churned with each step, the rhythmic pounding of her feet insufficient to silence the questions racing through her mind.

She resolved to make a decision once she was back inside, after catching her breath and gathering her thoughts. Then, if the gnawing unease remained, she would call the police to check on the Thompsons.

The sun had risen higher now, casting sharp beams

through the drawn curtains of Owen's bedroom. The boy sat cross-legged on the floor, his toys spread out around him in a haphazard arrangement, as if some great battle had taken place. His favorite action figures lay sprawled beside him, casualties in a war only Owen could see. But today, the boy was not playing. His face was a mask of concentration, his eyes vacant and unfocused, as if his mind was far away from the chaos of his toy soldiers.

In the stillness of the room, Owen suddenly tilted his head, as if listening to a sound that was not there. His eyes darted toward the corner, then back to the center of the room, widening slightly. A faint whisper seemed to flutter through the air, like the rustling of leaves, though the windows were shut tight.

"Yes?" Owen whispered to the empty room, his voice barely audible. "What do you mean? I don't understand."

There was a pause, a long silence that stretched, making the air thick with anticipation. Owen's small brow furrowed, and he nodded slowly, as if comprehending something only he could hear. His eyes grew wide with a mixture of curiosity and unease.

"You want me to... get what?" Owen asked, his voice rising just slightly, tinged with a hesitant curiosity. He glanced around his room, as though expecting something to appear from the shadows.

Another whisper, inaudible to anyone but the boy, seemed to drift through the room. Owen's expression softened, his features relaxing as if the unseen presence had soothed him.

"Daddy's...?" Owen's voice trailed off. "But... I don't know if I'm supposed to..."

The silence in the room felt heavy, almost oppressive, as if the very walls were holding their breath. Owen stood up slowly, his movements deliberate and almost mechanical. He glanced toward the door, then back at his toys, seemingly caught between two worlds. The whisper returned, firmer this time, insistent. Owen nodded, his face taking on a look of reluctant determination.

"Okay, I'll do it," he said softly. His voice was barely more than a breath. "But you promise it's for Daddy, right? It's something he needs?"

He waited, listening intently, and then nodded again. His small hands moved to push his toys aside, clearing a path on the floor. He walked across the room with a strange, almost hypnotic calm. His bare feet made no sound on the cool wooden floor, his steps light and careful, as though he were afraid of waking someone.

Owen's gaze was fixed on a small wooden step stool that sat in the corner of his room. He approached it slowly, as if it were something fragile. His fingers curled around the edges, and he dragged it behind him, the legs scraping softly against the floor, making a faint, rhythmic sound that seemed to echo through the otherwise silent house.

Reaching his parents' bedroom door, Owen hesitated, his hand hovering over the handle. He cast a quick glance down the hallway, his eyes flickering with a trace of doubt.

"But what if Mommy sees?" he asked quietly, looking over his shoulder. "She won't be mad, will she?"

The response he received, whatever it was, seemed to reassure him. He turned back to the door, grasped the handle, and pushed it open. The door swung inward with a low creak, revealing the dim, cool space beyond. Owen dragged the stool inside, positioning it carefully in front of his father's closet. He climbed up, his small frame balancing precariously on the step.

"Daddy's closet..." he murmured, his voice filled with a strange reverence. "Okay, I'm here. Now what?"

He reached out with trembling fingers and wrapped them around the cold, metallic handle of the closet door. With a slow, steady pull, he opened the door, revealing the neatly arranged clothes inside. The scent of his father's aftershave wafted out, familiar and comforting, but the comfort was tinged with an undercurrent of something darker.

Owen's eyes traveled up to the top shelf, where a plain,

unremarkable black metal box sat. To anyone else, it might have looked like nothing more than a forgotten storage container, but to Owen, it held a magnetic pull. His eyes widened, his breath quickening as he stared at it.

"There?" he asked, his voice filled with awe. "You want me to get that?"

He nodded as though someone had answered. Carefully, he reached up, his fingers stretching toward the box. His small hands just managed to brush against the cardboard, but it was out of reach. A frown of concentration furrowed his brow, and he stretched higher, wobbling slightly on the stool.

The box teetered on the edge of the shelf. Owen held his breath, his fingers trembling as they made contact again. The box tilted forward, the lid sliding off to reveal the dark, ominous shape within. The gun lay there, its black surface gleaming dully in the dim light.

Owen's eyes were fixed on it, his expression a mixture of fear and fascination. He reached into the box, his small hands shaking as they wrapped around the gun's handle. The metal was cool to the touch, heavier than he had anticipated. He pulled it down from the shelf with both hands, struggling to maintain his grip.

"I got it," Owen said, a hint of pride in his voice, though it was edged with uncertainty. "I found what you wanted. For Daddy, right? You said he needs it…"

The boy's voice wavered, as though some part of him was unsure, was still questioning the task he had been given. He held the gun awkwardly, cradling it as he might a toy, though his eyes were filled with the awareness that this was something far more dangerous.

As Owen stood there, clutching the gun, the bedroom door behind him creaked open. Jack appeared in the doorway, his expression shifting from mild curiosity to stark horror in an instant. The sight of his younger brother holding the gun sent a surge of panic through him.

"Owen!" Jack shouted, his voice breaking the eerie silence.

Owen turned toward the sound, the gun shifting in his hands. For a moment, everything seemed to move in slow motion. Jack's eyes widened, his body springing into action as he lunged forward. He reached for the gun, his hands colliding with Owen's just as the trigger was squeezed.

A deafening crack shattered the stillness, the sound of the gunshot echoing off the walls. The bullet zipped past Owen's head, embedding itself in the wall behind him. Owen stumbled backward, his eyes wide with shock. The gun slipped from his hands, clattering to the floor.

Owen's trance-like state shattered as he looked around wildly, the reality of what had just happened sinking in. His small body began to shake, and a scream tore from his throat, raw and terrified.

"Owen!" Jack cried again, rushing forward to pull his brother into his arms. He held Owen tightly, his own heart pounding, his mind racing with the horror of what had nearly happened.

The scream seemed to echo through the house, reaching Emily's ears down the hallway. She had been lying on her bed, earphones in, half-listening to music while scrolling through her phone. At the sound of the gunshot, she jerked upright, her phone slipping from her hands. She ripped the earphones out, Owen's screams reaching her, high-pitched and desperate.

Without hesitation, Emily bolted from her room, her feet pounding against the floor as she raced toward the noise. She skidded to a halt in the doorway of her parents' room, her eyes wide with shock at the scene before her. Jack was on the floor, clutching a trembling Owen. The gun lay a few feet away, its presence casting a long, dark shadow over the room.

"Oh my God," Emily whispered, her voice barely audible, her hand flying to her mouth. "What happened?"

Jack looked up at her, his face pale, his eyes filled with terror. "Owen had Dad's gun... It went off... I didn't think... Oh God, Emily, I didn't think..." His voice shook, and he struggled to maintain his composure.

"Is he okay?" Emily asked, her voice breaking as she dropped to her knees beside them. "Owen, are you okay?" Her hands hovered over Owen, her eyes filled with fear and concern.

Owen's sobs wracked his small frame. "I... I don't know what happened," he whimpered. "I thought Daddy needed it... I didn't mean to..."

Emily's gaze met Jack's, and they shared a moment of silent understanding, both realizing the gravity of what had just occurred. The tension in the room was palpable, the air thick with fear and unspoken questions.

Outside, Emma had just returned from her run. She was approaching the front door when the sharp crack of the gunshot reached her ears, followed by Owen's frantic scream. Her heart leapt into her throat, and she sprinted to the door, flinging it open and racing inside.

"Owen! Jack! Emily!" she shouted, her voice tinged with panic as she took the stairs two at a time. Owen's cries grew louder as she neared the bedroom, each step heightening her sense of dread.

Emma burst into the room, her eyes wide with horror at the sight before her. Her children were huddled on the floor, Owen trembling, Jack and Emily clutching him protectively. The gun lay abandoned nearby, its presence ominous and accusatory.

"What... what happened?" Emma's voice shook as she dropped to her knees, pulling all three of her children into a tight embrace, her heart pounding wildly in her chest.

Jack's voice was shaky, laced with tears, as he tried to explain. "Owen had Dad's gun... I just got to him in time... It went off, but it missed him..." His voice faltered, the reality of what had nearly happened weighing heavily on them all.

Emma's heart ached as she looked at Owen, who was still shaking in her arms. "Owen, sweetheart, why did you have the gun?" she asked softly, trying to keep her voice calm, though it trembled with fear.

Owen shook his head, his eyes wide and filled with

confusion. "I don't remember, Mommy," he whispered. "I just... I thought Daddy needed it... Someone told me... they told me Daddy needed it..."

Emma's blood ran cold at Owen's words. She glanced at Jack and Emily, the same fear mirrored in their eyes. Her hand trembled as she reached for her phone, her mind spinning. She had planned to call the police about George Thompson's house, the image of the broken window vivid in her mind. But now, all thoughts of the Thompsons vanished. The sound of the gunshot still echoed in her ears, and the sight of Owen holding that gun replayed over and over.

Instead, she clutched her children close, her mind swirling with fear and uncertainty. Something was terribly wrong, and whatever dark force was at work, it had now found its way into her home.

After Emma and Emily took Owen downstairs to the living room, not wanting to let him out of their sight, Jack remained alone in his parents' bedroom. The silence felt suffocating, wrapping around him like a shroud. He stood in the doorway, his eyes scanning the room, the scene still vivid in his mind. His heart pounded in his chest, a relentless beat that matched the throbbing of his thoughts. The gun lay on the floor where it had fallen, a dark, malevolent shape that seemed to absorb the light around it. It looked like a void, pulling everything into its presence. He stared at it for a moment, his mind replaying the sound of the shot, the way Owen had looked at him, bewildered and afraid.

Jack's throat tightened, his mouth dry. He swallowed hard, forcing himself to move. He crossed the room in a few quick strides, his footsteps muffled against the carpet. He knelt down and picked up the gun, its cold metal biting into his palm. The weight of it felt heavier than before, as if it carried not just its physical mass but the burden of what had almost happened.

Jack turned the gun over in his hands, his fingers tracing the hard lines of the barrel and grip. He felt a mixture of fear and anger welling up inside him. Fear for Owen, and anger at his father for being so careless, for leaving something so dangerous unlocked and where a child could find it. His father's neglect had nearly led to disaster. Jack's jaw tightened with resolve.

He had to hide the gun. He had to make sure Owen never found it again. Jack knew he couldn't rely on his parents to keep his brother safe - not after today. He had seen the way his father had brushed off the seriousness of the situation with Emily, how his mother had been too shaken to think clearly. It was up to him now.

Jack glanced around the room, his eyes landing on the closet where Owen had found the gun. His father's clothes hung neatly, his shoes lined up in an orderly row. A plan began to form in Jack's mind, a place he knew where the gun could be hidden, out of reach, out of sight. Somewhere even his father wouldn't think to look.

He opened the closet door further, and grabbed a shoebox from the top shelf, shaking out the pair of dress shoes inside. He placed the gun into the box, its black form standing out starkly against the pale cardboard. Jack closed the lid, securing it with a strip of packing tape he found on the closet shelf. He tested the weight of the box in his hands, nodding to himself in grim satisfaction. Finally, he returned the now-empty metallic black storage box to its place on the top shelf of the closet, careful to avoid drawing his father's attention to anything amiss.

With the shoebox under his arm, Jack moved quickly, his footsteps light as he left the bedroom. He headed down the hallway, toward the narrow door that led to the attic. His fingers fumbled with the latch for a moment before it gave way, the door creaking open to reveal the wooden stairs leading up into the darkness.

Jack hesitated, a flicker of doubt passing through him. The attic was a place full of shadows and dust, a space where the forgotten and the unused gathered. But it was the safest place he could think of. He took a deep breath and started up the stairs, each step creaking beneath his weight.

The attic was dim, the only light coming from a small,

dusty window that let in a thin beam of sunlight. Dust motes danced in the air, swirling in the faint glow. Jack's eyes adjusted to the gloom, picking out the shapes of old boxes and discarded furniture. He moved to a far corner, where a stack of old suitcases were placed. He pulled one of the suitcases aside and slid the shoebox into the space behind it.

Jack stood back, his eyes scanning the area. The shoebox was hidden, tucked away where no one would think to look. He felt a small measure of relief, knowing the gun was out of reach. He turned, making his way back to the attic stairs.

Back in the hallway, Jack closed the attic door behind him, his hand lingering on the latch. He pulled out his phone and opened a new message. His fingers hovered over the keys, his thoughts spinning. He wanted to tell someone, anyone, about what he had done. About what had almost happened. But he knew there was no one he could trust with this secret.

Jack sighed and slipped the phone back into his pocket. He turned toward the stairs, heading down to where he could hear the soft murmur of his mother's voice, trying to soothe Owen's lingering fears. Jack's steps were slow, his mind heavy with the burden of what he now carried. He knew he had done the right thing, but the feeling of unease lingered, like a shadow that refused to be shaken.

As he reached the bottom of the stairs, Jack resolved that he would keep a closer watch on Owen. He wouldn't let anything like this happen again. He couldn't. The thought of losing his brother, of coming so close to tragedy, was more than he could bear.

Jack walked into the living room, where his mother sat with Owen, holding him close. Emma looked up as Jack entered, her eyes meeting his with a mixture of gratitude and worry. Jack nodded to her, a silent promise passing between them. He wouldn't let anything happen to Owen. He would do whatever it took to keep him safe.

For now, the gun was hidden, and Jack had taken the first step in protecting his family. But he knew, deep down, that this was only the beginning. The events of the day had left a mark, a darkness that seemed to linger in the corners of their home, waiting. And Jack knew that he would have to be ready when it returned.

The kitchen was filled with the warm, soothing aroma of chamomile tea, a vain attempt to bring some comfort to the tense household. The soft clinking of a spoon against a ceramic mug was the only sound, interspersed with Owen's occasional sniffles as he sat at the kitchen table, cradled in Emma's arms. She stroked his hair gently, her face pale and drawn, eyes distant as she replayed the events of the past hour over and over in her mind.

Jack hovered at the edge of the kitchen, his hand resting on the doorframe, eyes flickering between his mother and brother. He had waited until Owen's breathing had steadied, and the boy's trembling had subsided. Now, Jack felt a gnawing need to share the burdens that had been weighing on him, like stones tied around his neck. He looked over his shoulder to see Emily standing just behind him, her face a mask of worry and confusion.

With a deep breath, Jack stepped into the kitchen. The floor creaked under his weight, and Emma looked up, her eyes meeting his. There was a tiredness in her gaze, but also a flicker of something else - hope, perhaps, or maybe just the desperate need for answers.

"Mom," Jack began, his voice wavering slightly. He cleared his throat and tried again, his tone firmer. "I need to talk to you about something. It's... important."

Emma nodded, gesturing for him to sit down. She released Owen, who had dozed off with his head resting on the table, exhaustion overtaking him. Jack pulled out a chair, sitting down heavily, feeling Emily take a seat beside him. Her presence was a small comfort, a reminder that he was not alone in his fears.

"What is it, Jack?" Emma asked, her voice soft but edged with concern. She glanced at Emily, sensing that something serious was going on.

Jack hesitated, his hands twisting in his lap as the memories of the night rushed back to him. The words felt heavy in his throat, but he knew he had to say them. "Mom... something's been happening. Something's not right with the house," he began, his voice shaky but determined. "At first, I thought it was just my imagination, but it's not. I've been hearing things at night - footsteps outside my room. And it wasn't just once. Every night, they stop right outside my door."

Emma's eyes widened slightly, the concern deepening. "What do you mean, footsteps?" she asked, her voice lowering.

Jack swallowed hard, feeling a chill creep up his spine. "Footsteps, clear as day. At first, I thought it was just my imagination, but then it happened again. They just come closer and closer. And then... there was a knock. A soft knock on my door. But that's not all, Mom. The door - it rattled, like something was trying to get in. I know I wasn't dreaming. It was real."

Emma's expression darkened, her lips parting slightly in disbelief, but the fear in Jack's voice was undeniable. She opened her mouth to speak, but Jack pressed on.

"I thought it couldn't get worse, but then I saw something. Red eyes. Outside my window, in the woods. They were staring at me - watching. I know it sounds insane, but I swear it wasn't my imagination. Something's out there."

Emma's face paled. She listened intently, her fingers still absentmindedly stroking Owen's hair. Jack took a breath, pushing on. "And it's not just the footsteps, Mom. Emily almost drowned in the pool. She said something pulled her under, something she couldn't see. It wasn't just an accident."

Emma turned to Emily, her eyes wide with shock. Emily nodded, her own face drawn with anxiety. "It's true, Mom. I know it sounds crazy, but I felt something grab my ankle. I tried to fight it, but it was so strong... I don't know what it was, but it wasn't normal."

Emma's hands trembled slightly as she took in her children's words, a chill settling over her. "But why didn't you tell me before?" she whispered, her voice strained.

Jack shifted uncomfortably, his gaze dropping to the table. "Because Dad told me not to. He said you'd get upset, that you didn't need to know. But there's more, Mom. Last night, I followed Dad. I saw him arguing with one of the neighbors. It wasn't just an argument - it was... violent. Like he wanted to hurt him." Jack's voice broke, his fear and confusion spilling over. "Mom, I think this house is haunted. I think something's here, and it's doing things to us. And Dad... he's changing. He's not himself anymore."

Emma's mind immediately flashed back to the broken window at the Thompson house. The sight of the jagged glass, the eerie stillness that had settled over the home, and George's mysterious absence suddenly felt more ominous in light of Jack's revelation. Could John have been involved? She had dismissed the thought earlier, but now, with Jack's words echoing in her ears, it seemed harder to ignore. The argument Jack mentioned, the violence he described - it lined up too closely with her uneasy feeling that morning. She thought of John's recent mood swings, his late nights, the way he had grown distant, almost like a stranger in his own home.

Emily, who had been listening quietly, leaned forward, her voice cutting through the tension. "Mom, Jack and I have been looking into this. We did some research, trying to find out if there was anything about this place - anything that could explain what's happening." She paused, gathering her thoughts, then continued. "But there's nothing, Mom. No one else ever lived here before us. This house is brand new. And before they built Briar Vale, this was just a dirt trail. People used to come here to go mudding or ride their ATVs. That's it. There's nothing remarkable about this area. No history, no stories, no legends. It's like whatever's happening, it just started when we moved in."

Emma's eyes widened as Emily spoke, her heart beating faster with each word. Her mind raced, trying to piece together the fragments of information. The lack of any history, any reason for the strange occurrences, only deepened the mystery. It was as if the darkness had sprung up from nothing, an unseen force that had chosen their home, their family, to torment.

She reached out, taking Jack's hand in her own, squeezing it gently. "Jack... Emily... I believe you," she said softly, her voice trembling with the admission. "I've felt it too. I've seen things, heard things that don't make sense. I thought it was just me, that maybe... maybe I was imagining it, or that my mind was playing tricks on me. But if you've seen it too..."

Emma's voice trailed off, her eyes searching Jack's face, then Emily's. They both looked back at her with a mixture of relief and fear, knowing they weren't alone in this.

"We have to figure this out, together," Emma continued, her voice gaining strength. "Whatever's happening, we can't let it tear us apart. We'll get to the bottom of this, I promise. But for now, I need you both to keep this between us. Especially from Dad. He's... he's under a lot of stress, and I don't want to make things worse."

Jack nodded slowly, though his heart ached with the weight of the secret. He glanced at Emily, who nodded as well, her lips pressed into a thin line. They both knew that their father's behavior was more than just stress. The man who had once been their protector now seemed like a stranger, someone who might be as much a threat as whatever haunted their house.

Emma sensed their hesitation, the doubt in their eyes. She leaned forward, her voice softening. "I know you're worried about your dad. I am too. But we have to give him some space. He's going through something, and pushing him might make things worse. I'm not saying we ignore what's happening, but let's be careful, okay? We'll keep an eye on him, and on each other. We'll get through this."

Jack swallowed hard, nodding again. The tension in the room seemed to ease slightly, the shared understanding a fragile comfort. He reached out, taking Emily's hand under the table, squeezing it. She squeezed back, a silent agreement to the pact they had just made.

CHAPTER 7

Revelations

August had come at last, its sultry breath stirring only faintly the air in Briar Vale, heralding the children's first school year since the move. Ordinarily, this would have been a season of joy, the house alive with the bright anticipation of new beginnings. But that usual fervor was curiously absent, its place taken by a dread that seeped through the very walls of the home. Emma felt, if anything, a flicker of relief. The arrival of school meant a reprieve - for the children, at least - from the suffocating atmosphere that clung to the household like a shadow. Time away from the house - away from the unseen strain - was what they all so desperately needed.

The morning had unfolded in a flurry of hurried motions, a frenzy barely contained. Breakfast had been served, the children ushered out the door to catch the bus that awaited them just beyond the conservation area that loomed over Phase 2 of Briar Vale. With John off to work, the house stood eerily silent. Emma, now alone, laced her shoes, the only sound the rasp of her breath as she prepared for her morning run.

A spectral mist hung low over the earth, tendrils of it weaving through the grass, while the air itself seemed to throb with the lingering damp of the previous night. Emma set out, her steps muted by the peculiar hush that wrapped the streets. The sky overhead bore the pallor of the dead, a sickly gray, as though the sun had forgotten its strength, unable to banish the night's gloom. The air was thick - cloying in its heat - each breath heavy and oppressive, clinging to her like some unseen force. It was too quiet, a stillness that seemed unnatural, as though the world was waiting for something, a secret poised to reveal itself just beyond the periphery of her senses.

Emma's heart matched the cadence of her hurried strides, her mind a swirling tempest of unease from which there seemed no escape. She had hoped this run might bring her solace, a chance to dispel the creeping fears that gnawed at her. Yet, no matter how swiftly she moved, the dread remained, crawling in her belly like a living thing. The horrors of the day before lingered, pressing down upon her: Jack's pale face and trembling voice as he spoke of footsteps in the night, Emily's harrowing brush with death, Owen's eerie talks of imaginary friends, and John - John, who had grown stranger with each passing day. All of it weighed upon her mind, an unrelenting chorus of dread that chased her through the mist.

As she rounded the corner, her pace slowed as the Thompson house loomed ahead. Something wasn't right. The broken window she'd seen on her last run had been eerily fixed, the glass now pristine.

Emma's gaze swept over the front porch. George Thompson's usual spot - vacant. The old wicker chair sat like a forgotten relic, untouched, as if it had been abandoned to time. His absence struck her as deeply wrong, a void in the fabric of her routine. She stopped in front of the house, her hands resting on her hips as she caught her breath. The silence felt like a weight, pressing down on her.

A sudden rustling broke the quiet. Her eyes flicked toward the bushes along the house. The leaves shivered, stirred by an invisible force. For a fleeting second, she thought she saw a shadow pass through the gloom, but when she blinked, it was gone. She swallowed hard, trying to steady her breath. You're imagining things, she told herself. But the chill crawling down her spine wouldn't let go. Not after what Jack and Emily had confided - their stories of ghostly footsteps, sinister shadows, and John's unnerving behavior gnawed at her, like the edge of some unspeakable truth. The weight of it was suffocating.

As she left the Thompson house behind, she cast one last glance over her shoulder. The house seemed to sag beneath some unseen burden, its presence heavy and brooding, like a shadow stretched unnaturally long in the fading light.

Her thoughts twisted inward, toward her own home, her own unraveling life. Briar Vale was supposed to be their escape, a fresh start free of the shadows of the past. Instead, it felt as if a darkness had followed them or, rooted itself deep in the very ground beneath their feet. John's strange obsession with the garden, his furtive glances, the cold distance in his voice - it was as though he had become someone else entirely. The house, once a promise of peace, now felt like a prison closing in on her, the air inside growing thinner with every passing day.

Emma's feet pounded the pavement harder, her breaths sharp and desperate. As she neared Agatha's place, a wave of relief washed over her. The strange old woman wasn't outside today. But something else was wrong. The usual throng of cats that patrolled Agatha's yard had vanished. Maybe she'd finally rehomed them. Or maybe something worse had happened.

She pushed forward, past the unfinished, skeletal homes that lined the street. They groaned as they always did, though the air was unnervingly still. It felt as if the empty houses were aware of her, watching her. The thick humidity pressed against her, each breath growing heavier, as if the very atmosphere were suffocating her. She ran faster, desperate to escape the growing dread wrapping itself around her chest like a vice. She could no longer deny it - something was horribly wrong with Briar Vale, with the house, and with John.

As she reached her own driveway, her legs burned and her chest tightened. She slowed, coming to a stop at the edge of her lawn, her eyes drawn to the perfect, manicured grass. A few dead leaves clung stubbornly to the hedges, swaying in the stillness. The front door loomed ahead, and Emma found herself hesitating, as if crossing that threshold would mean surrendering to the darkness that waited inside.

She inhaled deeply, trying to steel herself. She had to be strong - for herself, for the kids. Jack and Emily had turned to her, trusting her to protect them from whatever was creeping into their lives. And Owen... his odd behavior, the way he'd fetched John's gun as if under some unseen command - whatever malevolent force had invaded their home, she had to confront it. She had no choice but to fight. To save them all.

Wiping the sweat from her brow, she fixed her gaze on the house. In the soft light of morning, it looked so peaceful, so normal. But beneath that calm façade, Emma could feel it - the darkness lurking, waiting, watching. She clenched her fists, her nails biting into her palms.

It's just a house, she tried to tell herself. But she knew the lie as soon as she thought it. Briar Vale was not just a house. This was no ordinary place. Something far more sinister had taken root here - something that whispered in the stillness and moved in the shadows. And whatever it was, it had already sunk its claws into her family.

Emma set her phone on the kitchen counter, her thoughts spinning like the blades of the ceiling fan above her. The remnants of her morning run clung to her: a faint sheen of sweat on her forehead, the deep, steady ache in her calves, the taste of something metallic at the back of her throat. She had hoped the run would bring clarity, a momentary escape from the sense of dread that had settled over her like a shroud. Instead, it had only made the weight pressing on her chest feel heavier.

The image of George Thompson's window lingered in her mind. Though it had been repaired, the house still radiated an eerie sense of abandonment. And George's absence - paired with Jack witnessing that argument between John and George, and the emptiness of his porch - gnawed at her in a way she couldn't quite name. It reminded her of the hollow spaces slowly creeping into her own life, into her marriage

Emma picked up her phone again, scrolling through her contacts until she found Mary Kendrick's name. The real estate agent had been nothing if not accommodating when they bought the house, painting Briar Vale as the perfect community, ideal for families like theirs. She had promised stability, security - a fresh start. Now, Emma needed to know if there was something Mary hadn't told them. If there was more to this place than the polished façade of new homes and freshly paved streets.

Her thumb hovered over Mary's name for a moment, then she tapped the call button. The phone rang, each buzz echoing the thud of her pulse, and then Mary's voice came through, bright and efficient.

"Mary Kendrick speaking," she said, her tone professional, with that underlying cheer Emma had always found slightly forced.

"Mary, hi, it's Emma Miller," Emma began, trying to keep her voice steady. "I hope I'm not bothering you, but I've been meaning to ask you something about the house. It's probably nothing, but..."

"Not at all, Emma," Mary interrupted, her voice smoothing into a more personal warmth. "How can I help? Is everything all right?"

Emma hesitated, glancing out the window toward the Thompsons' house. "I've just noticed some strange things lately. Not just with our house but around the neighborhood. It's probably just my imagination, but I can't shake this feeling that something's... off. Have you heard of anything unusual happening around here?"

There was a brief pause on the other end of the line, a hesitation that made Emma's heart skip. Then Mary laughed softly, the sound brushing aside Emma's concerns like so many cobwebs.

"Oh, Emma, I'm sure it's just the stress of the move," Mary said lightly. "Briar Vale is a new community, after all. Everyone's still settling in, getting used to things. There's always a bit of an adjustment period. But I assure you, there's nothing unusual about the house. The only thing different with this transaction was the disclosures, but those were all standard procedure given the circumstances."

Emma's grip tightened on the phone, her knuckles turning white. "Disclosures?" she echoed, a knot forming in her stomach. "I don't remember any disclosures being mentioned. What do you mean, 'standard procedure'?"

Mary's voice took on a slightly more guarded tone. "Well, it's nothing to worry about, really. Just some paperwork about the lumber used in the construction. You know how it is with new developments - sometimes materials have to be sourced from different places. There were some supply chain issues due to the pandemic. I thought John went over all of this with you."

Emma's mind reeled. John had never mentioned any disclosures. He hadn't said a word about the lumber or any issues with the house's construction. She felt a flicker of anger beneath her growing unease. "John didn't tell me anything about this," she said, her voice tightening. "I didn't see any disclosures."

A moment of silence hung between them, thick and uncomfortable. Then Mary's tone softened, a hint of concern creeping in. "I'm sorry, Emma. That's surprising. The disclosures should have been part of your closing documents. Perhaps there was a mix-up, or maybe John just forgot. I can send you a copy right away if you'd like. But please, don't worry. Everything was cleared with the county. There's no danger. The homes are perfectly safe."

Emma closed her eyes, feeling the tension coil in her chest. Safe. The word felt hollow, devoid of any real comfort. "Yes, please send them," she said quietly. "I'd appreciate that."

"Of course," Mary replied quickly. "I'll email them to you shortly. And if you have any other concerns, feel free to call me anytime. Really, Emma, there's nothing to be alarmed about. I'm sure everything will be just fine."

Emma forced herself to mutter a few pleasantries, thanked Mary, and ended the call. She stood there for a moment, the phone still in her hand, staring blankly at the counter. The smell of coffee suddenly seemed too strong, turning her stomach. A deep sense of betrayal mixed with the unease she had been feeling. Disclosures. John had known something was wrong. He had kept this from her. The thought of his secrecy, his lies, made her feel as though the ground beneath her feet was slipping away.

Emma walked back to the kitchen counter, her eyes unfocused as she stared at her phone. She knew Mary would send the disclosure, but the dread gnawing at her was more than just about the wood. It was about the secrets, the lies, the creeping realization that her life was no longer her own. She checked her phone again, her eyes glancing at the time, and then at her email icon, waiting for the telltale ding of a new message.

It only took about thirty minutes for her phone to buzz. Emma snatched it up, her eyes skimming over the screen. As promised, there it was: an email from Mary with an attachment. Emma opened it, her breath catching as she read the title: *Disclosure of Materials Used in Construction*. She scrolled down, her eyes narrowing at the words stamped in bold: *Notice of EPA Action*.

Title: Disclosure of Materials Used in Construction

To: John and Emma Miller
From: Sunshine Homes Co.
Property Address: 124 Whispering Pines Road, Briar Vale Community, Jupiter, Florida 33458
*Subject: Notice Regarding Construction Materials and Regulatory Actions***

Date: April 16th, 2024

Dear Mr. and Mrs. Miller,
This letter serves as a formal disclosure concerning the

materials used in the construction of your property located at the above address within the Briar Vale community. As the current owners of this property, it is important that you are fully informed of certain regulatory issues that have arisen in connection with the construction materials used by the original developer, Collin Homes.

1. Use of Non-Compliant Lumber: It has come to our attention that Collin Homes, the original developer of the Briar Vale community, utilized lumber in the construction of several homes, including yours, that was not compliant with U.S. environmental regulations. This lumber was sourced from suppliers that failed to meet the legal standards set forth under the Lacey Act and other applicable regulations. As a result, the use of this lumber constitutes a regulatory violation.

2. Regulatory Actions and Compliance Measures: Following an investigation by the Environmental Protection Agency (EPA) and other regulatory bodies, it was determined that Collin Homes had violated federal environmental laws by using non-compliant lumber. Consequently, Collin Homes was subjected to significant fines and sanctions, leading to its eventual bankruptcy.

Upon acquiring the assets of Collin Homes, including the Briar Vale development, Sunshine Homes Co. has taken the following steps to ensure compliance and maintain the safety of our homeowners:

Payment of Fines: Sunshine Homes Co. has settled all outstanding fines and penalties associated with the use of non-compliant materials.

Regulatory Agreements: Sunshine Homes Co. has entered into agreements with the EPA and other relevant authorities to ensure continued compliance and oversight.

Continued Construction: Under these agreements, Sunshine Homes Co. has been permitted to continue construction of Phase 2 of the Briar Vale development and to sell homes that have already been built, including your property.

3. Property Inspections and Safety Assurance: To ensure the safety and integrity of homes constructed with non-compliant lumber, Sunshine Homes Co. conducted comprehensive inspections

of all affected properties. These inspections have confirmed the following:

Structural Integrity: There are no detected structural defects or immediate safety hazards associated with the use of the non-compliant lumber in your home.

Safety Compliance: The property meets all local and state building code requirements and is deemed safe for residential occupancy.

4. Homeowner Options and Recommendations: Sunshine Homes Co. is committed to maintaining transparency and addressing any concerns you may have. As such, we are offering the following:

Independent Inspection: Homeowners are entitled to request an independent inspection of their property, conducted by a third-party inspector at no cost. Please contact our customer service department to arrange this service.

Ongoing Support: Our customer service team is available to address any questions or concerns you may have regarding this matter. We are dedicated to ensuring your peace of mind and satisfaction as a homeowner.

5. Contact Information and Further Assistance: If you have any questions or require additional information, please do not hesitate to reach out to. We are here to assist you and provide any further clarification you may require.

Sunshine Homes Co. deeply regrets any inconvenience or concern this situation may cause. We remain committed to upholding the highest standards of safety, integrity, and transparency in all our operations. Rest assured, we will continue to monitor the situation closely and provide you with updates as necessary.

Thank you for your attention to this matter. We appreciate your cooperation and understanding.

Yours sincerely,
Sarah T. Wheeler
Director of Homeowner Relations

Sunshine Homes Co.

Emma's hands trembled as she placed her phone back on the counter, the email still open, its words blurring as her eyes stung with unshed tears. Her home - a place she had hoped would be a sanctuary for her family - was tainted, its very walls a product of deceit and illegality. And why was the Environmental Protection Agency involved? The realization that John had known about this, had kept it from her, gnawed at her insides. How could he have let them move into this house, with its hidden past, without so much as a word of warning? A wave of anger surged through her, mingling with the bitter taste of betrayal.

She felt like the ground beneath her was cracking, the stability of her marriage, of her life, giving way to something dark and unseen. Her mind raced with questions, her thoughts tumbling over one another in a chaotic swirl. Was this why the house had been so discounted? She remembered feeling surprised at how affordable such a seemingly perfect home had been. If everything was fine, then why had it been sold at such a low price? If there were no issues, why the need for a steep discount? And the thought of the EPA being involved made her stomach turn. Could it be a chemical issue with the materials? Something hazardous that they were now living in the midst of? What if the very walls of their home were infused with toxins? Could that be the source of the strange behaviors - even her own hallucinations?

She didn't know if or how these things connected, but deep in her gut, she felt an undeniable link. The sense of foreboding that had been growing within her, that something sinister lurked beneath the surface of their seemingly perfect life, now seemed justified.

Her eyes drifted to the kitchen window, looking out toward the row of immaculate houses lining the street. Each one appeared pristine and orderly, yet she knew they could be hiding secrets just like hers.

She could no longer ignore it. She couldn't wait for John's vague reassurances or evasive answers. Whatever was happening in Briar Vale, whatever John had kept hidden, she needed to confront him. Now. She felt a determination solidify within her, a resolve she hadn't felt in weeks, pushing her out of her paralysis. Emma grabbed her phone, her fingers moving quickly, almost instinctively, over the keys.

Emma: I got the disclosures from Mary. We need to talk. NOW.

She hit send, her heart pounding in her chest as she stared at the screen, waiting for a reply. Moments later, her phone buzzed in her hand, the response coming almost immediately. Her stomach clenched as she read the message.

John: At work. Later.

Emma's jaw tightened, her teeth grinding in frustration. John's refusal to address the issue head-on only confirmed her fears. Whatever was happening, he wasn't ready to deal with it, and maybe he never would be. She set the phone down with a thud, feeling the creeping sensation of isolation wrapping around her like a cold fog.

As she stood in the kitchen, a chill settled in her bones. She realized with a sinking heart that if she was going to uncover the truth about their home, about the discount, about the EPA involvement, and about John, she would have to do it on her own.

Emma paced back and forth, her steps quick and agitated. Her heart drummed a frantic rhythm, her mind still reeling from the day's revelations. She had spent the afternoon scrutinizing every inch of the disclosure documents, hoping to find some explanation that made sense, something that could soothe the unease that gnawed at her. But the words on the screen offered no solace, only more questions. The house was built with non-compliant lumber. The EPA had been involved. John had known all along and kept it from her.

She saw John's car pull into the driveway, the headlights casting elongated shadows against the walls of the living room. Her heart pounded even harder, a mix of anger and apprehension coursing through her veins. She turned towards the staircase and called up softly to the children, who were lingering near the top step, sensing the tension in the air.

"Go to your rooms," she said, her voice trembling slightly. "I need to talk to your father when he gets in. Please, just stay upstairs for a bit."

The children exchanged glances, hesitating. Jack's brow furrowed with concern, and Emily opened her mouth as if to speak but then closed it, deciding against saying anything. They turned and walked back to their rooms, the sound of their footsteps fading as they retreated down the hallway.

The familiar sound of the front door opening and then closing with a soft click snapped Emma out of her thoughts. She turned to see John stepping into the hallway, his face partially obscured by the dim light. He dropped his keys on the side table, his shoulders slumped with the weariness of the day, but there was an air of tension about him that hadn't been there before. Emma felt a surge of anger rise within her, a hot flush that traveled up her neck and into her cheeks. She crossed her arms over her chest, trying to steady her breathing as she stepped into the doorway.

"John," she called, her voice sharper than she intended.

John looked up, his eyes narrowing slightly in confusion. "What is it?" he asked, a note of irritation creeping into his voice as he moved further into the living room. She noticed his steps were unsteady, his movements sluggish. He reached up to loosen his tie, then spotted the bottle of whiskey on the sideboard. Emma noticed his eyes flicker to the bottle, and she knew this was not going to be the calm discussion she had hoped for. He poured himself a glass, his hand shaking slightly as he raised it to his lips. He took a long sip, his gaze meeting hers over the rim of the glass, his eyes challenging.

"We need to talk," Emma said, her words clipped, the anger bubbling just beneath the surface. "Now."

John's expression hardened, his irritation deepening into annoyance. He took another sip of whiskey, then set the glass down with a deliberate thud, his eyes still locked on hers. "About what?" he replied, his tone already defensive.

Emma took a deep breath, holding up her phone. The email was still open, the words glaring at her from the screen. "About this," she snapped. "About the house. The wood. The EPA. All the things you decided not to tell me!"

John froze for a moment, his face expressionless as he processed her words. Then his eyes darkened, a muscle twitching in his jaw. "What the hell are you talking about?" he muttered, though there was a flicker of something in his eyes - guilt, maybe, or fear.

"Don't play dumb, John," Emma retorted, her voice rising. "You knew about the disclosure. You knew about the EPA involvement. And you didn't tell me! You let us move into this house without a word of warning! What else are you hiding? Is there something wrong with this house? Should I be worried about our health, about the kids?"

John's jaw tightened, his eyes narrowing into a hard glare. He took a step toward her, his fists clenching at his sides. "You're blowing this out of proportion," he growled, his voice slurred slightly. "There's nothing wrong with the damn house. If there was, I wouldn't have bought it. I wouldn't have moved my family in."

"Then why didn't you tell me?" Emma shot back, her voice shaking with emotion. "Why did you keep it a secret? If there's nothing to worry about, why hide it from me?"

"Because you're paranoid, Emma!" John exploded, his voice echoing through the room like a clap of thunder. "You're always looking for something to be scared of, something to panic about. I knew you'd blow this out of proportion, just like you're doing now. If you weren't so fucking crazy, I might have told you. But no, you have to make a big deal out of everything!"

Emma staggered back, his words hitting her like a slap. The sharp smell of alcohol on his breath stung her senses. "Crazy?" she whispered, her voice barely audible. "You think I'm crazy?"

John sneered, taking another step toward her, his face contorted with anger. "Yes, Emma. Crazy. This is why I didn't tell you. Because you're always overreacting. I got us this house at a great price. The kind of house you've always wanted. You should be grateful. Instead, you're throwing a tantrum over nothing."

Emma felt the blood drain from her face, her back pressed against the wall as he loomed over her. Her heart was racing, fear clawing at her throat. She had never seen him like this, so angry, so... unrecognizable. For a moment, she thought he might hit her, the look in his eyes was so wild, so filled with rage.

"John, you're scaring me," Emma said, her voice trembling. She could feel her own hands shaking, her body reacting to the fear that gripped her. "I don't even know who you are anymore."

John's eyes flashed, and he raised his hand as if to strike, then seemed to catch himself. He lowered his hand, his fists still clenched, his breathing ragged. "You're the one who's changed, Emma," he hissed. "You're the one making this into something it's not. There's nothing wrong with the house, and there's nothing wrong with me. The only thing wrong here is you, with your paranoia and your fucking accusations!"

With that, he turned on his heel, his movements jerky and aggressive. He grabbed his glass of whiskey from the sideboard, draining it in one gulp before slamming it down. The sound of glass hitting wood echoed through the living room as he stormed toward the front door. He yanked it open, his movements rough and unsteady, the alcohol clearly having an effect.

"Where are you going?" Emma demanded, her voice rising

with panic as he stepped out onto the porch.

"Out," John snapped, not bothering to look back at her. "Away from this insanity."

He slammed the door behind him with a force that rattled the walls, the sound reverberating through the house. Emma stood frozen, the echo of the door slamming still ringing in her ears. Her chest felt tight, the panic rising like a wave threatening to drown her. She sank down onto the couch, her legs suddenly too weak to support her.

Her mind whirled, replaying the confrontation over and over. The venom in John's words, the look in his eyes - it was as if he had become a stranger, someone she no longer recognized. The smell of alcohol still lingered in the air, mingling with the faint scent of fear. Tears welled up in her eyes, but she blinked them back, refusing to let them fall. She had to be strong. For herself. For her children. She had to figure out what was happening in her home, in her marriage.

As she sat there in the dimming light of the evening, Emma knew one thing for certain: the man who had just stormed out of the house was not the man she had married. And she was no longer sure if he ever would be again. She wiped a tear from her cheek, standing up and heading toward the garage door.

She opened it, the faint smell of oil and sawdust hitting her nose. The sight of John's makeshift bed, a cot pushed against the wall, made her heart ache. She knew she had to put some distance between them, to protect herself and her children. Steeling herself, she texted him a final message.

Emma: Don't come back in the house tonight. Sleep in the garage. I don't know who you are anymore, John.

Emma hit send, her hands still shaking. She closed the door to the garage, locked the dead bold, and leaned against it, her body trembling. She was alone in this fight, and the realization of John's deceit and her growing isolation was sinking in, pressing on her chest like a heavy weight. As she made her way to the bedroom, the darkness of the evening deepened, mirroring the dark uncertainty that had settled over her life.

The walls of the Miller house seemed to vibrate with the echoes of Emma and John's argument, their voices reverberating through the hallways like the rumble of distant thunder. The tension that had simmered throughout the day had finally erupted into a full-blown confrontation, and the sound of it filled the air, heavy and oppressive.

Upstairs, in the dimly lit sanctuary of Emily's bedroom, the atmosphere was thick with fear. The room was cast in shadows, the only light coming from a small lamp on Emily's nightstand, its glow casting a faint, comforting circle around the siblings. Jack sat cross-legged on the floor next to Emily's bed, his eyes wide, darting towards the door as the argument downstairs reached a fevered pitch. Owen, their youngest brother, sat at the foot of the bed, absently fiddling with one of his toy cars, his expression distant, as if he were in another world entirely.

"They're really going at it," Jack whispered, his voice trembling. He glanced up at Emily, who was sitting on the bed, her back against the headboard, her arms wrapped around her knees. She bit her lower lip, her face pale in the lamplight. "I've never heard them fight like this."

Emily's gaze was fixed on the door, her fingers twisting the edge of her blanket. The shouting from below was muffled, but the anger in their father's voice was unmistakable. Each word hit her like a physical blow, causing her to flinch. She had always looked up to her father, admired his strength, but the man she heard now was a stranger - angry, venomous. It terrified her.

Jack leaned closer, his eyes wide with a mixture of fear and excitement. "Oh my god, I know what this is," he said, his voice barely a whisper, as though speaking louder might summon the thing he feared. "I think this is The Shining."

Emily's head snapped around, her eyes narrowing. "What?" she asked, her voice tight. "What are you talking about?"

Jack swallowed hard, his voice trembling as he spoke. "You know, like in the movie. The father goes crazy and tries to hurt his family. What if that's happening to Dad? What if this house is making him crazy?"

Emily's heart skipped a beat, a cold shiver running down her spine. She had heard Jack talk about his scary movies before, had seen him try to scare Owen with stories of ghosts and monsters, but there was something in his eyes now, something that made her blood run cold. He wasn't trying to scare them. He was scared.

"Don't be stupid, Jack," Emily whispered, her voice shaking. "This isn't some horror movie. Dad's not... he's not like that."

"But what if he is?" Jack insisted, his voice rising with panic. "What if the house is doing something to him? What if it's making him angry, making him... dangerous?"

Emily shook her head, trying to push the thought away. "No," she said firmly, though her voice wavered. "Dad's just stressed. He's been drinking, that's all. He's not going to..."

A loud crash from downstairs made them both jump, cutting off her words. They stared at each other, their faces pale. Emily's hands were trembling now, her knuckles white as she gripped the blanket. The sound of a door slamming shut echoed through the house, followed by a heavy silence that seemed to stretch on forever.

Jack's eyes were wide, filled with a fear that mirrored her own. "Did he just leave?" he whispered.

Emily nodded, her throat tight. She could hardly believe it herself. The thought of their father, always so strong and steady, storming out into the night filled her with a sense of unreality. It was as if the foundation of her world had been shaken, the ground beneath her feet turned to quicksand.

"What do we do?" Jack asked, his voice small and scared.

Emily shook her head, her mind racing. "I don't know," she admitted, her voice barely a whisper. She glanced over at Owen, who had been silent through it all. He was still sitting on the floor, his back to them, staring blankly at his toy car. He seemed oblivious to the chaos that had erupted around him, lost in his own world.

"Owen," Emily called softly, trying to draw his attention. When he didn't respond, she reached out and touched his shoulder. "Owen, are you okay?"

Owen looked up at her, his eyes dull, unfocused. For a moment, he seemed to look through her, as if she were a ghost. Then he blinked, his gaze clearing slightly. "Huh?" he said, his voice flat, disconnected.

"Are you okay?" Emily repeated, her heart aching at the emptiness in his eyes.

Owen shrugged, his shoulders barely moving. "I guess," he mumbled, turning back to his toy. There was no fear in his voice, no anger, no emotion at all. It was as if he had shut down, detached himself from the reality of what was happening.

Emily felt a pang of worry, a gnawing fear that something was wrong with Owen, that he was slipping away from them. She glanced at Jack, who was watching Owen with a concerned frown. He opened his mouth to say something, but Emily shook her head, silently pleading for him to leave Owen be. She didn't know how to reach him, how to pull him back from whatever place his mind had retreated to.

The three of them sat in silence, the air around them heavy with tension. The house seemed to hold its breath, the echoes of the argument fading into a stillness that was almost oppressive. Emily could hear her own heartbeat, the sound loud in her ears, and she wondered if Jack could hear it too.

"What's happening to us?" Jack whispered finally, his voice trembling.

Emily shook her head, feeling the weight of his question pressing down on her. "I don't know," she said softly. "But we have to stay together, okay? We have to take care of each other."

Jack nodded, his eyes filling with tears. "What if... what if Dad..."

Emily reached out, taking his hand in hers, squeezing it tightly. "We'll figure it out," she said, trying to sound braver than she felt. "We're going to be okay. We just have to be strong."

She wished she could believe her own words, wished she could shake the feeling that they were standing on the edge of a precipice, about to fall into a darkness from which there was no return. The sound of John's car starting outside shattered the silence, and they heard the tires screech as he sped away. The noise faded into the distance, leaving only the quiet of the house, and the three siblings, huddled together in the dark.

The house was quiet, the kind of stillness that only comes after a storm. The argument that had shattered the evening had left an eerie silence in its wake, a silence that seemed to seep into every corner, every crevice, pressing against the walls of the Miller home like an unwelcome presence. Emma lay in bed, staring up at the ceiling, her mind racing despite the late hour. The room was dark, the only light a thin sliver of moonlight filtering through the curtains, casting a pale glow across the bedspread.

John was out in the garage, and the house felt different without him. Lighter, in a way, as though the oppressive tension he carried with him had dissipated, leaving only the soft hum of the refrigerator and the occasional creak of the house settling. Emma closed her eyes, trying to will herself to sleep, to find some respite from the tumult of thoughts that swirled in her mind.

She drifted off slowly, the exhaustion of the day finally overtaking her. But her sleep was not restful. Almost immediately, she found herself standing in a place that was both familiar and alien, a place that existed on the edges of her consciousness. She was in a forest, the air thick and heavy with humidity, the scent of damp earth filling her nostrils. Tall trees loomed overhead, their branches intertwining to form a canopy that blocked out the sky, casting the forest floor in deep shadow.

Emma moved forward, the ground beneath her feet soft and yielding. The trees seemed to close in around her, their trunks thick and gnarled, the bark rough beneath her fingertips as she brushed past them. The air was still, yet it seemed to hum with a hidden energy, a pulsing undercurrent that set her nerves on edge. She could feel eyes on her, watching from the shadows, though she could see no one. Her heart began to beat faster, the hair on the back of her neck standing on end.

She could hear whispers, faint and indistinguishable, like the rustling of leaves in the wind. They came from all around her, surrounding her, yet she couldn't make out the words. The language was foreign, the sounds guttural and ancient, resonating with a power that sent a shiver down her spine. Emma turned in a slow circle, her eyes scanning the darkness, but the shadows seemed to move with her, keeping just out of sight.

A figure emerged at the edge of her vision, half-hidden in the darkness. Emma squinted, trying to make out the features, but the figure was indistinct, as though it were made of the very shadows that surrounded it. Another figure appeared to her left, and then another to her right, all of them hovering at the periphery of her vision, never fully coming into focus. She could feel their eyes on her, their presence heavy and oppressive, suffocating.

Panic began to claw at her throat, and she stumbled backward, her feet tangling in the underbrush. As she turned to run, she saw them: faces, distorted and grotesque, leering at her from the darkness. They were the faces of her neighbors - George Thompson, his eyes hollow and lifeless, roots winding their way from his mouth, encasing his head in a grotesque wreath; Agatha Cartwright, her mouth twisted into a cruel smile, vines slithering from her eye sockets, creeping over her cheeks. Ethel's face was barely recognizable, her features consumed by dark tendrils that twisted and pulsed as if alive. And then she saw her husband, John, his face contorted with rage, his eyes blazing. From his scalp and jawline, vines erupted, winding around his neck, slowly dragging him into the earth.

Emma's breath caught in her throat, her chest tightening with fear. She stumbled through the forest, the whispers growing louder, more insistent. The ground seemed to shift beneath her feet, the trees closing in, their branches reaching for her like skeletal hands. She could feel the weight of the shadows pressing against her, their presence thick and stifling, making it hard to breathe.

She broke through the trees and found herself standing in front of her house, but it was not as she remembered it. Vines had overrun the exterior, thick tendrils of greenery winding their way up the walls, choking the windows, creeping over the roof. Moss covered the stone steps, and the front door was nearly obscured by a tangle of foliage. The house seemed to pulse with a dark, malevolent energy, its walls alive with a slow, steady rhythm, like the heartbeat of some great beast.

Emma stepped forward, her feet moving of their own accord. She reached out, her hand brushing against the vine-covered door, and felt a shock run through her, as though she had touched a live wire. The whispers rose to a crescendo, the voices all around her now, pressing in on her, suffocating her. The figures moved closer, their shadows stretching out toward her, their presence like a dark cloud, thick and suffocating.

As she watched in horror, the faces of her neighbors and her husband began to merge with the house itself, their features stretching and distorting, becoming part of the very walls. Roots and vines grew from their mouths and eyes, intertwining with the structure, as if the house were absorbing them, consuming them. The dark shadows around them seemed to stand in judgment, their forms tall and imposing, watching Emma with a silent, malevolent gaze.

The door swung open with a creak, revealing only

darkness beyond. Emma felt herself being pulled toward it, the shadows pressing against her, pushing her forward. She tried to scream, but no sound came out. Her mouth opened, but the darkness swallowed her voice, the air thick and impenetrable. The last thing she saw before the darkness consumed her was the face of her husband, John, grotesquely entwined with the vines, his eyes filled with a fury that chilled her to the bone.

Emma woke with a start, her heart racing, her breath coming in short, panicked gasps. She was in her bed, the sheets tangled around her legs, the pillow damp with sweat. Her hands were shaking, her fingers clutching at the fabric of the blanket. The room was dark, the only light a faint glow from the alarm clock on the bedside table, casting a dim red hue across the room.

She sat up, her body trembling, her mind struggling to separate dream from reality. The vividness of the forest, the oppressive weight of the shadows, the distorted, root-covered faces - they all clung to her like cobwebs that refused to be brushed away. She could still hear the whispers, faint and distant, echoing in the corners of her mind.

Emma swung her legs over the side of the bed, her bare feet touching the cool floor. She knew she wouldn't find peace here, not in this room, not alone. She needed to feel the presence of her children, to reassure herself that they were safe, that this nightmare hadn't seeped into the real world.

She stood up, her movements shaky, and quietly made her way out of the bedroom, her feet padding softly against the carpet as she headed towards Emily's room. She pushed the door open gently, the soft creak barely audible in the silence of the house. Inside, she saw the faint outline of her children huddled together on the bed, their faces turned toward each other in the dim light.

Emma slipped into the room, feeling a wave of relief wash over her as she moved closer to the bed. She carefully climbed in beside them, pulling the blanket over herself and wrapping her arms around Jack and Emily. They stirred slightly, murmuring in their sleep, but did not wake. Emma held them close, feeling

166

their warmth, their steady breathing, and the sound of their heartbeats against her chest.

For the first time that night, she felt a semblance of safety, a fragile barrier against the darkness that loomed on the edge of her consciousness. She closed her eyes, trying to shut out the remnants of her dream, the faces entwined with vines, the dark shadows standing in judgment. She pressed her face into Jack's hair, breathing in the scent of him, and tried to let that simple, familiar comfort drive away the terrors that lingered in the dark corners of her mind.

But even as she held her children close, Emma knew that the darkness was still out there, creeping ever closer, and that the safety she felt was only an illusion.

CHAPTER 8

Breaking Point

The morning light slanted through the half-drawn curtains, casting long shadows across the living room floor. The air inside the Miller house was heavy with a silence that seemed to press down on everything, a silence that had become an unwelcome resident. Emma moved quietly through the space, her footsteps soft on the polished wood, as if she feared disturbing the oppressive stillness.

She had learned to navigate that silence, slipping through the rooms without making a sound, careful to avoid the creaking floorboards that might announce her presence. John's mood lingered in every corner, a brooding, intangible weight. Even when he wasn't in the room, his presence infected the air, turning every inch of the house into a battlefield of tension. Emma moved with a kind of quiet desperation, as though her careful steps might somehow avoid setting off another storm of anger.

John was outside in the backyard, as usual, bent over his precious garden. The garden that seemed to consume him, that kept him out of the house and away from his family. Emma watched him through the kitchen window, his figure bent and intent, his hands moving rhythmically as he worked the soil. The garden had become his obsession, a silent testament to his withdrawal. He had retreated into the earth, finding solace in the rows of plants that now flourished under his care. It was as if he had transferred all his affection and attention to the garden, leaving none for her or the children.

Emma turned away from the window, her heart heavy with the weight of the distance that had grown between them. There had been a time when John's laughter filled the house, when his hands would reach for hers in the quiet moments of the evening, when they would share the small joys and struggles of their days. Now, there was nothing but silence and the angry set of his shoulders as he turned away from her.

She could still remember the first time she had felt the shift, the subtle but unmistakable change. It was after they had moved into Briar Vale, when the house was still new and full of possibilities. John had been excited about the move, eager to leave the city behind, to start fresh in a place where they could breathe. But soon after they had settled in, something had changed. He had grown distant, his temper quick to flare, his words edged with a bitterness that had not been there before. At first, she had told herself it was just the stress of the move, the adjustment to a new life. But as the weeks turned into months, and John's moods darkened, she realized it was more than that.

The sound of footsteps broke into her thoughts, and she turned to see Emily descending the stairs, her face pale and drawn. Jack followed close behind, his eyes dark with worry. Owen trailed after them, clutching his favorite stuffed toy, his thumb hovering near his mouth in a sign of his anxiety. The children moved quietly, as if they, too, feared disturbing the heavy atmosphere that hung over the house.

"Morning, Mom," Emily said, her voice low, almost as if she was afraid to speak too loudly.

"Morning, sweetheart," Emma replied, forcing a smile. "Breakfast is ready."

The children settled at the table, and Emma busied herself with serving them, trying to keep her movements brisk and cheerful, though it felt like going through the motions. Jack pushed his cereal around the bowl with his spoon, his eyes flicking to the window where their father was visible through the glass.

"Is Dad going to be like this forever?" Jack asked suddenly, his voice breaking the fragile quiet.

Emma paused, her heart aching at the question. She looked at her son, his young face lined with worry far beyond his years. "I don't know, Jack," she said softly. "Your dad is... going through something. We just need to give him some time."

"Time for what?" Emily snapped, her frustration boiling over. "He doesn't even talk to us anymore. It's like we don't exist."

Owen looked up, his small voice cutting through the tension. "Is Daddy mad at us?" he asked, his eyes wide and innocent.

Emma's breath caught, a pang of sorrow piercing her. She knelt beside Owen, taking his small hand in hers. "No, darling. Daddy's not mad at you. He's just... tired. He's dealing with a lot right now. But he loves you. Never doubt that."

Owen nodded, but the worry in his eyes remained. Emma squeezed his hand, trying to convey a reassurance she didn't feel. She glanced at the clock, noting the time. "Finish up, you three. The bus will be here soon."

The children ate in silence, their movements slow and reluctant. Emma could feel the dread building in her chest, a tightness that threatened to choke her. She had to keep it together, for their sake. She had to protect them from the darkness that seemed to be creeping into their lives. But how could she protect them when she didn't even understand what was happening? When the man she had trusted had become a stranger?

The sound of the school bus approaching broke her thoughts. Emma stood, ushering the children to the door, her hands moving automatically to smooth their hair, to adjust their clothes. They walked out to the porch, their steps heavy with reluctance. Emma watched as they climbed onto the bus, her heart clenching as the doors closed behind them.

As the bus pulled away, she stood on the porch, her arms wrapped around herself, trying to ward off the chill that had settled over her. The house loomed behind her, its dark windows like eyes staring out into the day. John was still in the garden, his back to the house, his figure bent and absorbed in his work. Emma watched him for a moment longer, then turned and went inside, the door closing with a soft thud that echoed through the silent rooms.

The silence was heavier now, more oppressive, as if the walls themselves were closing in. Emma leaned against the door, her eyes closing briefly as she took a deep breath. She felt the weight of it all pressing down on her, the sense of helplessness that threatened to overwhelm her. Her family was slipping away, piece by piece, and she didn't know how to stop it.

The house was quiet, the only sound the faint rustling of the trees outside, the whisper of leaves against the windows. Emma stood there, alone in the silence, feeling the shadows creep closer, and wondering how long she could hold them at bay.

The morning light seeped into the kitchen, casting a pale glow over the tiled floor. Emma stood at the sink, her hands plunged into the warm soapy water, the scent of lemon filling the air. She scrubbed at the dishes with a fury she could barely contain, each motion sharp and precise. The sounds of breakfast had faded into the silence, the clinking of silverware and the clatter of plates now replaced by the rhythmic splash of water and the dull thud of her heart.

John had left not long ago, looking more disheveled than she had ever seen him. His shirt was wrinkled, half tucked into his pants, and his hair was unkempt, sticking up in places as if he'd run his hands through it a dozen times. His eyes were bloodshot, the shadows beneath them dark and hollow. He had stood in the doorway, his briefcase hanging loosely from his hand, as if it were too heavy to carry. Emma had watched him from across the room, her arms crossed over her chest, a knot of anger tightening in her stomach. He hadn't looked at her, hadn't even acknowledged her presence.

"Are you going to work?" she had asked, her voice cutting through the silence.

He hadn't answered, just grunted, a sound more animal than human, and turned away. He had shuffled out of the house without another word, the door slamming shut behind him, the sound echoing through the empty halls. Emma had stood there, her heart pounding, the fury simmering just beneath the surface. She wanted to scream, to shout at him, to make him see what he was doing to them, to their family. But the words had lodged in her throat, and she had let him go, the silence swallowing her once again.

Now, as she stood at the sink, her hands moving mechanically, she felt the anger rising, a tide she couldn't hold back. Her fingers clenched around the dish she was holding, the porcelain slick and fragile under her grip. How long could she keep this up? How long could she pretend that everything was fine, that their life wasn't falling apart at the seams? She could feel the cracks spreading, the fractures deepening, each one a reminder of the lies and the secrets that had taken root in their home.

The phone rang, its sharp trill cutting through the quiet. Emma jumped, nearly dropping the plate she was holding. She wiped her hands on a dish towel, irritation flaring as she reached for the phone. The display showed an unfamiliar number, but she answered it anyway, pressing the phone to her ear.

"Hello?" she said, her voice taut.

"Mrs. Miller?" a man's voice said, polite but edged with concern. "This is Tom Anderson from Anderson & Co. I apologize for calling you at home, but we've been trying to reach John. He hasn't been in the office for several weeks, and we're getting quite worried. Is everything alright?"

Emma felt the blood drain from her face, her fingers tightening around the phone. "He hasn't been to work?" she repeated, the words coming out in a whisper.

"No, ma'am," Tom replied, his tone gentle. "He hasn't been in, and we've left numerous messages. We just want to make sure everything is okay. Is there something we should know?"

Emma's mind whirled, the room seeming to tilt around her. She gripped the edge of the counter, trying to steady herself. "Thank you for letting me know," she said, her voice trembling. "I'll... I'll speak with him. I'm sure there's some explanation. I'll make sure he gets back to you."

"Please do," Tom said. "And if there's anything we can do to help, please let us know. We're just worried about him."

Emma muttered a quick goodbye and hung up, the phone slipping from her fingers and clattering onto the counter. She stood there, her mind blank, her heart pounding in her chest. John hadn't been to work in weeks. He had been lying to her every day, walking out the door with his briefcase, pretending everything was normal. Her thoughts spiraled, a tangle of confusion and rage. Where had he been going? What had he been doing? The questions buzzed in her mind, each one more painful than the last.

Her eyes landed on her phone, lying on the counter. She snatched it up, her fingers flying as she quickly typed out a message:

Emma: Where are you?

She hit send, her breath coming in short, angry bursts. She stared at the screen, willing it to light up with a response. Seconds ticked by, each one stretching into an eternity. The silence in the kitchen pressed in around her, thick and suffocating. Her hands trembled as she set the phone down.

A thought struck her, and she grabbed the phone again, opening the Find Friends app. Her stomach dropped.

He wasn't sharing his location with her anymore.

She turned back to the sink, fury boiling inside her, threatening to spill over. Grabbing a plate, she scrubbed furiously, water sloshing over the edges. She couldn't believe he had been lying to her, hiding this. What kind of man did that? What kind of husband?

Her thoughts raged like a storm, each one fueling the flames of her anger.

Minutes passed, each one heavier than the last. The phone remained silent, no response, no explanation. Emma let out a shaky breath, her hands gripping the edge of the sink. She felt like she was standing on the edge of a cliff, looking down into a dark, yawning abyss. She couldn't keep pretending, couldn't keep living like this. She had to know the truth, even if it tore her apart.

She grabbed the phone again, staring at the screen, at the empty message thread. Her anger gave way to something deeper, a raw, aching pain that throbbed in her chest. She had trusted him, believed in him, and he had betrayed her. The man she had loved, the man she had built a life with, was slipping away, and she didn't know how to stop it.

The phone buzzed, and Emma's heart leapt. She snatched it up, her eyes scanning the screen. But there was no message, no response. It was only a notification, a reminder of an appointment. Emma's hand clenched around the phone, the tears burning in her eyes. She was alone, more alone than she had ever been, trapped in a house filled with silence and lies.

Emma turned off the faucet, the last of the water swirling down the drain. She stood there, her hands resting on the edge of the sink, her head bowed. She needed to think, to figure out what to do. Her life, the life she had known, was unraveling, and she didn't know how to hold it together. She took a deep breath, the sound echoing in the quiet kitchen.

She straightened, wiping her hands on a dish towel, her movements slow and deliberate. She would find out what was happening. She had to. For the sake of her children, for her own sanity. She couldn't let this silence, this darkness, consume her. She had to confront John, demand answers, force him to see the pain he was causing.

Emma set her jaw, a hard line of determination. The time

for silence was over. She would no longer wait in the shadows, hoping for the truth to reveal itself. She would seek it out, drag it into the light, no matter what it cost. She turned away from the sink, the kitchen, and walked toward the door, her steps firm, her heart burning with a fire that refused to be quenched.

The afternoon light in the Miller house had dimmed, shrouded by the gathering clouds outside. The study, a seldom-used room tucked away at the back of the house, seemed darker still, as if the shadows were deeper here, thicker, clinging to the corners like cobwebs. Emma entered, her steps tentative, as if she feared what she might find. She hadn't ventured into John's study in weeks, not since he had withdrawn into himself, leaving behind the man she had known.

The desk was cluttered with papers, bills, and old receipts, a fine layer of dust settling on the surface, a testament to the room's disuse. She moved to the chair, her hand brushing against the dust as she sat down. The computer's screen flickered to life with a faint whir, the glow of the monitor casting a pale light on her face. She hesitated, her fingers poised over the keyboard, her thoughts swirling. She needed answers. The call from John's office had left her shaken, her anger stoking the embers of her determination. If John wouldn't tell her the truth, she would find it herself.

Emma began to type, her fingers moving with a purpose, each keystroke a step deeper into the past of Briar Vale. She searched the name of the development, scrolling through pages of advertisements and local news pieces praising the modern amenities and beautiful homes. Her frustration mounted as each link led to more of the same: glowing reviews, real estate listings, photos of smiling families in front of their new homes.

As she continued to scroll, she passed by a recent news article titled *"Samuel Redford, Local Prominent Attorney Disappears."* The article was followed by a few other similar articles, but they were largely unrelated.

She continued scrolling, her focus sharpening.

Then, a headline caught her eye, buried among the praise

and promotion:

Controversy Surrounds Briar Vale: Investigation into Collin Homes for Illegal Lumber Use.

Emma clicked on the link, her eyes narrowing as she scanned the article. The words on the screen seemed to leap out at her, each line drawing her deeper into a narrative she hadn't known existed.

Collin Homes, the developer behind the newly built Briar Vale community, is under investigation by the U.S. Fish and Wildlife Service and Customs and Border Protection for the use of illegally imported lumber. Sources suggest that the company used wood from protected areas, raising concerns about environmental violations and potential health risks.

Her breath hitched, the knot of anxiety in her chest tightening. Illegal lumber. The phrase echoed in her mind, a warning bell that clanged louder with each sentence she read. She remembered the disclosure she had discovered, the one John had hidden from her, the one that mentioned the use of non-certified wood. He had dismissed it, assured her it was nothing, just a minor oversight. But now, the pieces were falling into place, painting a picture of deceit and recklessness.

She continued to read, her eyes flicking over the words as the story unfolded. The investigation had been ongoing for months, sparked by a tip from a whistleblower within the company. There were mentions of falsified documents, of shipments routed through different countries to evade detection. The deeper she delved, the more she realized that this was not just a simple case of cutting corners; it was a carefully orchestrated scheme to profit at the expense of the law, and possibly, the safety of those who lived in the homes built with that wood.

The name Rick Collin appeared frequently, the founder

and CEO of Collin Homes. He was described as a shrewd businessman, a man who had built his company from the ground up, who was known for his ambition and his willingness to take risks. Emma's jaw tightened as she read about him, her anger simmering beneath the surface. This was the man who had put her family at risk, who had turned their dream home into a potential nightmare.

Emma's fingers moved over the keyboard, searching for more information, more details about the investigation. She found reports from environmental agencies, statements from Customs officials, all pointing to a web of corruption and illegal activity. The more she read, the deeper her unease grew. This wasn't just about illegal wood; it was about a company willing to flout the law, to endanger lives, all for the sake of profit.

Her eyes landed on a link to a local news forum, where residents and former employees of Collin Homes had shared their experiences. She clicked on it, her curiosity piqued, her heart thudding in her chest. The posts were a mix of complaints about shoddy construction, rumors about the company's practices, and, more troublingly, accounts of strange occurrences in Briar Vale. One post, written by someone claiming to be a former employee, caught her attention:

"I worked for Collin Homes on the Briar Vale project. We all knew about the lumber, but no one said anything. The money was good, and Rick made it clear we should keep our mouths shut. But there's more to it. I don't know how to explain it, but something's wrong with that place. It's like it is cursed."

Emma felt a shiver run down her spine, her eyes widening as she read the words. Cursed. The word seemed to leap off the screen, striking a chord deep within her. She thought of the strange behavior of their neighbors, of the feeling she had sometimes, late at night, that she was being watched. She had brushed it off as paranoia, as the stress of moving and settling into a new place. But what if it was more? What if there was something wrong with Briar Vale, something that went beyond the realm of the rational?

Emma leaned back in her chair, her mind racing. She glanced at her phone, half expecting a message from John, but the screen was blank, a silent testament to his absence. She felt a wave of frustration and fear wash over her. She was piecing together a picture, but there were still too many missing pieces, too many unanswered questions.

The study had grown darker as the sun sank behind the tree line, casting long shadows along the walls. Most of the light now came from the computer screen, its glow throwing eerie patterns across Emma's face as she leaned in, her eyes scanning the text before her with such intensity that it made her head ache. The dimness of the room seemed to heighten the tension that gripped her, feeding the sense of unease that had been building ever since she discovered the truth about the illegal lumber. But now, she felt she was on the brink of uncovering even more.

She hesitated for a moment, her fingers hovering over the keyboard. She took a deep breath, then typed the name that had appeared again and again in her search results: "Rick Collin." The letters looked innocuous enough on the screen, but Emma felt a prickle of anticipation, as if she were about to open a door to a place she couldn't return from. She hit the enter key, and the search engine sprang to life, bringing up a series of articles, each more chilling than the last.

Emma had to sift through numerous mentions in various investigations, but eventually, her eyes caught sight of an article titled "Whistleblower at Collin Homes Speaks Out." She clicked on the link, feeling her heart begin to pound.

Whistleblower at Collin Homes Speaks Out
By Lisa Carrington, Senior Reporter
Palm Beach Gazette
August 22, 2023

JUPITER, FL – Diego Morales, a former site foreman for Collin Homes, has made serious allegations against the well-known South Florida developer. Morales, who is no longer employed by the company, claims that Collin Homes engaged in unethical practices, including the use of substandard and potentially illegal materials in its construction projects.

These claims surface just a month after the unexpected death of Rick Collin, the founder and CEO of Collin Homes, in what was reported as a tragic construction site accident. While no official link has been made between Morales's allegations and Collin's death, his statements have raised concerns about the company's internal practices.

"There was always pressure to cut corners," Morales said. "We were told not to question the source of our materials. After Rick's death, I believe the truth needs to be known."

Collin Homes has denied the accusations, calling Morales's statements baseless. A company spokesperson stated, "We adhere to all industry regulations and standards. These claims are without merit, and we remain committed to the high quality and integrity for which Collin Homes is known."

It remains unclear whether local authorities will launch an investigation in response to these allegations. As the community reacts to Morales's claims, questions about the practices at Collin Homes and the circumstances surrounding Rick Collin's death are growing.

The Palm Beach Gazette will continue to follow this developing story.

Curious about the circumstances surrounding Rick Collin's death, Emma typed "Rick Collin death" into the search bar. A moment later, another article appeared, this one dated slightly over two years ago. She clicked on it, her pulse quickening. The article began with a photograph of a man in his late fifties, his rugged, lined face radiating an air of confidence. The caption beneath read: Rick Collin, founder of Collin Homes, tragically dies in construction site accident.

Emma's eyes flicked to the text, reading quickly, the words a blur as she absorbed the details.

Tragic Accident Claims Life of Local Developer Rick Collin
By Michael Turner, Staff Writer
Palm Beach Gazette
September 18, 2022

JUPITER, FL – Rick Collin, the founder and CEO of Collin Homes, one of South Florida's prominent real estate developers, was tragically killed in an accident at a Briar Vale construction site yesterday morning. The incident occurred shortly after 9 a.m., while Collin was inspecting the progress of the development, a newly constructed residential community near Jupiter.

According to initial reports, Collin was found deceased at the construction site. Emergency services were called immediately, but it was clear upon their arrival that Collin had succumbed to site related injuries. The exact circumstances surrounding the accident remain unclear, and an investigation by local authorities is currently underway.

"This is a tragic loss for our community," said Sheriff Harold Monroe of Palm Beach County. "We are committed to determining how this accident occurred and ensuring that all safety protocols are thoroughly reviewed and enforced."

Rick Collin was well-known in the local business community for his ambitious real estate projects, which have contributed significantly to the housing market in Jupiter and the surrounding areas. His company, Collin Homes, has built numerous residential developments over the past decade, earning a reputation for quality construction and innovative design.

"Rick was a visionary," said Susan Price, a spokeswoman for Collin Homes. "He had a passion for creating beautiful communities where families could thrive. His dedication to his work and his employees was unmatched. We are devastated by his loss, and our thoughts are with his family during this incredibly difficult time."

Collin Homes has temporarily suspended all construction activities at the Briar Vale site as a safety precaution and to allow for a comprehensive investigation into the incident. The company has stated that it is fully cooperating with local authorities and *safety inspectors to understand what led to the tragic event.*

One worker at the site, Diego Morales, who served as the site foreman, offered a cryptic statement in the wake of the incident. "Rick is with the spirits now," Morales said, his eyes wide with apparent distress. "The forest has taken him back."

While the exact meaning behind Morales's remarks remains unclear, and some may interpret them as merely the emotional response of a grief-stricken employee, they have nonetheless fueled speculation among the crew. A few workers at the site, speaking on condition of anonymity, described Morales as superstitious and prone to sharing stories about the land and its supposed spiritual significance.

The site where the accident occurred, Briar Vale, is part of a larger development plan that aims to expand residential options in the rapidly growing Jupiter area. Despite this tragic event, Collin Homes has expressed its commitment to continuing Collin's vision for the community.

"He had big plans for Briar Vale," said Price. "Rick believed in creating places where people could build their lives and feel a sense of belonging. We will honor his memory by continuing his work with the same dedication and care that he showed every day."

As the investigation continues, local residents and employees of Collin Homes have come together to mourn the loss of a leader whose impact on the community will not be forgotten. A memorial service is being planned, and details will be announced in the coming days.

For now, the future of Briar Vale remains uncertain as authorities and the company work to ensure that all necessary safety measures are in place to prevent further tragedies.

Emma's breath caught as she read a quote from one of the workers, a man named Diego Morales. The article described Diego as the site foreman, someone who would had worked closely with Collin. He had been vocal about his belief that something otherworldly was at play. The article dismissed his claims, painting him as a superstitious fool, a man given to flights of fancy. But Emma felt a chill run down her spine as she read his words:

"Rick is with the spirits now."

The words were stark on the screen, a testament to fear that Emma could almost feel radiating from the text. She leaned back in the chair, her hands trembling slightly. Her mind raced, connecting the dots between the illegal lumber, the strange behavior of her neighbors, and now this - the idea that something ancient and vengeful had been disturbed. She could feel the threads of the story weaving together, forming a tapestry of dread.

Emma's thoughts raced as she stared at the computer screen, the light casting a ghostly pallor over her face. She needed to find him, to speak with him. Diego Morales might be the only person who could shed light on the shadows that haunted her home, the shadows with those piercing red eyes. He might be able to tell her why John had changed, why he had become a man she barely recognized, consumed by a darkness she couldn't understand. Perhaps Diego could explain the strange behavior of their neighbors, the eerie stillness that had settled over the community like a shroud.

Her fingers moved quickly over the keyboard, typing in Diego's name, her determination growing with each click. She searched through pages of records, articles, anything that might lead her to him. Her breath quickened, her heart thudding in her chest as she scrolled through the results. And then she found it - an address in Belle Glade, Florida. A small town, no more than forty minutes away.

Belle Glade. The name felt both foreign and strangely familiar, a place that held the promise of answers. Emma scribbled the address on a notepad, her hands trembling slightly. Diego Morales had retreated there after leaving Collin Homes, seeking solitude away from the whispers and accusations. He had tried to warn them, tried to speak out, but his voice had been lost amid the clamor for profits and progress.

She looked at the clock on the wall. It was late afternoon,

the shadows stretching long and thin across the floor. The kids would be home from school soon, their footsteps breaking the silence that had settled over the house. She didn't have much time. She needed to think, to plan. Diego's words had been a warning, and if she was going to find out the truth, she needed to be prepared.

Emma decided she would wait. Tomorrow, after John left for wherever he went during the day - certainly not work, as she now knew - she would drive to Belle Glade. She would seek out Diego Morales, ask him the questions that burned inside her, and find out what he knew about the forest, the spirits, and the shadows that had taken hold of her life. She would go alone, without telling John. He had become part of the darkness, and she could no longer trust him.

As she made her decision, a sense of resolve settled over her, like a steel thread woven through her thoughts. She stood up from the desk, the notepad clutched in her hand, and looked out the window. The sky was a bruised purple, the first stars beginning to blink into existence. The day was ending, but tomorrow would bring new possibilities, new answers.

She could hear the distant sound of the school bus approaching, the low rumble growing louder. Soon, Emily, Jack, and Owen would come through the door, their voices filling the silence with chatter and laughter. She would have to hide her fear, her plans, from them. She needed to be strong, to protect them from the shadows that lurked just out of sight.

Emma turned off the computer, the room plunging into near darkness. She stood there for a moment, her mind racing with all that she had learned, all that she still needed to uncover. She knew that she was on the verge of something, that the pieces of the puzzle were beginning to come together. She just needed to take the next step, to reach out to Diego Morales and hear his story.

Tomorrow, she would drive to Belle Glade. She would find Diego, and she would demand answers. She had to know what was happening in her home, what had taken her husband from her, what was stalking the shadows of Briar Vale. She needed to know how to fight the darkness that was closing in around her.

Emma slipped the notepad into her pocket, her mind set on the journey ahead. The answers were out there, hidden in the words of a man who had seen the truth and tried to speak it. She was no longer afraid of the shadows. She was ready to face them, to drag them into the light.

As she moved toward the door, the sound of the school bus stopping at the end of the street reached her ears, followed by the familiar clamor of children's voices. Emma paused, listening to the life that still existed outside, the normalcy that she clung to like a lifeline. She stepped out of the study, closing the door behind her, her thoughts focused on what lay ahead.

Tomorrow, she would find Diego Morales. Tomorrow, she would begin to uncover the truth. She took a deep breath, the air filling her lungs with a sense of purpose.

Hopefully, she would finally begin to get answers.

CHAPTER 9

Animalistic Instincts

The morning sun crept above the horizon, casting long shadows that stretched lazily across the Miller's front yard. The air was thick with humidity, a wet blanket that clung to Emma's skin, promising the onset of another sweltering Florida day. From her vantage point at the living room window, Emma watched her husband John emerge from the house, his movements slow, almost mechanical, as if each step required more effort than the last. He didn't glance back at the house as he crossed the driveway, didn't even seem to notice the faded chalk drawings Owen had etched on the concrete the week before. His eyes, dull and unfocused, stared straight ahead, locked onto some invisible point in the distance.

John's shoulders were hunched, his usual brisk stride replaced by a sluggish shuffle that betrayed his growing detachment. He moved with the somber air of a man condemned, a stark contrast to the confident husband she had once known. Emma could only watch as he climbed into the driver's seat of the car, the door slamming shut with a muted thud. For a moment, he sat there, hands gripping the steering wheel, head bowed as if in prayer. Then, without a backward glance, he turned the key, and the engine roared to life. The car eased out of the driveway, disappearing down the road that led out of Briar Vale, into whatever dark recesses John now inhabited.

Emma remained at the window; her gaze fixed on the empty driveway long after John's car had vanished from sight. The house felt hollow around her, an echoing shell filled with shadows. She let out a small sigh, rubbing her eyes with the back of her hand. The early morning quiet was a stark contrast to the turmoil inside her. John had been leaving before dawn, avoiding her, avoiding the children. He spoke little, his words clipped and cold, like a man who had already decided to sever ties with everything around him. Each morning, Emma woke up to the emptiness of his absence, his side of the bed cool, his presence reduced to the faint scent of his cologne lingering in the air.

The children hadn't seen him in days. They asked about him, but Emma had no answers to give, only reassurances that she barely believed herself. She turned away from the window, the familiar ache of isolation tightening in her chest. This was not the life she had envisioned when they moved to Briar Vale. This was not the fresh start she had hoped for.

Emma made her way to the kitchen, where the silence hung heavy, broken only by the quiet hum of the refrigerator. The morning had begun like any other, a ritual of orchestrated chaos that had once been a comfort in its routine. She set about preparing breakfast, the mundane tasks offering a brief respite from her spiraling thoughts. She poured cereal into bowls, arranged fruit on plates, all the while her mind racing with the unsettling reality of their lives. The children's return to school had brought a semblance of normalcy back, a structure to their days that felt almost reassuring. Even in a new school, with new faces and routines, the predictability of schoolwork, lunch breaks, and bus rides gave them a small escape from the strangeness of home.

The sound of footsteps above signaled the beginning of the morning rush. Owen was the first to descend, his small face still puffy with sleep, hair tousled in all directions. He slid into his chair at the table, reaching for his bowl of cereal without a word. His eyes were distant, the usual spark of curiosity dimmed, replaced by a weariness that seemed too heavy for his small frame. Emma offered him a smile, but he barely glanced up, his spoon moving mechanically.

Emily and Jack followed soon after, their presence filling the kitchen with a brief, comforting bustle. They bickered lightly over who would use the bathroom first, their voices overlapping in a familiar sibling rhythm. Despite their attempts to mask it, Emma could sense the underlying tension in their words, the glances they exchanged when they thought she wasn't looking. They were old enough to feel the strain, to notice the way their father's absence weighed on the house.

As they settled into their places at the table, Emma moved through the motions, pouring juice, reminding them to pack their lunches, and signing off on the school forms they had thrust at her last minute. She watched them eat, the clinking of spoons against bowls the only sound. Despite the tension at home, the children's return to school brought a semblance of normalcy back into their lives. Even in a new school, with new faces and routines, the structure and predictability of the school day offered them a reprieve from the strange happenings in their home. It was a small comfort, but one that Emma clung to in the chaos.

The school bus's arrival broke the silence, its engine rumbling outside. "Bus is here!" Jack called out, swinging his backpack over his shoulder. Owen and Emily hurriedly grabbed their things, the hurried shuffle of their movements a stark contrast to John's lethargic departure earlier. Owen hesitated at the door, turning to Emma with a look that had been almost pleading. She knelt to smooth his hair, her heart aching at the sight of his worried eyes. "It's going to be okay," she whispered, forcing a smile she didn't feel. "Just focus on your schoolwork, and we'll have dinner together tonight, alright?"

Owen nodded, his small shoulders slumping under the weight of whatever unspoken fears he carried. Jack and Emily, older and more attuned to the unspoken tensions between their parents, exchanged a glance but said nothing, their footsteps heavy as they followed Owen out the door. Emma stood at the threshold, watching them walk down the street, their figures growing smaller with each step. A sense of foreboding settled in her chest, the feeling that they were moving further from safety with each passing day.

Her eyes fell on the car keys resting on the kitchen counter, glinting in a shaft of sunlight that streamed through the window. A surge of determination flooded through her, momentarily dispelling the fog of despair that had settled over her mind. She had spent too long waiting, too long questioning her sanity, too long wondering what lay hidden beneath the surface of her husband's cold demeanor. It was time to find answers. Time to unravel the mystery that had ensnared her family and stolen the peace from their home.

Emma grabbed the keys with a resolve she hadn't felt in weeks. Each click of her heels on the tile floor echoed with purpose as she strode towards the front door. She swung it open, stepping out into the morning sun. The heat hit her like a wave, the thick air wrapping around her like a second skin. She hesitated for a moment, her gaze sweeping the quiet, tree-lined street of Briar Vale. The houses stood in neat rows, their identical facades hiding the secrets that lurked within. It was hard to believe that behind those freshly painted walls, something malevolent was at work.

For a moment, the idea of confronting whatever lay ahead filled her with dread. Memories of John's empty eyes, of Owen's whispered fears, of the shadows that seemed to move just beyond her vision, all pressed down on her. But as she stood there, the sun rising higher in the sky, casting its harsh light over the seemingly idyllic neighborhood, Emma felt a spark of something long forgotten - a sense of purpose. She was not powerless. She was not alone. Whatever darkness had crept into their lives, she would face it, not as a passive observer, but as a mother determined to protect her children.

She locked the front door behind her, slipping the keys into her pocket. The morning air was already thick with the scent of magnolias and fresh-cut grass, masking the undercurrent of something sour that had tainted her senses since they moved here. Emma made her way to the car, her mind set on the journey ahead. Belle Glade was an hour's drive away, a distance that seemed to stretch like an eternity given the urgency she felt. She needed to find Diego Morales. The man who knew the truth, the man whose name was a lifeline in the sea of uncertainty that had become her reality.

She slid into the driver's seat, her fingers gripping the steering wheel with a newfound strength. As she turned the key, the engine rumbled to life, the sound cutting through the morning stillness. Emma glanced at the rearview mirror, at the empty driveway that had once been a place of joy, of home. Now, it was a threshold to a place she barely recognized, a place where shadows whispered and walls seemed to close in around her.

As Emma eased her car into reverse, the engine's low rumble reverberated through the quiet morning air, momentarily disturbing the stillness that lay like a shroud over Briar Vale. She carefully navigated the vehicle out of the driveway, her mind focused on the journey ahead, when her gaze fell upon a figure further down the street, just outside the Cartwright house.

Her foot lingered over the brake pedal as she squinted into the blinding sunlight, only to be struck by a sudden, sharp jolt of recognition. It was Agatha Cartwright, her elusive neighbor, whom she had not laid eyes upon in weeks. Agatha had always been a figure of peculiar aspect - a frail woman of seemingly benign disposition, who had greeted them with a forced civility when they first took residence. Yet, there was ever something about her that stirred an inexplicable unease within Emma. Perhaps it was her unsettling fixation upon her wretched cats, or that abominable pie she brought forth upon their arrival, with a smell so foul it still lingered faintly in Emma's memory. And yet, despite it all, Agatha had always worn that unnerving, brittle smile.

But today - there was something horribly different. Emma felt her pulse quicken, a strange and dreadful mixture of concern and morbid curiosity overtaking her as she observed the elderly woman laboring beneath the weight of a large, unwieldy bag. The way she struggled with it... it seemed unnatural, as if the very air around her had thickened, conspiring against her. What could it contain, that it burdened her so?

The bag was enormous, sagging in the middle, and Agatha's frail frame seemed barely able to manage its weight. The plastic material of the bag glistened in the sun, but it was the dark, brownish liquid seeping from one corner that caught Emma's eye. A slow, steady drip left a trail along the driveway, originating from the woods across the way, where the bag must have been dragged from. Emma felt a shiver run down her spine, her instincts screaming that something was terribly amiss.

"Agatha?" Emma called out, her voice cutting through the stillness, tinged with a note of hesitation. "Agatha, do you need some help?" She hoped her voice sounded casual, though the sight of the brown trail and the awkward bulk of the bag made her uneasy. Her mind raced with questions. What was in that bag? And why did it smell faintly of something foul, a scent that was just reaching her now, carried on the light breeze?

Agatha did not respond. She did not even look up. Her face, turned slightly towards the garage, was pallid, almost ashen, and her eyes, usually sharp and filled with a kind of nosy vigor, now seemed dull, sunken into dark hollows. Her movements were slow, lethargic, as if she were underwater or in a trance. She continued to pull at the bag, oblivious to Emma's presence, her shoulders heaving with effort. A strand of gray hair had fallen loose from her bun, sticking to her damp forehead, but she made no move to brush it away. The world outside might have ceased to exist for all the notice she took.

Emma swallowed, a heavy knot forming in her throat. She stepped out of her car, her sandals clicking against the pavement as she approached cautiously, the acrid scent of the liquid growing stronger with each step. Agatha dragged the bag over the threshold of her garage, her feet shuffling on the ground, leaving streaks of brown behind. Emma could hear her own heart beating, a dull thud that seemed to echo in her ears.

"Agatha," she called again, louder this time, her voice carrying an edge of urgency. "Are you okay? Can I help you with that?" She took another step closer, her eyes fixed on the dark stain spreading across the garage floor, its color disturbingly reminiscent of old blood. The smell was stronger now, tinged with a musky, almost animal-like scent that made Emma's stomach turn

Agatha paused for a moment, her head turning ever so slightly towards Emma, but still, she did not speak. Her eyes flickered with something - recognition, perhaps, or annoyance - before she resumed her task, her back hunching under the weight of the bag. She gave a final heave, pulling the bag fully into the shadowed interior of the garage, where it landed with a soft thud. Emma caught a glimpse of its contents, a shapeless mass, concealed beneath layers of plastic, but there was no mistaking the outline of something rigid, something that seemed to bend awkwardly within its confines.

A chill ran down Emma's spine, her unease sharpening into a pointed fear. Agatha's fingers fumbled with the garage door control, and it began to descend with a low hum, cutting off the sliver of light that had illuminated the bag. Emma watched, frozen, as the door lowered, inch by inch, sealing the scene behind a metal barrier. Then the door clanged shut, and Agatha was gone, swallowed by the shadows of her home.

Emma stood at the end of Agatha Cartwright's driveway, her breath shallow, her heart pounding as if trying to escape her chest. The Florida sun beat down on her back, but she barely felt its heat. All her senses were focused on the scene before her, where the garage door had just shut, sealing whatever lay inside behind a veil of metal. Her car idled nearby, but Emma could not bring herself to leave. Something was wrong, terribly wrong. Every instinct screamed at her to go back, to turn away from the darkness that seemed to seep out of every crevice of Agatha's house. But curiosity had taken hold, a grim curiosity born of fear and a desperate need to understand.

She glanced around, ensuring that no one was watching, that no other neighbor was out to witness her next move. The street was deserted, the houses quiet, their windows reflecting the sun's glare. Emma took a deep breath, trying to steady her nerves. The sound of her own breathing seemed unnaturally loud in the still morning air. She noticed the small, square window set into the garage door, just large enough to offer a glimpse inside. A single bulb hanging from the ceiling cast a dim, flickering light within, barely visible through the dirty glass.

Emma felt a magnetic pull toward the window, an inexplicable urge to peer inside, to confirm the horrors her mind had already imagined. She took a few cautious steps forward, her sandals making a faint shuffling noise against the gravel. As she neared the garage door, the faintest sounds reached her ears - strange, wet noises, like something being dragged across the concrete floor, accompanied by a low, guttural growl. Emma's skin prickled with fear, her heart beating faster.

She moved closer, her eyes fixated on the window. The glass was dirty, smudged with dust and grime, but she could still see through it. Pressing her face to the pane, she squinted, trying to make sense of the shadowy forms inside. At first, her eyes struggled to adjust to the dim light, but gradually the scene took shape.

The interior of the garage was cluttered, a chaotic jumble of tools and debris scattered across the floor. The air seemed thick, almost tangible, vibrating with an unsettling energy. Emma's gaze swept over the space, taking in the piles of bones that lay haphazardly along the walls, their bleached white surfaces stark against the dark concrete. An assortment of jars lined a shelf, filled with unidentifiable substances that glimmered in the half-light.

In the center of the garage, Agatha Cartwright crouched

over the large black bag she had dragged inside. The sight of her made Emma's breath hitch. Agatha's back was to the door, her movements frantic and animalistic as she tore at the bag. Her thin, bony hands were slick with something dark and wet, fingers digging into the plastic, pulling it apart with a ferocity that sent chills down Emma's spine.

Emma's eyes widened in horror as Agatha's head dipped forward, her mouth moving in a gruesome, gnawing motion. Emma's heart hammered as she realized what she was seeing - Agatha was eating. Her lips were stained with blood, her jaw working to tear at the raw, unidentifiable mass that lay before her. Agatha's movements were jerky, frenzied, driven by a hunger that seemed insatiable.

Emma wanted to scream, to turn and run, but her body refused to obey. She remained rooted to the spot, her eyes glued to the grotesque scene before her. Then, as if sensing she was being watched, Agatha paused, her movements stilling. She turned her head slightly, and Emma caught a glimpse of her face - eyes wide and unseeing, pupils dilated, gleaming in the dim light. Her face was smeared with blood, the crimson contrasting starkly against her pale, gaunt skin. Her mouth hung open, a strand of flesh dangling from her lips.

A low growl emanated from Agatha's bag, a sound that was both human and not, sending a shiver of pure terror through Emma's body. She tried to back away, her feet stumbling over the gravel as she moved, but she couldn't tear her eyes from the sight. Agatha turned back to the bag, resuming her gruesome feast, her shoulders hunched over like a feral animal.

Emma's eyes drifted to the corner of the garage, where more bags were piled. Some lay still, dark and foreboding, but one of them twitched. Emma's breath caught in her throat. The bag shifted again, a subtle movement, as if something inside was struggling weakly, fighting against the confines of its plastic prison. Then, Emma heard it - a faint, drawn-out "yowl" emanating from within.

Emma clapped a hand over her mouth, stifling a gasp.

The nausea that had been building in her stomach surged, threatening to overwhelm her. She stumbled back from the window, her legs weak, her vision blurring with tears. She had seen enough, more than enough. She needed to get away, to escape the sight of Agatha's bloodied face, the sound of her gnawing and growling echoing in her ears.

She turned and fled, her feet slipping on the gravel as she ran. She reached her car, yanking the door open with trembling hands. Emma climbed inside, slamming the door shut, her breaths coming in ragged gasps. Her eyes flicked up to the rearview mirror, half-expecting to see Agatha standing in the driveway, watching her with those wild, gleaming eyes. But the street was empty, the garage door closed, the house silent. Emma shuddered, the image of Agatha's blood-smeared face and those twitching bags seared into her mind.

Then, a thought struck her like a bolt of lightning, making her stomach churn. The pie. She remembered with a revolting thought the pie Agatha had brought over on their first day in the house, its rancid smell masked by the sweet, fruity exterior. At the time, Emma had dismissed it as an old recipe gone wrong, but now, in the harsh light of what she had just witnessed, the memory took on a sinister edge. What had been in that pie? What kind of person, or creature, would offer such a thing as a housewarming gift?

The bile rose in her throat, the nausea overwhelming. She pressed a hand to her mouth, willing herself not to be sick. The thought of that pie, sitting in her kitchen trash, filled her with a new horror, as if the darkness that had consumed Agatha had been there from the very beginning, hidden in plain sight. Emma could almost taste the foul, cloying scent that had wafted up when she lifted the pie's cover, mingling with the acrid smell of rot and decay she had just encountered.

Emma squeezed her eyes shut, trying to block out the images that crowded her mind, the thought of Agatha's teeth tearing into raw flesh, her lips stained with blood, the twitching bags that seemed to pulse with life. The neighborhood she had thought was a haven had become a place of nightmares, and now, the darkness was closing in around her.

Her hands shook as she gripped the steering wheel, forcing herself to focus on the task at hand. She needed to get away, needed to find answers, to understand what was happening. With a deep breath, she started the engine, the familiar sound grounding her in the present. She threw the car into gear, her foot pressing hard on the accelerator, the tires screeching as she sped away from Agatha's house, from the horror she had just witnessed.

As the houses of Briar Vale blurred into a nondescript backdrop, Emma felt a hollow resolve fill her chest. She would find Diego Morales. She would get to the bottom of this. The road stretched out before her, straight and unending, each mile a barrier between her and the horrors that lay behind. But no matter how far she drove, she knew that the darkness of Briar Vale would follow, a shadow that clung to her, whispering of the secrets she had yet to uncover.

CHAPTER 10

Into the Darkness

Mary Kendrick's heels clicked against the stone pathway as she approached the Miller's house, a neat stack of papers clutched in her hand. The late morning sun filtered through the swaying palms that lined the street, casting dappled shadows across the manicured lawn. Briar Vale was quiet this time of day, with most residents either at work or keeping to the cool interiors of their homes, away from the oppressive Florida heat. The humidity hung in the air, thick and almost tangible, making the simple act of breathing feel like an effort.

Mary's mind raced with thoughts as she climbed the front steps. Her broker had just called that morning, reminding her that Emma Miller's signature was needed on the disclosure forms about the illegal lumber. *"How did I miss that?"* Mary muttered to herself, feeling a prick of anxiety. She was usually meticulous about paperwork, but the whirlwind of transactions and the rush to sell the remaining houses in Briar Vale had obviously led to some oversights. This could have legal repercussions, and Mary's reputation couldn't afford a mistake like this, especially not now.

Pausing on the front porch, Mary took a deep breath, trying to shake off her nerves. She smoothed the wrinkles from her blouse and rang the doorbell. The chime echoed through the house, a clear, melodic sound that seemed to hang in the air, unanswered. She waited, tapping her foot lightly against the stone step, glancing around the quiet street. The houses of Briar Vale, with their pristine facades and well-kept gardens, exuded an air of suburban perfection. Yet, there was something about the stillness that felt off, as if the entire neighborhood were holding its breath.

She rang the doorbell again, this time pressing the button a little longer, hoping the sound would reach any occupant inside. Still, there was no answer. Mary frowned, feeling a twinge of irritation mixed with concern. She had texted Emma only yesterday, explaining that she had some additional paperwork to review and would be by this morning. It wasn't like Emma to ignore a visitor, especially after expressing concern over the house. Mary sighed, pulling her phone from her purse. With a few quick taps, she sent a message to Emma.

Mary: I'm here at your house with some paperwork to sign. No one home?

The reply came almost immediately, the phone buzzing softly in her hand.

Emma: What paperwork? I'm out right now. Leave it on the porch, and I'll look at it later.

Mary hesitated for a moment before typing a response.

Mary: I need your signature on the disclosure about the lumber. I realized we only have John's, and my broker said we need yours too. It's really important. Can we meet later today?

The pause before Emma's reply felt longer than it probably was. Mary could almost feel Emma's confusion through the screen.

Emma: I am going to be out for the day. Can you leave the

paperwork, and we can meet later?

Mary bit her lip, feeling a little more flustered. She was hoping to wrap this up. She typed back quickly.

Mary: Sure, I'll leave the papers here. But it's urgent we get your signature soon. It's about the wood used in the house. We can discuss it more later.

Mary slipped her phone back into her bag, frowning slightly. Emma's confusion bothered her. Had John kept the details of the disclosure from his wife? The thought sent a ripple of unease through her. With a slight sigh, Mary placed the stack of papers on the small glass-topped table next to the wicker chair on the porch. The documents fluttered slightly in the breeze, the top page lifting as if attempting to take flight before settling back down.

As Mary turned to leave, her foot already on the first step, something caught her eye - a flicker of movement at the side of the house. For a split second, she thought she saw a shadow, a dark shape darting out of sight. But when she blinked, it was gone, leaving her to wonder if her eyes had played tricks on her. She hesitated, her gaze shifting towards the wooden gate leading to the backyard, which was swaying slightly ajar. A strange prickling sensation ran down her spine.

She glanced back at the street, as if expecting to see someone watching, but the quiet suburban landscape remained undisturbed. Taking a deep breath, she walked towards the gate, her heels clicking softly on the pathway. As she approached, she pushed the gate gently with her hand, the wood creaking slightly as it swung open. The hinges groaned, the sound echoing faintly in the heavy air, like a sigh escaping from the depths of an ancient, slumbering creature.

Mary peered into the backyard, her eyes adjusting to the sudden shift from bright sunlight to the dappled shade cast by the tall oaks that bordered the Miller property. The backyard was lush, overgrown almost, with a garden that seemed to have sprung up overnight. Flowers of every imaginable color spilled from the beds, their petals glistening with dew in the morning light. The air was thick with the sweet, almost cloying scent of blossoms, mingled with a more pungent, underlying odor that was less pleasant. It was a strange contrast to the carefully manicured front lawns of Briar Vale, and Mary found herself drawn forward, compelled by a mixture of curiosity and unease.

Mary Kendrick stepped through the gate, her senses immediately assaulted by the overwhelming scent of flowers mingled with something less pleasant, something that made her stomach turn. The backyard stretched out before her, a riot of colors spilling from every corner. Roses, lilies, and exotic blooms Mary couldn't name swayed gently in the breeze, their petals shimmering with dew in the morning light. The garden looked like a scene from a painting, vibrant and lush, as if someone had poured life into every inch of soil.

Yet, despite the beauty, an unease lingered in the air. Mary took a few cautious steps forward, her heels sinking slightly into the soft earth. As she walked closer to the heart of the garden, the unpleasant smell grew stronger, overriding the fragrance of the flowers. Her nose wrinkled in distaste, and she paused, looking around for the source. Flies buzzed lazily around the edges of the flower beds, their droning hum filling the quiet of the morning. Mary's gaze followed the path of a particularly large fly as it landed near a cluster of bright red flowers, crawling over the petals as if searching for something more enticing.

Mary took a step closer, her hand instinctively rising to cover her mouth and nose against the foul stench. Her eyes darted over the flower beds, searching for any sign of what could be causing such a morbid smell. Her mind raced with possibilities, each one more disturbing than the last. Perhaps it was just some elaborate gardening project gone wrong, she thought desperately, trying to convince herself that she was overreacting. Maybe John had been experimenting with fertilizer or had buried organic waste too close to the surface.

As she contemplated this, Mary suddenly heard the crunch of footsteps on the gravel behind her. She spun around, her eyes wide with surprise and fear. John Miller stood a few feet away, holding the stack of papers she had left on the front porch. His expression was dark and unreadable, his eyes fixed on her with an intensity that made Mary's skin crawl.

"You did this," John said, his voice low and simmering with barely controlled anger. He held up the papers, shaking them slightly. "You brought this chaos into my house."

Mary's heart pounded, and she took a step back, her heel sinking into the soft earth. "John, I - I just came to drop off the documents," she stammered, trying to keep her voice calm. "I needed Emma's signature. It's about the lumber used in the house. I didn't mean to - "

"You didn't mean to?" John cut her off, his voice rising with a sharp edge. He took a step closer, his eyes narrowing. "You didn't mean to cause trouble? You didn't mean to tear my family apart?"

Mary shook her head, bewildered. "John, I don't understand. I'm just doing my job. There's nothing - "

"Nothing?" John's voice was almost a snarl now. He took another step closer, his face contorted with anger. "You've been meddling, stirring things up. You and that damn company. You think you can just come into people's lives, into my life, and make demands?"

Mary felt a wave of fear wash over her. John's mood seemed unpredictable, swinging from quiet menace to outright fury. She could see his hands shaking, the papers crumpling in his grip. "John, please," she said softly, trying to placate him. "I'm not here to cause any problems. I just need Emma's signature, that's all."

"Emma's signature?" John repeated, his voice dripping with sarcasm. He threw the papers onto the ground between them, where they landed in a scattered heap. "Emma didn't need to know about this. Emma didn't need to know anything. You think you can come here, dig into our business, tell us what to do?"

Mary took a cautious step back, her eyes flicking to the garden gate, calculating the distance. She needed to stay calm, needed to find a way to defuse the situation. "I'm just following up on some legal requirements," she said, her voice trembling slightly. "It's nothing personal, John. I promise."

"Nothing personal?" John echoed, a bitter laugh escaping his lips. "Everything is personal. You think you're just doing your job, but you don't see the consequences, do you? You don't see the chaos you leave behind."

He took another step forward, and Mary instinctively stepped back again, her heel hitting the edge of one of the freshly dug patches. She wobbled slightly, catching her balance, her eyes never leaving John's. The scent of decay filled her nostrils, and she felt bile rise in her throat. She needed to get out of there, needed to put distance between herself and John's mounting rage. She needed to get away.

It was a day of breathtaking beauty in Briar Vale, the kind that seemed to suspend time itself. The sky, a vast expanse of endless blue, was dotted with soft, puffy clouds, drifting lazily across the horizon like silent ships upon a gentle sea. The sun hung high, its warm, golden light spilling over the neighborhood, casting everything in a soft, honeyed glow. Each house stood proudly in the sunlight, their freshly painted facades gleaming, their windows reflecting the brilliance of the day.

The trees, old and wise, lined the streets with their thick, leafy branches that swayed gently in the breeze. Their leaves, a vibrant green, rustled softly, like a thousand whispers carrying secrets only the wind knew. Beneath them, the grass was a lush carpet, deep emerald and cool to the touch, meticulously trimmed and free of blemish. Flower beds overflowed with color: the bright yellows of marigolds, the deep purples of irises, and the soft pinks of petunias. Their fragrance mingled in the air, sweet and heady, filling the senses with the promise of summer.

Birds flitted from branch to branch, their songs a symphony of trills and chirps, echoing joyously through the clear air. Occasionally, a squirrel darted across a lawn, its bushy tail flicking as it disappeared into the safety of the underbrush. Even the insects seemed at peace, bees moving from flower to flower with a lazy hum, their movements unhurried, as if time itself had slowed to savor the perfection of the day.

The gentle breeze carried with it the distant sounds of suburban life. The murmur of a lawnmower somewhere down the street, the faint laughter of children playing a game of tag, their voices high and carefree, and the rhythmic creak of a porch swing. All these sounds blended into a soothing background, a lullaby of contentment that wrapped around Briar Vale like a soft, comforting blanket.

Then, only for a moment, a scream tore through the tranquil air, sharp and jarring, like a jagged crack in a flawless pane of glass. It was a cry of terror, raw and visceral, that seemed to reverberate through the stillness, slicing through the serenity of the day. The sound rose high, reaching out desperately, before fading just as swiftly, swallowed by the warm summer air. It hung there for the briefest of instants, a note of discord in the symphony of peace, before dissolving into the ether, leaving no trace that it had ever been.

Yet, as quickly as it had come, it was gone. The birds continued to sing, their melodies undisturbed, a sweet chorus of life that flowed on as if nothing had happened. Their chirps and trills carried no hint of alarm, only the joyous, carefree tones of creatures at home in their world. The wind continued to blow, a gentle, soothing caress that rustled the leaves in the trees and swept over the manicured lawns, whispering through the branches as if sharing a secret with the sky.

If anyone had been around, if any ears had been attuned to the subtleties of the day, they might have noticed the faint, distant sound of unearthly laughter carried on the breeze. But that too, went unheard.

Emma's hands gripped the steering wheel tightly as she drove through the quiet streets of Belle Glade, her knuckles white from the strain. The landscape was a stark contrast to the pristine, manicured lawns of Briar Vale. Here, the roads were narrower, flanked by fields stretching out to the horizon, the earth dark and fertile. The houses she passed were modest, some weathered by time and the elements, their paint peeling and roofs sagging. The air was heavy with the scent of soil and distant cane fields, mingling with the faint aroma of smoke from a nearby burn.

As she navigated through the small, rural town, Emma felt her anxiety mounting. She glanced at the address scribbled on the piece of paper beside her, then back at the houses lining the street, searching for the numbers. Her heart pounded in her chest, a mixture of fear and determination driving her forward. She had to know what was happening to her family. She had to find out what Diego Morales knew about Rick Collins and the cursed wood that had found its way into their home.

Finally, she spotted the house: a small, single-story structure set back from the road, partially hidden by a large banyan tree whose gnarled roots clawed at the ground. The house was painted a faded blue, its windows covered with simple, white curtains. A dusty truck was parked in the gravel driveway, and a small, neatly kept garden bordered the front porch, where a few potted plants stood like silent sentinels.

Emma pulled into the driveway, the crunch of gravel beneath her tires loud in the stillness. She turned off the engine and sat for a moment, her hands still gripping the steering wheel. Taking a deep breath, she forced herself to let go, to unclench her fingers and open the car door. The air outside was warm and still, heavy with the promise of the approaching afternoon. She walked up the path to the front door, her footsteps slow and hesitant, each step echoing the uncertainty she felt.

Emma paused at the door, raising her hand to knock, but hesitated. She glanced at her phone, considering sending a quick message to Jack, but decided against it. She had told him she would be out for a while, and she didn't want to worry him or the others. This was something she needed to do alone. With a final deep breath, she knocked on the door, the sound of her fist against the wood sharp in the quiet.

For a moment, there was no response. Emma stood on the porch, feeling the weight of the house pressing down on her, the banyan tree's branches swaying gently overhead. She was about to knock again when she heard the sound of footsteps from within, slow and cautious. The door creaked open a few inches, revealing a man in his late sixties, his face weathered and lined, his eyes dark and wary. He wore a simple shirt and faded jeans, his hair a mix of gray and black, pulled back into a loose ponytail.

"Can I help you?" he asked, his voice gruff and guarded. His eyes flickered over Emma, taking in her appearance, the uncertainty in his gaze clear.

"Mr. Morales?" Emma said, her voice trembling slightly. "Diego Morales?"

The man's eyes narrowed, suspicion deepening the lines of his face. "Who's asking?"

"My name is Emma Miller," she said, summoning all her courage. "I live in Briar Vale. I've come to ask you about Rick Collins and the wood he used to build the houses there."

At the mention of Rick Collin, Diego's expression hardened. He stepped back, shaking his head. "No. Please, go away," he said, his voice low and firm. "That part of my life has passed. I don't want to relive it."

He began to close the door, but Emma reached out, placing her hand against the wood to stop him. "Please, Mr. Morales, I'm begging you," she said urgently. "My family is in danger. My husband is changing, my neighbors are acting strangely, and I keep seeing shadows... things I can't explain. You're the only one who can help me. Please, I need to know what's happening."

Diego hesitated, his hand on the doorknob. He looked at Emma, his eyes narrowing, as if searching her face for some sign of deceit. The desperation in her voice seemed to reach him, and he sighed heavily, the sound like the air escaping from an old tire. He opened the door a little wider, the resistance fading from his stance.

"All right," he said, his voice resigned. "Come in."

Emma nodded, stepping inside. The interior of the house was simple and sparsely furnished, a far cry from the polished, curated spaces of her own home. The walls were painted a light yellow, the furniture old but well-kept. A small, round table stood in the center of the living room, surrounded by a few mismatched chairs. The air inside was cool, a fan in the corner whirring softly, stirring the heavy scent of incense that hung in the air.

Diego closed the door behind her, locking it with a firm click. He motioned for Emma to sit at the table, his movements careful and deliberate. Emma sat down, her hands resting in her lap, her eyes following Diego as he took a seat opposite her. He leaned back in his chair, crossing his arms over his chest, his gaze never leaving her face.

"What do you know about Rick Collin?" Diego asked, his voice flat, devoid of emotion.

Emma took a deep breath, gathering her thoughts. "I know he was the developer who built Briar Vale," she began. "I know he used illegal lumber, and that wood was used to build my house. And I know he died... in an accident." She hesitated, unsure how much to reveal, then decided to be honest. "My family... strange things have been happening since we moved in. My husband's behavior has changed, and... and there's something wrong with the house."

Diego's expression remained unreadable, but Emma saw a flicker of recognition in his eyes. He nodded slowly, as if confirming something to himself. "You're right about the wood," he said after a moment. "It came from a place in the Amazon. A sacred place, one that was never meant to be disturbed. Rick...

he didn't care. He just wanted the cheap lumber, didn't believe in the old stories. But I knew. I saw the signs. I heard the whispers."

Emma leaned forward, her pulse quickening. "What stories? What whispers?"

Diego glanced away, his eyes distant as if seeing something far off. "The Anhanga," he said quietly. "Spirits of the forest. Guardians. They protect the land, and they don't take kindly to those who defile it. Rick didn't believe. He laughed at the warnings, said it was all superstition."

Emma felt a shiver run down her spine. The pieces of the puzzle were falling into place, but they painted a picture far darker than she had imagined. "What happened to Rick?" she asked softly.

Diego leaned forward, his voice dropping to a whisper. "I should probably start from the beginning," he said, his eyes boring into hers. "You need to know everything... if you are to understand."

CHAPTER 11

Sins of the Land

Early **Spring 2021, Jupiter, Florida:** The afternoon sun streamed through the tall windows of Rick Collins's office, casting sharp angles of light across the dark, polished mahogany of his desk. The room, once a place of calm and orderly conduct, now reflected the turmoil that had gripped its occupant. Stacks of papers, blueprints, and financial reports cluttered every available surface, creating a landscape of controlled chaos. The air, thick with the lingering aroma of cigar smoke and fresh coffee, felt oppressive, as if it too were burdened by the weight of the looming deadlines.

Rick sat behind his desk, his fingers tapping restlessly on the armrest of his leather chair. His eyes were fixed on the screen of his laptop, the glow of the monitor casting a cold light on his lined face. The numbers on the spreadsheet blurred before him, a tide of red ink threatening to overwhelm the black. The familiar churning in his gut told him that he was out of time. The CDD loan, the lifeline he had so confidently secured for the Briar Vale development, was now a noose tightening around his neck. If he missed the next deadline, if the construction did not continue as scheduled, he stood to lose everything.

His mind raced, weighing the options, each more bleak than the last. The U.S. lumber shortage had crippled the industry, the COVID-19 restrictions making matters even worse. Mills were shut down, supply chains disrupted, and prices had soared beyond reason. The local suppliers, once reliable partners, now offered nothing but excuses and inflated costs. The reality was stark: without wood, there could be no building. And without building, Briar Vale would collapse, taking Rick and his company with it.

He leaned back in his chair, a weary sigh escaping his lips. His gaze drifted to the photographs that lined his desk, images of his wife and children, their faces bright with smiles from happier times. A pang of guilt struck him, a sharp reminder of the stakes. This wasn't just about business. It was about survival - his family's future, their security. He had worked too hard, sacrificed too much to see it all slip away now.

The phone on his desk rang, cutting through his thoughts like a knife. Rick snatched it up, his voice sharp with irritation. "Collins here," he barked.

"Rick," came the voice on the other end, smooth and low, a voice Rick recognized immediately as one of his more discreet contacts. "I heard you're having some trouble sourcing lumber."

Rick's jaw tightened. "You heard right. The local mills are useless, and I've got a project that's going to go under if I don't find a solution fast."

There was a pause, and then the voice continued, "I might have a lead for you. It's not exactly above board, but it'll get you what you need. There's an operation out of Brazil. They're sitting on a supply of hardwood that can be ready to be cut and shipped quickly. It's not legal, and it's not cheap, but it'll get you your wood."

Rick was silent for a moment, his mind turning over the possibilities. Illegal wood. The words alone should have set off alarms, should have brought up images of raids, fines, and headlines. But the thought of failure, of losing everything, overshadowed any concerns for legality or ethics. His reputation had been built on taking risks, on making the hard choices that others shied away from. And this was just another decision in a long line of them.

"How much?" Rick asked, his voice steady, betraying none

of the turmoil inside him.

"It'll take a month to get the full supply to you," the voice said, "but you'll have enough to keep things moving in the meantime. As for cost, let's just say it's competitive, considering the circumstances. You'll be able to keep your project afloat."

Rick nodded, more to himself than to the voice on the phone. "And no one will know where it came from?"

A soft chuckle came through the line. "Rick, you know how these things work. As long as you pay, no one asks questions. The wood will show up, and that's all anyone needs to know."

Rick's fingers drummed on the desk, his eyes narrowing as he weighed the decision. It wasn't the first time he had bent the rules, but this felt different, more dangerous. The stakes were higher. But then, so were the rewards.

"Do it," Rick said finally, his voice hardening with resolve. "Get me the wood. And make sure it stays off the radar. If anyone asks, it's business as usual."

"You got it," the voice replied smoothly. "I'll make the arrangements."

Rick ended the call and set the phone down, a sense of grim satisfaction settling over him. The tension in his shoulders eased slightly, replaced by a cautious optimism. He had a plan, a way out of the trap that had been closing around him. Briar Vale would continue. The deadlines would be met. The investors would be kept happy. And he would emerge unscathed, just as he always had.

He stood up, moving to the window that overlooked the city below. The streets, quieter now under the weight of the pandemic, stretched out before him. He watched as people moved like ants, tiny and insignificant, each with their own worries and fears. Rick felt a flicker of contempt. They would never understand the pressures he faced, the sacrifices he made to keep things running. It was easy to judge from a distance, easy to cling to ideals when you had nothing to lose.

For a moment, a shadow passed over his thoughts, a

whisper of doubt. The image of the dense, ancient Brazilian forest came unbidden to his mind. He imagined the trees, tall and silent, standing sentinel over the land undisturbed for centuries. Their vast canopies reached skyward, their roots buried deep in the earth, forming a world apart, untouched by the hands of time or progress.

Rick shook his head, dispelling the thoughts like cobwebs. What mattered was here and now, the real world, the world of deals and deadlines, of profit and progress. He had no time for sympathy or tree huggers. The romanticized vision of an untouched wilderness was a luxury he could not afford. His concerns were immediate, pressing, grounded in the cold reality of financial statements and the ever-present threat of ruin. He had a project to complete, a company to save.

The fleeting images of the forest receded, replaced by the familiar numbers and figures on his laptop screen. Rick's jaw tightened as he steeled himself against the pangs of conscience that had surfaced. He was not a man to be swayed by sentimentality or vague notions of environmentalism. The world moved forward, driven by the demands of industry and growth, and he would move with it, ensuring his survival and success, no matter the cost.

He turned from the window, the golden light casting his shadow long and dark against the floor. His decision made, he moved back to his desk, ready to make the necessary calls, to set the wheels in motion. The future was waiting, and Rick Collins was a man who always seized it with both hands.

Outside, the sun dipped lower in the sky, the shadows lengthening, the light fading. The city, with its silent streets and shuttered shops, held its breath, waiting. And in his office, Rick Collins worked on, his thoughts already on the next challenge, the next hurdle to overcome, oblivious to the darkness gathering just beyond the edge of his vision.

Pará, Brazil: The Brazilian sun blazed down from a cloudless sky, casting the once-majestic jungle in a harsh, unforgiving light. What had once been a verdant sanctuary, alive with the whispers of ancient trees and the calls of unseen birds, was now a scene of devastation. The earth, scarred and gouged by the relentless advance of heavy machinery, lay strewn with the fallen giants of the forest. The air was thick with the scent of sap and sawdust, mingled with the acrid stench of diesel. The noise of chainsaws and bulldozers filled the clearing, a constant, discordant drone that set Diego Morales's teeth on edge.

He had been here for two weeks, sent by Rick Collins to oversee the logging operation and expedite the shipment of timber. The delays had become unacceptable, and Rick had hoped that Diego's local knowledge and fluency in Portuguese would help smooth things over. Yet, as Diego stood amidst the chaos, a growing sense of unease gnawed at him. The forest, once a place of life and tranquility, now felt wrong. There was a heaviness in the air, a sense of foreboding that he could not shake.

Diego made his way toward a group of workers taking a break under the shade of a makeshift canopy. Their faces were drawn and weary, their movements slow and deliberate. As he approached, he caught fragments of their conversation, their voices low and filled with a tension that matched his own unease.

"...three men gone now, without a trace..."

"...heard screams in the night..."

"...the Anhanga do not forgive..."

Diego's heart quickened at the mention of the Anhanga. These were not words to be spoken lightly. He had grown up with the chilling stories of these vengeful trickster spirits, the unseen guardians of the forest who drive even the most rational men to madness, and make them see horrors they couldn't escape. His grandmother had told him these tales in a voice both fearful and reverent, as if simply uttering their name might summon them. The Anhanga weren't just protectors of the ancient trees - they were ruthless punishers of those who dared to desecrate the land. As a child, Diego had been fascinated by these stories, sensing a truth in them that went beyond the simple lessons of respect for nature. Now, standing in the heart of the devastation, those tales seemed to take on a new, ominous reality.

He approached the group, his eyes meeting those of the elder among them. The old man's face was lined with the marks of a hard life, his skin weathered and tanned by years under the sun. His eyes, however, were sharp and clear, filled with a wisdom that came from experience and a deep connection to the land. He looked up as Diego approached, his expression one of resignation mixed with the faintest hint of hope.

"Señor Morales," the old man said, his voice low and steady, "you should not be here."

Diego hesitated, then stepped closer, lowering his voice so the other workers would not hear. "What is happening, Señor?" he asked. "I have heard the men talking. They say the Anhanga are angry. What have you seen?"

The old man's gaze flickered to the forest, his eyes narrowing as if he could see beyond the trees, into the very heart of the jungle. "This forest is sacred," he said quietly. "It has been protected by the Anhanga for centuries. The spirits do not take kindly to those who come with machines and saws, to tear down what has stood for longer than any of us have been alive. The men feel it, even if they do not speak of it. They know they are being watched, judged."

Diego nodded, a chill running down his spine. "And the men who have gone missing?" he asked. "What happened to them?"

The old man sighed, his shoulders sagging as if the weight of the forest itself pressed down upon him. "Three men have disappeared, Señor. They were strong, brave, not the kind to run from shadows. Yet they vanished without a trace. One night they were there, the next morning, gone. No one heard them leave, no one saw anything. But there were signs..."

"What signs?" Diego pressed, his voice tense.

The old man hesitated, then continued. "There were strange markings in the earth, as if something had been dragged away. And the forest... it was different. The trees seemed to close in, as if trying to hide something. The air was thick, heavy, like the breath of a sleeping beast. And there were the sounds."

Diego's brows furrowed. "Sounds?"

The old man nodded. "At night, when the machines are silent and the men sleep, there are noises. Whispers on the wind, like voices speaking a language no one understands. Sometimes, there is laughter - soft, but not human. And then, there are the screams. They are distant, but they carry on the wind, echoing through the trees. They chill the blood, Señor. They sound like the cries of men in pain."

Diego felt a shiver run through him, despite the heat. He glanced around, as if expecting to see eyes watching from the shadows. "You believe this is the Anhanga?" he asked.

The old man's eyes were grave. "I know it is. My father spoke of them, and his father before him. They are the guardians of the forest, and they do not forgive easily. We have disturbed their home, Señor Morales. We have brought this upon ourselves."

Diego's thoughts raced. He had known there were risks in this operation, but he had thought only of the physical dangers - the heavy machinery, the potential for accidents. He had not considered the possibility of something beyond the tangible, something ancient and vengeful. He looked at the old man, sensing the depth of his belief, his connection to the land.

"What can we do?" Diego asked, feeling a rising sense of urgency.

The old man shook his head slowly. "The Anhanga are not easily appeased. They demand respect, a return to the ways of old. But you, Señor, can make a difference. You can speak to those who brought us here, who see only profit and not the price to be paid. Tell them to stop, to leave this place, before more are lost."

Diego turned and walked away, his hand drifting to the

back of his neck as he wrestled with his thoughts. Rick Collins would never believe in spirits, in old legends - his world was far from this - built on contracts, profits, and deadlines. But Diego had grown up here, among the whispers of the forest, where the stories of the Anhanga were more than mere superstition. The signs were unmistakable, and as much as he tried to push away his fear, he felt the weight of unseen eyes on him, watching, judging, warning. The fear of what might come, of what had already begun, was far too real for him.

He hesitated, the conflict twisting in his chest. But deep down, he knew he had to act, even if it meant appearing as a fool. A man like Rick - someone not from here, unfamiliar with the land and its stories - would never understand. But he would have to try.

Diego nodded, his resolve hardening. He reached into his pocket and pulled out his phone, dialing Rick Collins's number with a sense of purpose. The phone rang twice before Rick's voice, sharp and irritated, came through the line.

"Diego, what is it? I've got a lot on my plate right now."

Diego took a deep breath, steadying himself. "Rick, I need you to come down here," he said, his voice firm. "There's something you need to see. The men are scared, and there are things happening that I can't explain. They're talking about the Anhanga, the spirits of the forest. I think we're in over our heads."

There was a pause, then a sigh on the other end of the line. "Diego, I don't have time for this. I sent you down there to get things moving, not to buy into local superstitions. We've got deadlines to meet. I don't care about spirits or ghosts."

"I know how it sounds," Diego insisted, his voice steady but urgent. "But this isn't just folklore to these people. Even if you don't believe, there's something real happening here, something that could threaten the whole operation. If you don't come down and see for yourself, you're risking more than just delays. You're risking workers walking off. Maybe even lives. I've seen the look in the men's eyes. They won't stick around much longer if this keeps up."

Rick's voice was edged with frustration. "Are you seriously asking me to fly all the way to Brazil to chase after ghost stories, Diego? I've got a company to run. We can't afford to waste time on this."

Diego's grip tightened on the phone. "Rick, I wouldn't be asking if I didn't think it was important. I've been here two weeks, and I'm telling you, there's something wrong. I've felt it myself. The forest... it's not just trees and soil. There's something alive here, something that doesn't want us here. You need to see it, to understand what we're dealing with."

There was a long silence, broken only by the faint hum of the line. Diego waited, his heart pounding, willing Rick to see reason. Finally, Rick spoke, his voice resigned, a note of irritation still lingering.

"All right, Diego," he said. "I'll come down. But this better be worth my time. I'm not in the mood for wild goose chases. If this turns out to be nothing, you'll be the one explaining to the investors why we're behind schedule."

Diego nodded, relief flooding through him. "Thank you, Rick. I'll make the arrangements. Just... keep an open mind. There are things here that I don't think we fully understand."

The line went dead, and Diego slipped the phone back into his pocket. He turned to the old man, who watched him with a knowing gaze.

"Is he coming?" the old man asked.

Diego nodded. "He's coming."

The old man's eyes shifted to the forest; his face lined with worry. "The Anhanga are patient, Señor Morales. They have waited centuries. They can wait a little longer. But they will not wait forever."

Diego felt a chill as he looked into the dark shadows beneath the trees. The forest seemed to pulse with a life of its own, the air thick with a presence that he could almost feel pressing against his skin. He had done what he could, but he knew that whatever forces were at work here, they were beyond his control. The Anhanga were watching, and they would not be denied.

The next few days were oppressively hot, the kind of heat that wrapped around the body like a suffocating shroud. The air was thick with the scent of earth and sap, and the noise of the jungle was overlaid by the grating sounds of industry: chainsaws growling, trees crashing, and men shouting orders. The once-pristine sanctuary of the sacred forest had been transformed into a scene of desolation. The ground was scarred with the tracks of heavy machinery, and the once-majestic trees lay in fallen ranks, their leaves already beginning to wither in the relentless sun.

Rick Collins, having just arrived in Brazil, made his way through the chaos, his expression a mask of irritation. His face was flushed, partly from the heat, partly from the frustration that had been gnawing at him for weeks. His shirt, once crisp, was now plastered to his back with sweat, his collar loose and wilting. He clutched a clipboard in one hand, the other swiping angrily at the mosquitoes that buzzed persistently around his head.

Rick spotted Diego Morales near a cluster of workers; his foreman's broad shoulders set in a posture of deep unease. Diego was speaking to one of the local men, his voice low and urgent, his face lined with worry. Rick's mouth twisted in a scowl as he approached, irritation sparking in his eyes.

"Diego!" he called, his voice cutting through the noise like a whip. Diego looked up, his expression tightening as he saw Rick striding towards him. The worker he had been speaking to backed away, casting a nervous glance at Rick before hurrying off into the forest.

"What the hell is going on?" Rick demanded as he came to a stop in front of Diego. "We're weeks behind schedule, and I find you chatting instead of working. Do you have any idea what this delay is costing us?"

Diego's face was a mask of concern, his eyes dark under the brim of his hat. He hesitated for a moment, then spoke, his voice low but firm. "Señor Collins, there is something you need to know. The men... they are afraid. There have been too many accidents, too many things that cannot be explained. They say the forest is cursed, that the Anhanga spirits are angry. We should not be cutting these trees."

Rick's face flushed a deeper red, his patience fraying. "Cursed?" he snapped. "I've heard enough of this superstitious nonsense. Spirits, curses - it's all bullshit! We have a job to do, Diego. We're here to clear this land, not to play at ghost stories."

Diego held his ground, his expression earnest. "It is not just stories, Señor. There have been whispers, strange voices in the wind. Men have seen shadows moving through the trees, heard laughter where there should be none. Some have been injured, others have... changed. It is as if the forest itself is fighting back."

Rick's eyes blazed with anger, his hand tightening around the clipboard. "You think I'm going to let a few ghost stories stop this project? We are in too deep. We've got deadlines, contracts, investors breathing down our necks. If we don't deliver, we're finished. Do you understand that? Finished!"

Diego's eyes flickered with frustration. "Señor Collins, you must listen. The Anhanga are the guardians of this forest. They bring madness to those who defile their home. We are playing with forces we do not understand."

Rick let out a bark of bitter laughter. "Madness? The only madness here is letting these idiotic superstitions derail the entire project! I don't care about your Anhanga or your curses. I care about getting this job done. Now, either you get these men back to work, or I'll find someone who can. We've wasted enough time as it is."

Diego's shoulders slumped slightly, the fight draining out of him. He looked at Rick with a mixture of sadness and something that might have been pity. "You are making a mistake, Señor," he said softly. "The forest will not forgive this."

Rick turned away; his jaw clenched. "The forest can go to hell," he muttered. "We're here to cut wood, not to make friends with trees. Now get back to work. I don't want to hear another word about spirits."

He stalked away, his steps heavy with anger, his thoughts already turning to the next set of problems he needed to solve. Behind him, Diego watched him go, his face drawn with worry. He turned back to the ancient tree that loomed over the clearing, its dark bark twisted and gnarled. He touched it lightly, as if seeking comfort, feeling the rough texture under his fingertips.

A breeze stirred the leaves, and for a moment, Diego thought he heard a sound like a sigh, a low murmur that seemed to come from deep within the earth. He closed his eyes, whispering a silent prayer, hoping that the spirits would show mercy, though he feared it was already too late.

Rick continued through the site, barking orders, oblivious to the growing unease among the workers, the shadows that seemed to gather at the edge of his vision. His thoughts were focused solely on deadlines, profits, and the promises he had made to far-off investors, men who had never set foot in a jungle nor felt the weight of ancient eyes upon them.

He noticed the hesitant movements of the men, their glances toward the forest lingering a little too long, the conversations growing quieter when they thought he wasn't listening. His frustration surged. Enough was enough.

With a sharp motion, Rick turned and stalked toward the group of workers, forcing them to stop what they were doing and look his way. Diego, standing nearby, watched with the same grave expression, though there was a flicker of something else - maybe pity.

Rick's voice cut through the murmur like a whip. "Alright, listen up!" He glared at them, scanning their faces. "I know some of you are spooked by these stories, but here's the deal. If we finish this job on time, there's a hefty bonus in it for everyone. Double your usual pay for the month. We clear this land, and you walk away richer. Simple as that."

The workers exchanged uncertain glances, whispers passing between them, but the mention of double pay began to shift the mood. Rick could see some of them weighing the money against their fear. He crossed his arms, his scowl deepening.

"There's no room for ghost stories out here," he continued, his voice hard. "You want to walk away from this job with more cash in your pockets than you've ever seen? Then do your part and get it done."

He didn't wait for a response. Turning sharply, he stalked off again, his temper barely held in check. Behind him, the workers murmured amongst themselves, the promise of wealth hanging in the humid air, fighting with the dread that still clung to the edges of the clearing.

Rick did not see the way the forest watched him, silent and patient, the ancient trees standing like sentinels, waiting. He did not hear the whispers that drifted through the leaves, the soft, mocking laughter that seemed to come from nowhere and everywhere all at once.

And he did not notice the way the light seemed to dim, just slightly, as though a shadow had passed over the sun, a shadow that lingered in the corner of his vision, just out of sight. The forest was watching, and it was waiting.

Jupiter, Florida: The afternoon sun beat down upon the Briar Vale construction site, casting harsh shadows that stretched across the half-finished houses and piles of lumber. Two months had passed since the first foundations were laid, and the site now bustled with activity. The air was thick with the scent of sawdust and fresh paint, mingled with the acrid fumes of gasoline. The constant hum of machinery filled the air, underscored by the steady pounding of hammers and the occasional bark of orders. It was a scene of industry and progress, a testament to human ambition carved out of the wilderness. Yet beneath the veneer of activity, there was a tension, a subtle unease that clung to the air like a shadow.

Rick Collins moved through the site with the purposeful stride of a man on a mission, frustration evident in the tight lines of his jaw. The Briar Vale project was already behind schedule, and every delay felt like another goddamn nail in his career's coffin. He spotted Diego Morales, clipboard in hand, checking off inventory by a stack of lumber.

"Diego!" Rick barked, his voice cutting through the hum of machinery and the thud of hammers. Diego turned, his expression serious, lines of worry etched across his face.

"Rick," Diego said, nodding in acknowledgment.

Rick didn't slow his pace as he approached. "The lumber," he said bluntly. "What's the status? Are we still waiting on that damn delivery?"

Diego hesitated for a moment, glancing at the stack of wood behind him. "Yes," he replied. "It just arrived. We're on schedule with that, at least."

Rick let out a harsh, short laugh. "Well, thank fuck for that," he muttered. "At least something is fucking on schedule." He ran a hand through his hair, already looking away from Diego and toward the commotion at the far end of the site.

Diego opened his mouth as if to say something but then closed it. Against his better judgement, he had pushed for this lumber delivery, insisting it was essential to get things back on track. But now that it was here, he felt a knot of regret in his stomach. Something about today felt off, as if the air itself were charged with a dark energy.

Rick was about to continue his tirade when he noticed a group of workers gathered around the industrial woodchipper at the far end of the site. The machine was silent, smoke curling from its maw, and the men stood in a loose circle, their postures tense, eyes flicking between Rick and the chipper.

"What now?" Rick grumbled, his irritation flaring anew. "If it's not one fucking thing, it's another."

Diego followed Rick's gaze, his expression darkening. He could sense the unease in the men's stances. "I'll check it out," he offered, but Rick was already striding toward the scene, his steps quick and determined. Diego sighed and followed, his own pace slower, as if trying to delay the inevitable.

As Rick approached, the workers parted like a somber, unwilling audience. Their faces were masks of strained frustration, but something darker lurked in their eyes - an apprehensive fear that seemed to seep into the very air around them. The silence was almost tangible, clinging to the scene like a heavy shroud, and the only sound was the occasional rustling of leaves stirred by a hesitant breeze.

"What's going on here?" Rick's voice sliced through the quiet, its sharpness accentuating the tension that crackled in the air.

A burly worker, his thick beard flecked with grime and his hands streaked with oil and sweat, stepped forward. His face was ashen, eyes wide and nervous. "It's the chipper, boss," he stammered, his voice quavering. "Damn thing's jammed up again. We can't get it to start."

Rick's jaw clenched, a muscle twitching erratically as he glared at the machine. "Again?" he barked. "What the hell are you idiots doing with this thing? It's supposed to cut wood, not take a fucking nap!"

The worker's shoulders slumped; his helplessness evident. "We've checked everything, boss. The blades, the motor. It just... stopped."

Rick's face twisted into a scowl as he pushed past the men, his anger evident in every step. The woodchipper loomed before him, its metal casing smudged with a thick layer of grime and sawdust that hinted at the violence it could unleash. The tangled mess of branches trapped in the blades looked grotesque, like a snarled mass of hair caught in a sinister trap.

Rick seized a long, sturdy branch from a nearby pile, his movements sharp and impatient. He jabbed it into the chipper's gaping maw, his aggression palpable as he tried to dislodge the obstruction. The air was filled with the acrid scent of engine oil and the faint, unsettling sound of the chipper's internal workings groaning with resistance.

Diego, watching from a distance, felt a tightening in his chest - a gnawing sense of dread that seemed to grow heavier with each passing moment. His eyes were fixed on Rick, his hands clenched into tight fists as he watched the scene unfold with mounting anxiety.

"Come on, you piece of shit," Rick growled, shoving the branch deeper into the chipper. His face was a mask of determination, but there was a flicker of something else - an underlying edge of fear that he fought to suppress. He leaned in, using his full weight to force the branch into the tangle, his body almost completely engulfed by the machine's shadow.

Suddenly, there was a horrifying metallic groan from deep within the chipper, a sound that reverberated through Rick's bones and made his heart skip a beat. He hesitated, his breath catching in his throat, before he thrust the branch in with renewed force.

The wood chipper roared to life with a deafening, feral growl. The blades spun with an uncontrollable frenzy, their violent whirring cutting through the air like a monstrous scream. The branch was swiftly drawn into the machine's maw, and with a sickening, brutal jerk, Rick was pulled forward. His body lurched, hands flailing wildly as he fought for balance. For a heart-stopping moment, his eyes widened in sheer, unadulterated terror, his mouth opening in a silent, desperate cry.

The chipper's blades caught Rick's sleeve, yanking him inexorably into the crushing, grinding maw. He struggled, his attempts to pull back futile against the relentless pull of the machine. The grinding, shredding noise grew louder, a grotesque symphony of metal and flesh that drowned out Rick's screams. Blood sprayed in dark, splattering arcs, staining the ground and the horrified faces of the men who had dared to stand too close.

The workers stood frozen, their expressions frozen in a mixture of shock and horror as they watched Rick being torn apart by the merciless machine. The chipper's roar seemed almost triumphant, a guttural, monstrous sound that reverberated through the clearing and echoed ominously among the trees.

And then, as quickly as it had started, it stopped. The chipper fell silent, its blades grinding to a halt. The air was thick with the metallic scent of blood, the echoes of the machine's roar fading into the oppressive heat of the afternoon. The only sound was the dull thud of Rick's remains hitting the ground, a twisted, broken heap at the foot of the machine.

The men stared, pale and trembling, the horror of what they had witnessed still sinking in. It was then that the laughter began. Soft at first, almost a whisper, it drifted through the site, carried on the breeze. It was a strange sound, soft, mocking and cold, as if the very air was alive with malice. The workers glanced around, fear creeping into their eyes, searching for the source of the sound. But there was no one there, only the distant rustling of leaves and the faint hum of machinery.

Diego stood at the edge of the clearing, his face ashen, his eyes wide with disbelief. He had heard the stories, the whispers of spirits and curses, passed down from the elders, but he had never truly witnessed anything beyond rumor. Now, as he stood there, the eerie laughter echoing in his ears, so faint and distant yet undeniable, he felt a chill run down his spine.

There was a presence here, something ancient and powerful, something that did not belong in the world of men. It had been awakened, and it was angry. Diego could feel it, a weight in the air, a darkness that seemed to press in from all sides. He knew, without a doubt, that Rick's death had not been an accident. It was a warning.

As the laughter faded, Diego turned and walked away, his steps slow and heavy. He did not look back at the scene of horror behind him, nor did he speak to the men who watched him go. He felt the eyes of the forest upon him, and felt the weight of ancient judgment. He had just brought death back to his home.

Belle Glade, Florida, Present Day: As Emma stepped out of Diego Morales's modest home into the fading light of late afternoon, her mind swirled with the echoes of his words. The oppressive Florida heat clung to her skin, thick and suffocating, mirroring the heavy burden that now weighed upon her heart. The air was pregnant with the scent of wet earth and impending rain, signaling an approaching storm that seemed to mirror the turmoil within her. She paused on the cracked concrete path leading from Diego's door, trying to steady her breathing, trying to make sense of the dark revelations that had just been laid bare before her.

"The Anhanga will not stop until what is theirs is returned," Diego had said, his voice low and rough, as if the weight of the truth was too much to bear. He had looked at her with haunted eyes, filled with a fear that had taken root deep in his soul. "They know who took from them, and they punish those who try to hold on to what was never theirs to begin with." Diego's face had been lined with guilt, his eyes distant as he spoke of his time at the logging site, his complicity in the theft. He had admitted, almost in a whisper, that he had been the one to alert authorities to the illegal logging operation after Rick's death, a desperate attempt to make amends for the wrongs he had helped to perpetuate.

"They drive men insane," Diego had continued, his voice trembling. "They can twist the mind, turn a good man evil, all in the name of revenge. They take away what you love most, piece by piece, until there's nothing left but despair." His words had resonated with a deep sense of regret, the kind that comes from a man who knows he has done wrong and seeks redemption, even if it's too late.

Emma's thoughts turned to her husband, John. Could it be that his increasingly erratic behavior was not just a symptom of stress or some midlife crisis? Could the cursed wood, the same wood that had brought Rick Collins to his gruesome end, be exerting its malevolent influence over him? She remembered the disclosures that had been withheld from her, the secret that John had kept hidden, that the house was built with illegally sourced lumber. He knew. Her heart pounded with a sickening realization. He knew, and he didn't tell her. Her hands trembled as she reached for her phone.

The silence of the street was interrupted only by the distant roll of thunder, a prelude to the afternoon storm that gathered strength in the darkening sky. Emma's fingers fumbled as she dialed her daughter's number. She needed to hear Emily's voice, needed the reassurance that her children were safe. The phone rang, each ring a nail in the coffin of her patience. At last, the ringing stopped, but instead of Emily's familiar voice, Emma was met with the crackling hiss of static.

"Hello? Emily?" she called out, her voice betraying the rising tide of her panic. The static persisted, a grating sound that sent a chill down her spine. She glanced up at the sky, dark clouds roiling in the distance, as if the heavens themselves were disturbed by the events unfolding below. She hung up and redialed, her heart pounding faster with each failed attempt. This time, the line connected briefly, and she heard a faint, distorted echo of what might have been her daughter's voice before the static swallowed it again. Emma's chest tightened. Something was wrong. Terribly wrong.

She pocketed the phone, her movements frantic and clumsy as she hurried to the car parked at the curb. Her mind raced, tangled in fear and confusion. The Anhanga. If what Diego said was true, they weren't just ancient spirits bound to a distant forest - they were here, in Briar Vale, in her home. A part of her home. And they knew. The realization cut through the fog clouding her thoughts, leaving a trail of icy clarity in its wake. The spirits knew, and they would stop at nothing.

John's growing obsession with the garden, the widening distance between them, the strange behavior she had noticed in their neighbors - it all began to make a dreadful, haunting sense. The disclosures they had signed. They all knew, and they had all accepted it - the theft from the Anhanga. And now, they were paying the price. She had to get her family out of that house, and far away from Briar Vale.

The car roared to life under her shaky hands, its engine sounding louder than usual in the quiet street. She pulled away from the curb, her gaze flitting to the rearview mirror, as if expecting to see some shadowy figure materialize in pursuit. The road stretched before her, leading back to Briar Vale, back to the house that now felt more like a trap than a home. She pressed her foot harder on the gas pedal, the tires spinning slightly on the rain-slicked asphalt.

The first drops of rain began to fall, splattering against the windshield, accompanied by the intermittent flashes of lightning that illuminated the gathering darkness. The storm was coming, fast and furious, and so was Emma's realization of the danger her family faced. Her thoughts were a tangled web of fear and determination. She had to get home. She had to get her children away from John, away from the house, away from the spirits that sought vengeance for their stolen legacy.

"Emily," she whispered to the empty car, her voice drowned out by the rising wind. "Jack. Owen." Their names were her anchor, pulling her back from the brink of despair. She would not let the spirits have them. She would not lose her family to the darkness that had already claimed so much. Her fingers tightened around the steering wheel, knuckles whitening as the rain came down in sheets, obscuring the road ahead.

The static on her phone was like the static in her heart, a signal that something was desperately wrong. She tried Emily's number one last time, the crackling noise a prelude to the disconnection she knew was coming. The storm raged outside, and Emma could feel its echo in her own heart, a storm of fear, guilt, and resolve. Whatever the cost, she would not let the darkness consume them. She would bring her children into the light, away from the cursed legacy that had ensnared them.

She drove through the rain, her thoughts a litany of desperation and hope, as the storm closed in around her, swallowing the world in its shadow.

CHAPTER 12

Fire and Blood

The Florida night roared like a heaving, storm-wracked beast, each peal of thunder echoing the crash of a celestial hammer. Sheets of rain lashed through the air, battering the rooftops of Briar Vale and transforming the ground into a mire of muck and water. Emma stood at the edge of her driveway, having parked her car in the shadows just down the street. She was drenched from the relentless downpour, her clothes clinging to her sodden frame. Her hands trembled as she peered through the rain-slicked windows into the front room. There, through the blurred glass, she saw John's silhouette cast by the flickering light of the TV. He was staring out the window, searching for her through the storm's veil.

Earlier, a harbinger of dread had struck her in the form of a text from John: "Where are you, Emma? Why are you not home with the kids?" The message had pierced through her like a cold blade, heightening her fear and pressing upon her a dire sense of urgency. Now, he was waiting, watching, for her.

With the storm as her cacophonous backdrop, the sight of him made her heart race with a mix of cold fear and urgency. She knew she had to get inside, but the presence of John so clearly visible through the front windows made her decision for her. With a determined nod, she turned and moved swiftly towards the detached garage, her feet splashing through shallow puddles as the storm roared around her.

Her breath came in shallow gasps as she skirted the edge of the garage, its darkened windows offering no solace. She hesitated only briefly before heading towards the back gate, a flimsy wooden barrier that stood slightly ajar, flapping weakly in the wind. Emma slipped through, the latch clicking softly behind her as she entered the backyard, shutting out the storm's cacophony.

The backyard was a tangle of shadows, with every blade of grass and flower petal swaying beneath the gusts. It was in the midst of one of these gusts that Emma first smelled the sickening scent of decay. Lightning illuminated John's garden intermittently, revealing its dark and malevolent presence at the heart of the yard. The garden seemed to throb with an unseen, sinister vitality, the flowers nodding rhythmically as if in some unholy communion with the storm. Emma's heart raced, caught between dread and an overpowering urge to uncover the source of the unsettling scent.

As she approached, she saw the heavy rain washing away the freshly laid soil, exposing the dark, shifting underlayers beneath. The odor hit her with a forceful assault - a sickening blend of sweet rot and raw earth that clawed at her throat. Emma gagged, her hand flying to her mouth as she neared the flower beds. Each step seemed to amplify the stench, growing more nauseating with every movement.

She stumbled forward, her foot catching on a clump of loose soil, and she fell heavily to her knees in the muddy ground. The rain had turned the soil into a slick, unnervingly soft sludge, causing her to slip further. As she struggled to regain her balance, her hands instinctively dug into the wet earth. Her fingers clawed desperately at the shifting soil, pulling at the ground as if trying to uncover the source of the putrid odor that filled the air.

Her nails dug into the wet soil, and something caught - fabric, rough and grimy. She pulled, and the earth gave way with a sickening squelch, revealing a mottled, decaying hand tangled in a web of dark, twisting roots. Emma shrieked, falling back onto her heels, her eyes wide with horror. The lightning flashed, illuminating the grinning, skeletal face of George Thompson, his eye sockets sunken and hollow, his once-human form grotesquely entwined with the very earth itself. Tendrils of roots snaked through his gaping mouth and coiled around his skull, pulling him deeper into the dirt as if nature itself was reclaiming his body in some nightmarish perversion of decay.

His skin was stretched taut like a leathery mask over brittle bones, riddled with the invasive roots that pierced through the flesh like grotesque veins, feeding on the rotting tissue. The remnants of his shirt hung in tatters, the fabric fused with the putrid flesh beneath, while patches of moss and fungal growth spread across his chest, thriving in the damp rot. The ground itself seemed to pulse with an unnatural hunger, slowly absorbing him into its clutches.

Next to George, half-buried beneath the same grotesque mass of roots and mud, Emma caught sight of another hand - smaller, frailer, and in an even more advanced state of decay. Its bones, stark white and brittle, poked through the earth like gnarled twigs. Emma's breath hitched in her throat. Ethel. The skeletal remains were nearly unrecognizable, yet there was something unmistakable in the delicate curve of the fingers, now wrapped in thick roots, as if the earth itself had claimed her long before her time.

Emma's stomach lurched violently, bile burning her throat as she scrambled backward, her hands slipping in the mud, now smeared with the earthy stench of decomposition. Her mind reeled, suffocated by the stench of death, and she gasped for air as desperation clawed at her senses. The bodies weren't just decaying - they were being devoured by the earth itself, pulled downward in a hideous mockery of burial.

She turned to flee, only to catch sight of another grave - this one freshly dug, but the roots were already spreading, as if eagerly awaiting their next victim. The earth there seemed unnaturally disturbed, the freshly turned soil writhing with the same invasive tendrils. And then another, and another - four gaping holes, lined up side by side, each one a silent, ominous promise of death, each one ready to swallow the living. The forest around her was alive, watching, hungry.

A scream tore from her lips, a sound of pure, unbridled terror that was swallowed by the storm. She stumbled to her feet, her gaze darting wildly around the garden. That's when she saw him. John stood at the edge of the darkness, his face a twisted mask of fury and insanity. Lightning flickered, casting his features in a grotesque tableau of light and shadow. His eyes gleamed with a cold, feral intensity, and a smile stretched across his lips, thin and cruel.

"Where have you been, Emma?" he demanded, his voice rising above the roar of the storm. "Out there plotting against me? Turning the kids against me?" His voice was a snarl, every word dripping with venom. He took a step forward, his hands clenched into fists at his sides. "You think you can make a fool of me? You think you can make me look weak?"

Emma backed away, her heart pounding in her chest. "John, please," she begged, her voice quivering with fear. "This isn't you. The John I know would never do this." Her words came out in ragged gasps, each one heavy with desperation. "It's the woods... the spirits - they're influencing you!" She forced herself to stay calm, her eyes locked on his, a final, desperate attempt to reach the man she once knew. "We can leave. We can escape this, John. Get help. We can fix it - just please, stop."

John's laughter cut through the air, sharp and twisted, void of any real joy. "The John you knew is gone, Emma. Dead. And it's because of you! Because of all of you! I did everything for you. Gave you everything you wanted. And what did I get? Emasculated. Humiliated. Cut off like I was nothing!" His eyes blazed with fury as his voice dropped to a low, dangerous growl. "But I'll show you. I'll show everyone what I can really do. And then... then I will get the respect I deserve." His voice rose to a fevered pitch, a manic, chilling roar that was beyond reason.

As John spoke, lightning flashed across the sky, briefly illuminating his face. Emma's heart froze at what she saw.

Beneath his skin, something horrifying writhed - small, root-like structures pulsing and twisting along his veins, as if alive. They coiled and spread through his body like a parasite taking root. Her breath hitched, the sight leaving her paralyzed with terror.

Emma's breath hitched, and she knew in that moment that there was no saving him. The John she loved was gone, consumed by the malevolent force that had taken hold of him. Panic surged through her, and she turned and ran, her feet slipping in the mud as she bolted towards the house. Her mind screamed for her to get to the children, but instinct drove her feet. She darted through the back door, her wet shoes sliding on the tile floor as she stumbled into the narrow hallway. John's footsteps were close behind, relentless in their pursuit. She reached out for the nearest door, yanking it open and rushing inside.

It was the utility room, a narrow, cramped space filled with the hulking forms of a water heater and a maze of pipes. A chest freezer sat against one wall, humming quietly, a grim reminder of the mundane reality that had once defined her life. The air was thick with the smell of dampness, metal, and a faint, musty odor. A cluttered shelf lined the opposite wall, crammed with cleaning supplies - bottles of bleach, disinfectant sprays, and old rags spilling over the edge. Mops and brooms were propped against the corner, their handles creating a shadowed lattice in the dim light. Emma squeezed herself into the narrow space between the freezer and the wall, her breath coming in short, ragged gasps.

Her eyes darted to the small, dirty window above the freezer, offering a narrow view of the storm outside. The rain lashed against the glass with a ferocity that matched the pounding of her heart. She could hear John's footsteps in the hallway, slow and deliberate, each one sending a jolt of fear through her. His voice was a low, mocking murmur, barely audible over the storm but unmistakably filled with malice.

"You can't hide from me, Emma," John called, his voice

seeping through the thin walls like poison. "I know you're in there. Do you really think you can keep me from my own children? You think you can turn them against me?" His words were a dark promise, echoing with a venom that sent chills down her spine.

The door handle rattled, and Emma held her breath, pressing herself tighter against the wall. The door creaked open, and John's shadow filled the doorway. His face was obscured in darkness, but his eyes glinted in the pale light, burning with a fevered intensity that was both terrifying and alien. In his hand, he held a heavy padlock, his fingers tightening around it with grim determination.

"You think you can hide from what's coming, Emma?" he said softly, his voice cutting through the darkness like a blade. "You can't hide from me. You can't hide from the truth." He took a step back, and Emma heard the padlock click into place, the sound resonating in the small room like a death knell.

He swung the door shut with a jarring finality, the metal frame clanging against the jamb, echoing through the small room. Emma heard the click of the padlock being fastened, the metallic scrape sending a chill through her entire body. The lock slid into place with a loud, definitive snap, sealing her inside. The sound resonated like a death knell in the confined space, cutting off the last thread of her freedom.

She heard John's footsteps retreating down the hallway, each step deliberate and unhurried, a stark contrast to the frantic pounding of her own heart. The silence that followed was suffocating, pressing in on her like the dark, damp walls of the utility room. Emma pressed her ear against the door, her breathing shallow and rapid. The reality of her situation settled over her, a cold weight in her stomach. She was trapped, locked away, powerless to stop whatever horrors John intended to unleash.

Emma's heart raced as John's footsteps faded into the distance, leaving her alone in the dim confines of the utility room. Her eyes darted to the small window above the freezer, the only possible way out. She had to reach the children, to protect them from the man John had become. But first, she had to get herself free. Her phone was lost, swallowed by the storm and chaos. The thought of her children, unaware of the looming danger, filled her with a desperate need to act.

She spotted the box of matches on the shelf and quickly grabbed them. If she could start a fire, the alarms would go off, warning the kids. It wasn't much, but it was all she could think of. She struck a match against the box, the flame flaring to life. With trembling hands, she gathered a pile of old rags from the shelf and held the match to them. The rags caught fire, and she watched as the flames began to grow, the smell of smoke curling up towards the ceiling. Within moments, the fire alarm blared to life, its piercing shriek cutting through the air. Relief washed over her. It would be impossible for the children to ignore that sound.

But she wasn't safe yet. She had to get out, to be with them, to get them out of the house. Her eyes fixed on the small window above the freezer. That was her way out. She hurried to the freezer, intending to push it beneath the window to use it as a stepping stone. She braced her hands against the cool metal surface and pushed, but it didn't budge. The freezer was heavy, far heavier than she expected. A cold dread crept into her stomach, her fingers hesitating on the edge of the lid. Something inside her knew, even before she opened it, what she would find.

With a sense of mounting horror, she lifted the lid. The smell of death hit her immediately, a foul, cloying stench that made her gag. Her eyes widened in shock as she saw Mary Kendrick's body crammed inside, her face pale and contorted in a grotesque expression of fear. Emma's breath caught in her throat, her mind reeling. Mary's lifeless eyes stared blankly up at her, the once vibrant woman now nothing more than a corpse, discarded like a piece of garbage.

Emma's stomach turned, bile rising in her throat. She stumbled back, her hand flying to her mouth to stifle a scream. She slammed the lid of the freezer shut, turning away, her heart pounding wildly. The knowledge of what John had done settled over her like a suffocating blanket, but she couldn't allow herself to be paralyzed by fear. Her children needed her. They were all that mattered.

Gritting her teeth, Emma returned to the freezer, her muscles tensing with determination. She braced herself against the side, planting her feet firmly on the ground. With a grunt of effort, she pushed against the metal, straining with all her strength. The freezer groaned, scraping against the floor as it slowly moved into position beneath the window. Her arms burned with the effort, her breath coming in ragged gasps, but she didn't stop. She shoved again, harder this time, forcing the heavy appliance into place.

Her body trembled with exertion, but she couldn't afford to rest. Emma climbed onto the freezer, her fingers reaching up to pry open the small, grimy window. Rain splattered her face, cold and relentless, as she managed to wedge it open wide enough to fit through. The storm's fury was a welcome contrast to the suffocating heat and smoke inside. She pulled herself up, squeezing through the narrow gap, her clothes catching on the rough edges of the frame.

With one final effort, she heaved her body through the window, tumbling out into the night. She landed on the wet grass with a heavy thud, mud splashing up around her. The rain poured down, drenching her to the bone, but she barely noticed. She staggered to her feet, her eyes darting toward the house. The fire alarm still blared, its shrill cry piercing through the storm. The urgency to reach her children propelled her forward. She had to get to them before John did. With her heart hammering in her chest, Emma sprinted toward the front of the house, her mind focused solely on saving her family from the nightmare that had consumed their home.

The smoke alarm's piercing wail reverberated through the

house, mingling with the frantic drumming of rain against the windows and the low rumble of thunder that rolled through the night. The acrid scent of smoke curled through the air, thick and pungent, clawing its way up from the utility room and spreading through the house like a poisonous fog. Shadows leapt and flickered across the walls, cast by the erratic dance of flames that licked hungrily at the edges of the room.

John burst into the kitchen, his eyes wild with fury, his breath coming in ragged gasps. His hands were clenched into fists, his knuckles white against the tan of his skin. His hair was damp, plastered to his forehead, and his clothes clung to his frame, soaked through from the rain. He kicked a chair out of his way, sending it clattering to the floor, and let out a low, guttural growl of frustration.

He stormed through the house, each step heavy, resounding through the floorboards like the footfalls of a beast. The blaring alarm grated against his nerves, amplifying the chaos in his mind. He knew Emma had started the fire, and the realization that she was defying him, even from her locked prison, filled him with a rage that bordered on madness. His thoughts were a maelstrom of anger.

Running up to his bedroom, John's fury blazed hotter than the flames beginning to lick up the walls. His breath came in short, rapid bursts, his chest heaving with the effort to contain the inferno of rage that threatened to consume him. He could hear the smoke alarm screaming, the sound piercing through the chaos, but he didn't care. All he cared about was finding the gun. The gun that would make everything right. The gun that would bring order back to his world.

Pushing the door open with a crash, John barreled into the room, his eyes wild as he scanned the space. The darkness was cut only by the erratic flashes of lightning that spilled through the window, casting long, jagged shadows across the floor. The storm outside seemed to echo the storm within, each flash illuminating the twisted expression on his face. He moved with a purpose, tearing open drawers and ripping through the closet, his hands throwing clothes and belongings aside in a desperate frenzy.

The bedroom was rapidly becoming a shambles, items strewn across the floor in a haphazard mess. John's fingers clawed through the piles, pulling at coats and sweaters, digging into boxes that held old memories and forgotten things. His hands shook with the need to find what he was searching for, his breath coming in harsh, ragged gasps.

"Where is it?" he snarled under his breath, his voice a guttural growl. His anger was a living thing, coiling in his chest, tightening with each passing second that he came up empty-handed. He moved to the bedside table, yanking open the drawer so hard that it nearly came off its hinges. Papers and small items spilled onto the floor, but no gun.

His eyes darted around the room, wild and frenzied, his frustration mounting. He turned to the dresser, jerking open the top drawer, his fingers rifling through socks and old receipts. A flash of lightning illuminated his face, the deep lines of his fury etched into his skin. He yanked out another drawer, emptying its contents onto the floor in a fit of rage. Still, nothing.

John's heart pounded in his chest, each beat echoing the pounding of the rain against the windows. His mind raced, thoughts jumbling together in a chaotic whirl. It had to be here. It had to be. He stormed to the closet, tearing through the hanging clothes, pushing them aside as he searched the shelves. His hands grasped the small metal box he had used to hide the gun. He pulled it down, his breath catching in his throat. But when he opened the lid, the box was empty.

He stared at it for a moment, disbelief flooding his senses. The gun was gone. Taken. Hidden from him. A slow, creeping rage began to fill the void left by his shock. Someone had moved it. Someone had dared to take his gun. His mind flashed to Jack. It had to be him. The little shit. A snarl formed on John's lips, his anger twisting his features into a mask of hatred.

His fist crashed into the closet door, the wood splintering under the force of his blow. The pain didn't register, not against the burning fury that consumed him. He threw the empty box across the room, the sound of it hitting the wall lost amid the roar of the storm and the blare of the smoke alarm. His eyes landed on the window; the sight of the garage barely visible through the sheets of rain. His shovel. The thought cut through his rage like a knife. The shovel would do. It was fitting. It was poetic.

John turned sharply, his movements swift and decisive. He had a new purpose now. The gun was gone, but it didn't matter. He had something better. Something that would make them see. He strode towards the door, his hands clenched into fists, the veins standing out on his arms. His footsteps were heavy, reverberating through the floorboards as he marched down the hallway.

The smell of smoke was stronger now, thick and acrid, filling his nostrils and stinging his eyes. But he barely noticed. His mind was fixed on one thing - retrieving the shovel. With it, he would show them. He would bring them all to heel. They would understand his power, his control. He would make them see.

John's footsteps faded down the hallway, the house falling into a temporary, uneasy silence. The fire alarm continued to blare, its shrill cry echoing through the rooms, mingling with the distant roll of thunder and the patter of rain.

The storm raged outside Owen's bedroom window, each crack of thunder shaking the house as if it were being assaulted by a monstrous, unseen hand. The walls seemed to tremble, shivering beneath the onslaught of nature's fury. The air inside the room was thick and oppressive, suffused with the low hum of rain, each drop a whisper of dread as it lashed the window in relentless torrents. Lightning would flash, splitting the sky in jagged streaks, casting fleeting, ghostly illumination across the room, then plunging it back into shadow.

Owen stood at the window, his small hands gripping the sill as if holding on for dear life, his wide, innocent eyes reflecting the chaos outside. The garden below, which by daylight had been a place of simple beauty, now churned with darkness and mud. The flowers swayed as if moved by some dark force, their vibrant petals bowed and beaten by the storm. It was no longer a garden but a battlefield, a place of unease, where something evil stirred beneath the surface.

Behind him, Emily and Jack watched with pale faces, their eyes locked on the scene unfolding through the sheets of rain. The wind howled, rattling the glass, as though desperate to break through and claim them too. But the true terror was not in the storm, not in the hammering thunder or the flashes of light, but in the figures below. Their mother, Emma, was hunched and small, a vulnerable shape against the looming presence of their father, John.

The twisted flower beds in the garden seemed alive with malevolent energy, as if the earth itself conspired against her. The children couldn't see the graves buried beneath the mud, but they felt them - felt the dark, pulsing dread that radiated from them, an unspoken horror hanging heavy in the air. The smell of rain and decay seemed to creep into the room, chilling them to the bone.

"Mom?" Owen's voice trembled, barely a whisper, as he leaned closer to the glass, his breath fogging the surface. His young mind couldn't grasp the full terror of what he saw, but his heart knew. The sight of John's furious face, distorted in the lightning's brief illumination, and the way their mother shrank before him, sent icy fingers of fear crawling down his spine.

Emily stood just behind him, her arms wrapped tightly around her body, as if to hold herself together. "Something's wrong," she murmured, her voice laced with dread. She didn't take her eyes off the scene below, her gaze fixed on their mother's trembling form.

John's voice rose through the storm, a distant, distorted shout that reached them in snatches, carried on the wind, torn apart by the rain. They couldn't make out the words, but the tone was unmistakable - rage, fury, a madness that turned their father into something unrecognizable. Owen shivered, feeling Emily's fear, feeling Jack's silent tension beside him.

Outside, through the flickering light of the storm, they saw their mother stumble backward, her feet slipping in the muck. A crack of lightning illuminated John's towering form as he stepped toward her, fists clenched, his posture brimming with barely-contained violence. Emma tried to speak, but her voice was swallowed by the roar of the storm, her fear visible in the way she recoiled from him, her body trembling.

"What's he going to do?" Jack whispered, his voice barely audible, strangled with fear. His eyes darted between his parents, heart racing as he watched his mother's desperate attempts to escape.

Lightning flashed again, and they saw it - the moment when Emma turned to run, slipping and stumbling in the mud. Her sharp cry pierced the storm, but was quickly devoured by the wind. She bolted toward the house, her feet slipping, her hands clawing at the ground for purchase. Behind her, John's furious shout echoed like a thunderclap, louder than the storm itself. His figure loomed large and terrible, a shadow of pure wrath against the tempest.

"He's coming inside," Emily gasped, her breath catching in her throat. Her voice broke, trembling with panic. "We need to hide. Now!"

Jack didn't hesitate. His hand shot out, grabbing Owen by the arm, pulling him back from the window. Panic surged through the three of them, their fear feeding off one another as the reality of the nightmare settled in. This wasn't just a storm. This wasn't just their father. This was something far darker, far more terrifying, and they had to escape.

Their footsteps were quick and frantic as they fled from the room, darting into the hallway, the weight of their terror pushing them forward. The sound of the storm faded behind them, but the dread lingered, clinging to their every step, following them into the dark recesses of the house. Up the narrow ladder they climbed, each rung creaking beneath their weight as they hurried into the attic, their refuge from the madness below.

In the oppressive gloom of the attic, the air felt thick with the weight of their fear. Each creak of the house, each distant groan of the storm outside, seemed magnified in the suffocating silence. The children huddled close together, their hearts racing, breath shallow, as they listened for the telltale sounds of John moving below them. Lightning flashed intermittently through the narrow attic window, casting long, jagged shadows that flickered across their pale, terrified faces.

Jack stood rigid, his eyes scanning the dusty space, thoughts racing as his mind grappled with a terrible decision. He could hear Emily's shaky breath beside him, her grip tightening around Owen's small hand, the young boy's wide, tearful eyes reflecting the turmoil that swirled inside each of them. Jack's own heart pounded in his chest, a fierce rhythm that seemed to echo in the silence.

"I have to do something," Jack whispered, his voice hoarse with tension. His eyes shifted toward the old chest in the corner, half-buried beneath layers of forgotten clutter. He knew what lay hidden there - something he had once considered their secret treasure, something meant to protect them. Now, it was their only hope.

Emily shook her head, her face pale. "Jack, no... it's too dangerous. He's not... he's not like before. He's gone crazy. You've seen it."

Jack looked down at her, his jaw clenched, the weight of his decision settling heavy on his shoulders. "I can't just stay up here and hide while he's out there - while Mom's out there, too. I have to distract him, Emily. I'll draw him away and check on her. You and Owen stay here. I'll make sure you're safe."

Owen whimpered softly, his small voice barely cutting through the tension. "But what if he hurts you, Jack? What if... what if you don't come back?"

The boy's words struck Jack harder than he wanted to admit, but he forced a small, tight-lipped smile. "I'll come back, I promise." His eyes softened for a moment as he glanced at Emily, then back to Owen. "But I need to do this."

As he knelt to unlatch the old chest, his hands trembling slightly, Emily's voice cut through the silence, softer now, tinged with a resigned sadness. "Remember... remember when we used to think it would be so cool to be in one of those horror movies? Like the ones we'd watch late at night when Mom wasn't looking?"

Jack paused, his fingers resting on the chest, the tension in his body easing slightly as a fleeting memory crossed his mind. Those late-night movie marathons, the thrill of the unknown, the excitement of imagining themselves as brave heroes facing down impossible monsters. They'd laugh and joke about how fearless they would be if anything like that ever happened to them. It had seemed fun then, a distant fantasy. Now, as the real horror unfolded around them, the dark reality of their situation crushed any trace of that childhood innocence.

"This isn't cool anymore," Emily continued, her voice barely above a whisper. She hugged her arms tighter around herself, her eyes pleading with Jack. "It's not fun or exciting... it's terrifying. And I don't want to lose you."

Jack swallowed hard, his throat tight with emotion, but he forced a grim smile onto his face. "I know, Em. I know it's not cool anymore. But I'll be careful. I'm not going to let him hurt you, or Owen. I'll get him away from here. And then..." He hesitated, glancing down at the chest. "Then we'll figure out what to do."

With a deep breath, he opened the chest, revealing the cold, metallic form of the gun. He reached for it, feeling its weight in his hands. His fingers curled around the grip, and for a moment, a wave of uncertainty washed over him. He had never held a real gun before - never imagined he would need to use one. The situation felt unreal, as though he had stumbled into one of those nightmare movies they used to watch, but this time, there was no escape, no rewinding the tape or turning off the screen.

Emily's voice was softer now, almost pleading. "Jack... be careful. Please."

He nodded, tucking the gun into the waistband of his jeans. He knew what he had to do, even if every fiber of his being screamed against it. He couldn't let the terror paralyze him - not now.

Without another word, Jack moved toward the attic stairs, his steps deliberate and slow, the sound of the storm outside barely registering as he descended into the darkened house below. Each step felt heavier than the last, as though the weight of their family's survival rested on his shoulders. His heart hammered in his chest, louder than the creaks of the stairs, louder than the rain drumming against the roof.

The shadows thickened as he approached the lower floor, the dim light barely enough to guide him through the hallway. His mind raced, picturing John's crazed face, the way their father had transformed into a stranger, consumed by something monstrous and violent.

As Jack reached the base of the stairs, he paused, steeling himself. He had to be ready for whatever awaited him in the depths of the house. One final glance back, a silent promise to Emily and Owen, and he disappeared into the darkness.

The air in the house had grown thick with smoke, curling in lazy tendrils through the hallway as the flames slowly claimed more of their home. Jack moved cautiously down the stairs, his heartbeat thundering in his ears, matching the frantic rhythm of the fire alarm's wail. The acrid scent of burning wood and plastic filled his nostrils, choking him, but he kept moving, one hand gripping the gun, the other brushing the banister for balance. Each step felt heavier, the dread mounting in his chest.

He reached the bottom of the stairs, his gaze darting toward the utility room. His mother had to be there. She had to be okay. The door was padlocked, the metal gleaming in the orange glow of the encroaching fire. Jack's hand trembled as he rattled the lock.

"Mom!" he shouted, his voice hoarse from smoke and fear. "Mom! Are you in there?"

There was no answer. His heart dropped, panic tightening around him like a vice. He banged on the door, harder this time, his knuckles white around the gun. "Mom! Please! Answer me!"

Silence.

Jack's breath hitched in his chest, his mind spinning with the worst possibilities. Had he been too late? Was she already? He shook the thought from his head, teeth gritting in frustration. His mind was screaming at him to keep moving, to get back to Emily and Owen, to find some way out of this nightmare.

Jack stood frozen for a moment, staring at the padlocked utility room door, his breath coming in ragged gasps. The fire alarm wailed overhead, and the smoke thickened in the air, searing his throat and eyes. He strained to listen for any sign of his mother, pressing his ear against the cold door, but there was only the ominous crackling of fire and the shriek of the alarm.

He pulled back, eyes darting around the house. His father - where was John? The hallway stretched out before him, empty and ominous, bathed in the flickering orange glow of the growing flames. The kitchen beyond was silent, the shadows dancing madly as the fire gnawed at the edges of the house.

But John wasn't there.

Jack's heart raced as his mind spun. Had his father left? Was he lurking somewhere, waiting? The silence felt suffocating, broken only by the occasional groaning of the house as the fire began to claim it. He took a cautious step forward, his shoes scuffing the floor, every muscle tensed, prepared for John to appear from the shadows at any moment.

Then, from upstairs, came the unmistakable sound of commotion - faint shouts, muffled through the thick smoke. Jack froze, his stomach twisting with dread. The voices - Emily and Owen. He couldn't make out the words, but the panic in them was unmistakable. And then there was another voice, low and menacing, rising above the others - John's voice.

The blood drained from Jack's face as realization hit him like a hammer. His father was upstairs, and his siblings were up there with him.

A wave of terror surged through Jack, his mind filling with worst-case scenarios. His father had gone mad, and now he was cornering them. Jack's heart pounded in his chest, his hand tightening around the gun's handle. He couldn't waste another second. His mind screamed at him to keep moving, to get back to Emily and Owen, to find some way out of this nightmare.

He turned, ready to head back upstairs, when a shadow fell across the hallway. Jack froze, his stomach knotting. The flickering light of the flames cast long, dancing shapes across the walls, turning everything into a distorted, hellish landscape. And there, at the foot of the stairs leading to the attic, stood his father.

John's figure loomed in the corridor, backlit by the growing fire, his face half-hidden in shadow. He held a shovel, its metal edge glinting with fresh blood, staining the handle where his fingers gripped it tightly. His eyes - once so familiar, so full of warmth - were now wild, feral. They gleamed with a sick intensity that chilled Jack to the bone.

"Where are you going, Jack?" John's voice was low, eerily calm, as if the flames licking at the walls around him were of no consequence. He took a slow step forward, dragging the shovel behind him with a soft scraping sound. "You don't get it, do you, Jack?" John's voice was low, a sickly calm creeping into his words. "This... this is what needs to happen. The garden, the earth - it calls for all of us." He paused, his eyes narrowing as his lips twisted into a cruel smile. "You and your siblings, you belong to it now, just like the others."

Jack's breath hitched, his hands tightening around the gun. "Dad, please," he begged, his voice barely above a whisper. His legs felt like they were made of lead, his body trembling uncontrollably. "This isn't you. You don't have to do this. We can help you, just - just stop. Please."

John tilted his head, the twisted smile deepening into something far more unsettling. "Help me?" he repeated, his voice dripping with mockery. A short, cold laugh escaped his lips, echoing eerily in the smoke-filled hallway. He took another step forward, the shovel glinting ominously in the flickering firelight. "You think you can help me? Fix me?" His eyes narrowed, burning with a feverish intensity. "I don't need to be fixed, Jack. I see things clearly now - clearer than ever."

Jack's heart pounded in his chest, each word from his father like a knife in his gut. He didn't recognize the man standing before him. This wasn't his dad - the man who had taught him how to ride a bike, who had sat with him late at night, comforting him when nightmares had shaken him awake. This man was something else, something monstrous, shaped by whatever evil had twisted its way into his heart.

Tears blurred Jack's vision as he took a shaky step back. "Please, Dad... I don't want to hurt you."

John's eyes narrowed, and the smile vanished from his lips. His grip on the shovel tightened, his knuckles turning white. "You think you can hurt me, Jack? You think you have any power here? You're just a weak child!" His voice rose to a shout, echoing through the smoke-filled house. "You can't touch me. No one can."

Jack's chest tightened with fear as John lifted the bloodstained shovel, his face twisting into a snarl of fury. "Dad, don't - " Jack's voice cracked, his hands shaking as the tears streamed down his face. His father raised the shovel higher, advancing with a slow, deliberate menace, eyes burning with a madness Jack had never seen.

"Time is up, Jack," John growled, taking another step forward.

The gun felt cold and heavy in Jack's hands. He didn't want to shoot. Every part of him screamed against it - this was his father, the man he loved, the man he had trusted. But as John took one more step, raising the shovel with murderous intent, Jack knew he had no choice. His legs shook as he lifted the gun, tears blurring his vision.

"I'm sorry," Jack whispered, his voice breaking. "I'm so sorry."

John lunged forward, the shovel arcing through the air, aiming straight for Jack. In that split second, Jack's finger tightened on the trigger, and the gun went off. The sound of the gunshot cracked through the air, louder than the storm, louder than the fire.

John staggered, the shovel slipping from his grasp and clattering to the floor with a dull thud. He looked down at his chest, where a dark stain of blood was spreading across his shirt. His eyes widened in shock, disbelief flickering across his face.

Jack's heart clenched as he watched his father fall to his knees, his expression twisting with a mixture of pain and betrayal. "Jack..." John's voice was barely a whisper now, weak and broken, as he crumpled to the floor.

The gun slipped from Jack's trembling hands, clattering to the floor as he stared at his father's body. His chest heaved with sobs, the weight of what he had done crashing down on him like a wave. He sank to his knees, unable to tear his eyes away from the man who had once been his hero, now lying motionless in a pool of blood.

"I'm sorry, Dad," Jack whispered again, his voice barely audible over the roar of the fire. "I'm so sorry..."

The storm continued to rage over Briar Vale, the sky a swirling cauldron of black clouds split by jagged streaks of lightning. Rain lashed down in torrents, but it did nothing to quell the inferno that had engulfed the Miller house. Emma stumbled out from the back of the house, her body drenched and her chest heaving with the strain of her escape. The air was thick with smoke, its acrid stench filling her lungs and stinging her eyes. She rounded the corner to the front yard, her heart sinking at the sight before her.

The house was fully consumed by flames, great tongues of fire licking the sky as they devoured the roof, walls, and everything inside. The storm had taken on a more sinister aspect, as if the wind and rain were feeding the fire rather than extinguishing it. Thick black smoke billowed upward, swirling into the night, casting an eerie glow against the storm clouds. The fire roared like a living beast, crackling and snapping, its fury unchecked.

"Jack! Emily! Owen!" Emma cried, her voice barely carrying above the roar of the fire and the howl of the wind. Her chest tightened with fear as she scanned the scene, searching for any sign of her children. The front of the house was ablaze, the flames consuming the walls in seconds, windows shattering under the intense heat. The front door, now scorched and sagging, hung loosely from its hinges, ready to collapse at any moment.

Then, through the thick smoke, she heard them.

"MOM!"

The voices came, faint but unmistakable. Emma's heart leapt into her throat as she saw movement near the front door. Her eyes widened as she saw Emily first, stumbling out of the doorway, her hand clutching Owen's as they coughed and gasped for air. Jack followed close behind, his face pale, his clothes singed by the flames. His arms were outstretched, guiding his siblings forward, shielding them from the searing heat.

Emma sprinted toward them, her breath catching in her throat as the weight of relief and terror crashed over her. The rain pelted her face, mixing with the tears that spilled freely from her eyes. She reached out, pulling them into her arms the moment they reached her. She held them fiercely, her fingers trembling as she pressed their bodies close to her own, feeling their ragged breaths and pounding hearts.

"I've got you, I've got you," Emma whispered frantically, her voice choked with sobs. "You're safe, we're safe."

Emily buried her face in her mother's shoulder, her body shaking with silent sobs. Owen clung to Emma's side, his small hands gripping her shirt as though he feared she might disappear. Jack stood a little apart, his gaze fixed on the house, his expression hollow and haunted. The weight of what had just transpired clung to him like a shroud.

Emma, too, looked back toward the house. Flames leapt higher and higher, consuming everything in their path with ravenous intensity. It was more than just fire - it was something alive, something old and malevolent. It spread unnaturally fast, as though the very air was feeding it, its tendrils reaching outward like claws.

"We have to go," Jack muttered, his voice thick with exhaustion, his face streaked with soot. "It's spreading too fast. We can't stay here."

Emma nodded, her mind clouded with both terror and urgency. She turned, pulling her children with her as they began to move down the street, the heat from the flames searing their backs as they fled. But as they moved, Emma couldn't resist one final glance over her shoulder.

To her horror, she saw that the fire had leapt all the way to Agatha's house. Bright orange flames danced along the roof, consuming it with unnatural speed, as if the fire was sentient - hungry. Agatha's windows shattered from the heat, sending shards of glass raining down. Flames snaked through the walls, devouring the home like it had been waiting for this moment. And then the Thompsons' house erupted as well, fire bursting from its windows like a scream from the dead.

It wasn't just their house. The fire was spreading in all directions, licking at the surrounding properties, racing toward the new homes still under construction. The wood of the frames, damp from the rain, shouldn't have caught so easily, but the flames devoured them with unnatural hunger. The entire neighborhood seemed to be alight, the flames moving with a malevolent energy that defied the storm's fury.

Emma's heart pounded in her chest as she pulled her

children along faster, the flames crackling and roaring behind them, devouring everything in their wake. They stumbled down the street, their feet slipping on the slick pavement, the fire's eerie glow casting long shadows ahead of them.

Then came the sound - a sound that pierced the very heart of the night. It started as a low murmur, a strange, inhuman noise that rose above the wind and the fire. Faint at first, but growing louder with each passing second. Laughter - gleeful, high-pitched, and chilling. It echoed through the night, mingling with the hiss of the flames and the howling wind.

Emma's blood ran cold. She looked back once more, and through the inferno, she saw them - shadowy shapes, indistinct figures dancing in the flames. They moved with unnatural grace, their forms flickering like the fire itself, their laughter mixing with the crackle of the blaze. The Anhanga. The spirits, freed from their prison, were dancing in the destruction they had wrought, their long-awaited vengeance unfolding before her eyes.

The house began to collapse in on itself, the roof crumbling under the weight of the fire, the walls buckling inward. With a deafening crash, the Miller house fell, the flames rising in a final, triumphant blaze before consuming it entirely. And with it, John. The cursed legacy of the Anhanga, the twisted madness that had gripped him, was swallowed by the inferno.

Emma tightened her grip on her children, her breath coming in ragged gasps. The sound of the laughter continued to echo, faint but unmistakable, carried on the wind as they fled the neighborhood. The flames danced in the distance, their terrible light casting the streets in an otherworldly glow. But Emma did not look back again.

She couldn't. The past was burning behind her, and there was nothing left to save.

CHAPTER 13

After the Flames

The acrid stench of smoke clung to the night air like a heavy shroud as Emma stood outside the remains of their home, watching the orange glow of the fire flicker and die. The flames had gutted everything, leaving behind nothing but charred skeletons of what was once a life they had dreamed would be a fresh start. The ground beneath her feet was slick with the rain from the sudden storm, a stark contrast to the inferno that had raged mere moments ago. The storm had brought relief, but only after the destruction had taken its toll.

The wail of sirens cut through the silence, the red and blue lights of fire trucks and police cars casting strange, wavering shadows across the ruins. Briar Vale, once pristine and orderly, now resembled a battlefield, its neat rows of houses marred by ash and ruin. The firefighters moved with grim efficiency; their faces obscured by masks as they doused the last of the flames. But it was too late. The house - her house - was gone, swallowed by the fire that seemed almost unnatural in its hunger, as if it had been alive, seeking to devour everything in its path.

She stood there, numb, her arms wrapped tightly around Jack and Emily, who clung to her sides, their faces pale and streaked with soot. Owen, silent and distant, stood a little apart, staring into the distance with an unsettling stillness that made Emma's heart twist. His wide eyes reflected the flashing lights, but his gaze seemed fixed on something beyond the here and now, something far darker.

"Ma'am," a voice broke through the fog of her thoughts. A paramedic, his face kind yet worn with the weight of long hours, gently touched her arm. "We need to get you and the children checked out. You're all lucky to be alive."

Lucky. The word felt hollow. Emma glanced down at Jack, whose hands still trembled in her grip. He had been the one to pull the trigger, the one who had saved them all from John's madness. Her husband - no, the man he had become - was gone, consumed not only by the fire but by the rage and malevolent forces that had twisted him into something unrecognizable.

She nodded absently, allowing the paramedic to guide her toward the waiting ambulance. The children followed, dazed and silent, their steps heavy with the weight of the night's horrors. As she climbed into the vehicle, the cold metal of the ambulance floor sent a shiver through her, a reminder that they were still flesh and blood, still alive, though she could scarcely comprehend how.

Hours passed in a blur. The sterile lights of the hospital, the brief sting of antiseptic, the muted murmurs of doctors and nurses - none of it seemed real. Emma answered their questions mechanically, her mind only half-present, her thoughts turning again and again to the house, the fire, the things she had seen buried beneath the garden. It felt as if a fog had settled over her mind, the details of the night slipping through her grasp like sand through her fingers.

It wasn't until days later, when they were moved to a cramped hotel room, that the reality of their situation began to sink in. The police had come, asking their questions, prodding her for answers about John's behavior, about the fire, about the missing neighbors. Emma had given them the barest details, knowing full well that the truth - that the fire had been the final act in a tragedy wrought by supernatural forces - would never be believed. Instead, she spoke of John's paranoia, of the strange occurrences in the house, of the growing dread that had seeped into their lives long before the flames.

The story had taken on a life of its own, the press dubbing it the "Briar Vale Curse." The headlines screamed of mystery and murder, of unsolved disappearances, of strange happenings linked to the land itself. The media circled like vultures, hungry for any morsel of sensation. But even as they speculated, even as the neighborhood became the stuff of local legend, the police had found nothing. Not a single body. Not John's. Not Mary Kendrick's. Not even the neighbors Emma had seen with her own eyes, buried in the twisted remains of John's garden.

"They found nothing," Jack said quietly one morning, sitting at the small table by the window with a newspaper spread before him. His voice was calm, but there was a tremor beneath it, a fear that hadn't left him since that night. "Not a single body. It's like... they disappeared."

Emma sat on the edge of the hotel bed, the thin, floral comforter wrinkled beneath her as she unfolded the local paper she had picked up from the front office. The children were quietly watching TV, their faces still pale and distant after the traumatic events of the past few days. She had hoped the news wouldn't touch them here, but it was impossible to escape.

Her eyes fixed on the headline, the stark black letters almost jumping off the page:

Briar Vale Curse? Mystery Surrounds Devastating Fire and Missing Residents
Byline: James Parker, Senior Reporter
Date: August 14, 2024

Jupiter, FL - What was once a peaceful suburban community has now become the center of a growing mystery that has captivated local residents. In the early hours of Monday night, a devastating fire tore through Briar Vale, a relatively new housing development in Jupiter, leaving several homes destroyed and the neighborhood shaken. But as the investigation unfolds, questions remain about the fate of those who lived there - and the cause of the blaze.

While the fire's origins are still under investigation, authorities are puzzled by the rapid spread of the flames, which seemed unaffected by the heavy rain and winds of a passing summer storm. Witnesses described the fire as behaving "unnaturally," leaping from house to house with alarming speed. "It was like something was pushing it, feeding it," said one firefighter, who spoke on the condition of anonymity. "We've never seen anything like it." Investigators are looking into the possibility of an accelerant, possibly tied to the materials used in the construction of the homes.

Adding to the mystery, no bodies have been recovered from the fire, despite residents being unaccounted for. Among the missing is John Miller, a father of three, who was reportedly involved in a violent altercation with his family shortly before the fire broke out. Additional residents are also missing, but authorities have withheld their names until families are contacted. "It's like they just vanished," said Detective Liza Hayes of the Jupiter Police Department. "We've got no leads, no remains - nothing."

In a surprising development, police found a driver's license belonging to Samuel Redford in a shed behind John Miller's home. Redford, a prominent local real estate figure, is best known for representing Sunshine Homes, the developer behind Briar Vale. His role in brokering a controversial deal with the Environmental Protection Agency (EPA) to allow sales of homes in the development - despite environmental violations - had previously drawn scrutiny. The discovery of Redford's license has raised more questions, as he has not been seen publicly in months. His unexplained absence has added another layer of mystery to the situation, fueling speculation about his possible involvement.

John Miller's wife, Emma, and their three children - Jack, Emily, and Owen - narrowly escaped the fire and are currently receiving psychological counseling. Mrs. Miller has declined to comment publicly, but sources close to the family say she had been concerned about her husband's mental state in the weeks leading up to the incident.

In a stranger twist, many of the homes destroyed in the fire had ties to a now-defunct scandal involving Collin Homes in 2022. The company had faced a legal battle over using illegally imported lumber, allegedly taken from sacred lands, in the construction of houses. Rumors of a curse have swirled around the development ever since, with some local residents now referring to the events as the "Briar Vale Curse."

Former residents have shared eerie stories of odd behavior in the neighborhood before the fire - unexplained noises, and sightings of shadowy figures in the trees. Some have speculated that the fire was part of a larger, supernatural event linked to the illegal materials used in constructing the homes.

As authorities continue their investigation, the community of Jupiter is left wondering: Was this a tragic accident, or is there something more sinister at play?

Emma's stomach turned as she placed the paper down. She continued folding a shirt into her suitcase, her back to him. She hadn't wanted to tell the children, hadn't wanted to burden them with more than they'd already endured. But Jack was older now, too old to be sheltered from the truth. Still, she couldn't bring herself to respond, couldn't give voice to the dark thoughts that gnawed at the edges of her mind.

Owen, sitting cross-legged on the bed, glanced up from the toy he was absentmindedly turning in his hands. His eyes, far too knowing for a child of his age, fixed on Jack. "They were taken," he said softly, his voice barely a whisper. "Taken to the dark place."

Emma turned, her heart lurching in her chest. "Owen, what do you mean?"

But he only shook his head and returned to his toy, his small fingers tracing the outline of it with a strange, mechanical rhythm. Emma's gaze lingered on him, her mind drifting to the haunting dream she had several nights before everything burned - the twisted vines creeping over their home, the whispers from unseen figures drawing closer, consuming all in their path. Diego's words echoed in her thoughts: The Anhanga will take back what is theirs, along with those who transgressed against them.

She swallowed hard, her throat tightening as the pieces began to fall into place. The Anhanga hadn't simply destroyed Briar Vale. They had reclaimed it, dragging those who had wronged them - the bodies buried in the garden, John, all the others - into the darkness where they could never return. The cursed wood, the stolen life from sacred land... it had all come full circle.

Emma exchanged a glance with Jack, who shrugged, though his wide, fearful eyes betrayed his calm exterior. She knew he was trying to be strong, to make sense of everything just like she was. But how could they ever explain what had happened in Briar Vale? How could anyone understand the dark force that had consumed their father and their home?

Sighing deeply, Emma sank onto the bed beside Owen, pulling him close, though the gesture felt as much for her comfort as it was for his. The boy's small frame felt so fragile in her arms, as if the weight of everything that had happened might shatter him if she didn't hold him tight enough. She stroked his hair absentmindedly, her thoughts drifting back to John.

She missed him - the real John, the man he had been before Briar Vale and the curse. The man who had loved their children, who had laughed with her, who had once been her partner in every sense of the word. But that man had vanished long before the fire, consumed by something ancient, something dark. In his place, there had been a monster, a twisted reflection of the person she once knew, a shadow driven by madness and vengeance.

Now, that shadow was gone, and with it, a part of her life she could never reclaim.

Now, there was only one thing left to do: leave Briar Vale behind. She had already arranged for their departure. Tomorrow, they would drive away, start fresh, find a place where the memories of that cursed neighborhood couldn't reach them. She didn't care where, as long as it was far from here.

The End

EPILOGUE

Environmental Protection Agency
Office of Regulatory Compliance and Investigation
1200 Pennsylvania Avenue, NW
Washington, D.C. 20460

Date: March 15, 2024

To: Mr. Daniel Price
Chief Executive Officer
Sunshine Homes Co.
789 Horizon Drive
Jupiter, Florida 33458

Subject: Reopening of Case Number EPA-2023-01482

Dear Mr. Price,

The Environmental Protection Agency (EPA) is writing to inform you that Case Number EPA-2023-01482, previously closed on January 12, 2024, has been reopened due to new and concerning developments.

The recent fire that rapidly destroyed the residential neighborhood known as Briar Vale associated with Sunshine Homes Co. has raised significant safety concerns. The unnaturally accelerated spread of the fire strongly suggests the presence of one or more chemical accelerants in the construction materials, particularly in the wood used for building the homes. This concerning development has prompted the EPA to launch a renewed investigation to assess whether hazardous substances contributed to the rapid fire progression, and to determine whether the prior safety analysis provided by Sunshine Homes Co. was conducted properly and in full compliance with EPA standards.

Immediate Action Required:

1. In response to these developments, Sunshine Homes Co. is directed to take the following actions immediately:

2. Suspend all further sales or transfers of properties in the affected neighborhood until the EPA completes its investigation.

3. Provide full remediation by removing all unoccupied homes and other structures from the affected land in their entirety. This requires the complete demolition and disposal of all structures in the impacted area to eliminate any potential environmental or health hazards.

4. Excavate and remove the top foot of soil from the affected land. Due to the potential contamination of the soil with hazardous substances from the fire, this top layer of ground soil must be removed and treated as toxic waste. The soil must be disposed of in accordance with federal and state hazardous waste regulations to prevent further environmental contamination.

5. Treat all materials removed from the site as toxic and environmentally hazardous. As part of the remediation process, the dismantled materials must be disposed of in accordance with federal and state regulations for hazardous waste to ensure that no potential contaminants remain on the site or are improperly disposed of.

6. Fully cooperate with EPA inspections and investigations, providing all necessary documentation, access to the site, and any

requested materials that will aid in the investigation.

Failure to comply with these directives will result in regulatory enforcement actions, including but not limited to fines, penalties, and further legal measures.

Next Steps:

The EPA will be coordinating with local fire departments, environmental agencies, and hazardous waste specialists to conduct further inspections and sampling. Until the EPA investigation is completed and the remediation process is verified, no further construction, sales, or transfers of the affected properties are permitted.

For further inquiries or assistance, please contact Ms. Laura Jenkins, Senior Environmental Compliance Officer.

We appreciate your immediate cooperation in addressing this critical safety and environmental matter.

Sincerely,
Laura Jenkins
Senior Environmental Compliance Officer
Environmental Protection Agency

CC: Samuel Redford, Counsel for Sunshine Homes Co.

Six Months Later

The sun hung low in the pale sky, casting long shadows

across the dusty construction site. The rhythmic clatter of hammers and the deep rumble of machinery filled the air, underscored by the faint hum of chatter among the workers. It was an ordinary day, the kind that would blend into the dozens of others that marked the progress of yet another suburban development in Florida. But the air here carried an oppressive weight, something almost imperceptible, like the calm before a storm.

At the center of the site, a large stack of lumber lay piled haphazardly, waiting to be used. Thick beams, some still rough-hewn, were marked with various stamps and labels - ordinary signs of where they had come from, as far as the workers were concerned. Yet amidst the routine noise and activity, none of them noticed the particular branding that adorned the wood at the very base of the pile.

It was faint, half obscured by mud and dust kicked up from the workers' boots. But if one looked closely enough, the words could still be made out, etched into the wood like a brand left from some forgotten, cursed past: Collin Homes.

A gust of wind swept across the site, rattling loose tarps and sending a swirl of grit into the air. One of the workers, a broad-shouldered man with a weathered face, paused to wipe the sweat from his brow. He glanced down at the pile of wood, his gaze lingering on the faded stamp, though it held no meaning for him. He had never heard of the name or its history. The wood had been repurposed, salvaged from a bankrupt sale of materials - nothing more than the bones of an old project now being given new life.

It was just wood.

The worker shrugged, hefting one of the beams onto his shoulder and carrying it toward the half-built frame of a new house, its skeletal walls rising against the bright sky. As he set the beam into place, the wind picked up again, this time carrying with it a faint sound - so soft, so distant, that at first, it seemed no more than the whisper of leaves rustling through the trees at the edge of the site. But it grew louder, and with it came a sound that made the hairs on the back of his neck stand on end.

Laughter.

A child's laugh, high-pitched and gleeful, carried on the wind like an echo from far away, though no children were near. The worker frowned, glancing over his shoulder toward the source of the sound. His fellow workers continued their tasks, oblivious to the eerie noise, their faces etched in concentration as they went about their day.

He turned back to the house, his mind telling him it was nothing - just the wind playing tricks, stirring up some distant noise. But deep down, a cold unease coiled in his chest, a sense that something unseen had brushed against him, that the air itself had thickened with a presence he could not name. His hands trembled slightly as he hammered the beam into place, the sound of wood on wood strangely hollow.

The laughter faded, swallowed by the steady grind of construction, but the unease lingered, an invisible thread that wove itself into the very foundation of the new house. The worker cast one more glance at the pile of lumber, the faded **Collin Homes** stamp now obscured by shadows.

In the distance, beyond the sounds of progress and the chatter of men, there was a shift. The wind picked up once more, and as it swept through the construction site, there came again that faint, eerie sound - a sound that would have been easily dismissed if not for the quiet dread it left in its wake.

It was the sound of soft, distant laughter, receding into the wind, as if something long buried, long forgotten, had been stirred from its slumber.

The worker shivered, but he didn't stop. He had a job to do, after all. He set the next beam into place, oblivious to the quiet stirrings in the earth beneath his feet, and the chill that lingered in the air long after the laughter had died away.

High above, the clouds moved languidly across the sky, casting their long, creeping shadows upon the earth below. They seemed to bide their time. Ever watchful, as though possessed of some silent patience. Waiting... waiting for their moment, heedless of the toils and lives of those beneath them.

All while remaining unnoticed by those below.

Made in United States
Troutdale, OR
04/23/2025

30847897R00156